Love and Miss Fortune

HEARTS OF LOUISIANA, BOOK THREE

MAGGIE PRESTON

CYPRESS PRESS, LLC

Title: LOVE AND MISS FORTUNE / Maggie Preston
Description: Paperback First Edition
Publication Date: September 21, 2023
Cover Design: Fantasia Frog Designs
Formatting: Samantha Moran, Obsidian Inkwell Publishing, LLC

Paperback ISBN-13: 978-7356234-5-0
Also available as an ebook edition.

About the Purchase of This Book

Contents

In memory of my dad, who taught me the secret to a good drink is good company.

Chapter One

Charlotte Fortune was born bass-ackwards on the unluckiest day of the year according to the family history kept by their long-time housekeeper, Miss Perla. Things had gone downhill from there and weren't looking particularly bright this morning.

Harley jerked the car to the shoulder of Highway 70, careful not to plow down the rubberneckers jostling for first position in the disaster that passed for her life. Spilling herself from the car to the pavement, she shouldered her way through the weekend campers then slinked around a woman taking a selfie with the scene of the accident in the background. She turned just as Harley drew even, holding up the picture to examine it closer.

"Rainbow filter," Harley deadpanned in the woman's ear, then craned her neck to see the subject of the photo - a demolished pallet of her distillery's signature product swirling into the cracks of the blacktop road. "Nice touch."

The woman jumped and swiveled her head like an agitated bobblehead doll. "I know, right?" Classic Valley California dripped from her accent and bottled tan. "With the lake in the background? Someone in the crowd said the company's nickname is *Misfortune's* Brew so the rainbow seems, like, I don't know, *apropos*? It's like that dude Confucius says, everything has beauty; you just sometimes, I don't know, gotta fake it." Her fingers danced over the screen. "My followers will love it."

"Glad we could provide entertainment for your day," Harley snapped, her voice drowning beneath the bitterness crawling up her throat.

Miss California's jaw dropped and she clutched the phone to her chest, eyes wide. "They are *soooo* right. You southerners are just the sweetest. Thank you!"

On cue, Brownell Belle Tower chimed a slow, haunting peal. To Harley, the funeral dirge pounded home the last nail in the coffin of her five year struggle to rebuild her dad's distillery. They even had a dead body: one pallet of her great-great-great-great-great granddaddy's finest corn liquor, crushed nearly beyond recognition in the middle of the highway.

Misfortune's Brew, Harley repeated the name bitterly, biting her tongue and blending further into the spectators huddled along Lake Opelousas a few miles north of Belle Terre, Louisiana. *Mix one part Harley Fortune with two parts bad luck. Stir until it foams over the rim.*

She was out of time.

She was out of money.

She was out of options.

She was going to lose Fortune's Brew.

Harley struggled to remember how to breathe. Panic pulled at the last threads of her sanity, hope already as frayed and worn as her favorite jeans in the ongoing battle against family and fate.

"Can my life get any better?" she asked herself, hoping

there was no one paying attention to her talking to herself. No sense being known as unlucky *and* slightly touched, as her Granny would say. The family had enough of a reputation to live down.

Pity party, table for one. She blinked back the burn of tears and when that failed, Harley closed her eyes.

"Are you alright?"

The calm voice, a cocktail blended of concern and a sexy rumble, flowed through Harley like the twelve-year-old Dewar's her Uncle Everett brought to Thanksgiving last year. She snapped to attention and opened her eyes to find the source.

The mid-morning sun blinded her for a moment, or perhaps it was the glint of copper and honey in the fringe of hair waving at her from the man who'd managed to move silently into her personal space. At just five foot two, Harley was used to people standing over her. But this guy didn't loom. He just... was.

She couldn't see much against the glare. Just the solid male form, broad shoulders squaring out the frame and tapering down to long legs.

"No," she forced out the word then turned her back on the accident where her future *literally* spiraled down the drain, stomping further away from the crowd and back to her car to grab her phone. Hopefully she'd remembered to grab it. Had she charged it last night? She needed to take pictures for the insurance claim.

Her steps faltered, skidding across the gravel. A groan creaked out of her throat. She'd cancelled the collision policy last week. To save money and give them more time until her birthday.

The blood drained from her body leaving her skin cold in the wake.

"You really don't look good," the man said, following her movement, worry raising the pitch of his voice. "Kind of pale. Like you've eaten bad sushi or had to pull a coyote ugly over a bad one-night stand."

Harley narrowed her gaze, feeling the brows over her eyes knit into a single line. He was near enough the aroma of his cologne mingled with the scent of the sweet peas blooming at the Tower gardens, the intoxicating fragrance of expensive champagne and sandalwood carried by the early March breeze off the lake.

"You don't have much luck with women, do you?"

Mr. Helpful shrugged, those very broad shoulders looking solid enough to lean on. But there was a mischievous tilt to his mouth as he whipped off the sunglasses and gazed at her down the bridge of his nose. "Depends on the woman."

A heavy dose of invitation laced his voice, like a generous dollop of cream in her coffee to sweeten the bitter chicory brew. Was he flirting with her? Her face burned beneath the awareness in his light brown eyes. But what did he see? Did he see beyond the dirty ballcap and wrinkled button down? What put that glint in his eyes, crooked that grin just so? It sure as hell couldn't be *her*. Not today.

She didn't need to know. Harley had enough problems.

Harley tugged on the brim of her ballcap and continued to her car, searching the crevices of the front seat for her missing phone. No luck. She lost that thing more than her patience lately. Propping one hip against the dented bumper of her twenty-year-old Mercedes, she eyed the car with a mixture of pride and nostalgia. The car had belonged to her father, just like the distillery. At least it was still running.

What am I going to do now? she wondered. Harley dropped her forehead into her palm. If they didn't deliver this purchase order, they wouldn't qualify for the Crescent City MicroLiquor Spirits Competition in May. Of course, to get to that she had to get past her family and her birthday-slash-do-or-die deadline on April 13th, which was on a Friday this year. She'd been born on Friday the 13th. How appropriate her future would be decided on the same day.

The sound of footsteps crunched against the gravel. Harley squinted between her fingers. Shiny loafers appeared in her field of vision as she counted the blades of grass.

"Nice car. Mercedes F-class. The fastest coupe they ever made for the public but the first with side airbags." The facts rolled off his tongue in an absent-minded flood. Would that tongue sweep across her mouth as easily? Bring the same warmth as his voice?

Harley looked up with a roll of her eyes. He scrubbed the windblown hair from his forehead and tilted his head left as he examined the car.

Then he refocused on her, a sharpening that constricted in his pupils. "Seriously, though. If you're not feeling well the ambulance is still here. Would you like to let them check you out? The truck driver seems to be, uh —" he paused, looking back toward the flashing red lights, the slow smile tilting up one corner of a very nice mouth to flash the perfect amount of straight white teeth, "well, just using up oxygen if you want to know the truth."

Harley huffed out a laugh before she could stop herself. "He's not going to get a bill for it, so I guess he figures why not?"

Mr. Helpful mulled over her bitter remark but must have decided to ignore it. Instead, he repeated, "I'm sure the EMT would be happy to check you out." Either amusement or too much sun crinkled the corners of his eyes.

More innuendo for Harley to decipher. "The EMT likely has his hands full right now. The driver looks to be a bit of a drama queen."

She propelled herself off the hood as a thought filled her head. Maybe they could salvage a few boxes to keep the customer happy until they could distill another batch. She eyed the crushed pallet then scooted around the ancient Mercedes to open the trunk.

The Good Samaritan followed. "True, but I think he's worried about facing his boss. He said a hungry gator is nicer and more fun to work with."

That stopped her short and she pivoted, her eyes dragging up from the shiny loafers to the pleated grey slacks and simple black t-shirt fit snugly across the chest and what Harley suspected were washboard abs. She'd never dated a guy with washboard abs. Damn. She needed to stop thinking about that.

Dating. Not washboard abs.

Thoughts of dating again made her nauseous.

There was probably a jacket somewhere nearby waiting for this guy. Harley would bet it had one of those little hankies folded precisely in the front pocket. Her life was filled with people like this guy. With quick motions, she opened the trunk. "Yeah, I hear she's a real piece of work."

"Oh, do you know her?"

Again, that huff of sound cracked from her lungs. "Belle Terre is a small town. Everyone knows everyone." *And everything about everyone*, she added to herself.

Anyone local probably knew the details of Harley's life. And what was at stake. She'd dropped five grand into the mail less than an hour ago in the hope of changing the expected outcome. As usual, it was the wrong decision. *Sorry, mom and dad.*

Add to that her aunt had rather publicly picked another distillery and whiskey to call out on her cable reality TV show... now the world knew what the Fortune family thought of Harley Fortune and her chance for success.

"I'm hoping to meet up with her today." The man's attention zeroed in on the wrecked truck, the front end sitting *cattywhompus* in the ditch. The Fortune's Brew logo displayed prominently on the tailgate. *Fortune's Brew. Where good fortune meets good whiskey.*

"There's some business I'd like to discuss with her."

Just another salesman, Harley figured, slamming the trunk closed. They were always coming out to the property, most trying to convince her to sell the hybrid corn her daddy and granddaddy had developed with their supplier. As if that was the only thing that made Fortune's Brew special. Even an expensive steak could be ruined by a bad chef.

"From the sounds of it you might want to avoid her," Harley warned. "Especially today. She doesn't sound like a really nice person."

That lazy smile again; Harley had to admit it was a damn good smile. If she had time to think about such things, and she didn't, she'd definitely see the appeal of being on the receiving end of a smile like that. A person would want to let that smile carry them away to dark places where naughty things could happen that had never happened before. Maybe holding out for true love made as much sense as trying to keep the distillery in operation.

"I'm not worried." Mr. Helpful slipped the pair of designer sunglasses back on his perfectly aquiline nose. He pointed a key fob over Harley's shoulder and beeped open the door to a sporty little number the color of a Tuscan sun she'd seen on the slideshow from her granny's computer. One of those car deodorizers hung from the rearview mirror in the shape of a four-leaf clover. "If you're sure you're feeling alright then I'm going to head out."

"Watch out for hungry gators," she warned as he started to turn.

The grin stretched back across his face, sharpening the angle of his cheeks without making his face appear hard. "I can hold my own against any wild creature I might meet today."

Harley didn't doubt that. He could likely charm the clouds from the sky.

He gave her one final lopsided grin. "Best of luck to you."

Harley rolled her eyes. Luck. If she had any luck she'd have listened to her instincts and driven this order to the supplier herself. But Uncle Everett had called a family meeting at lunch and she needed to be there.

What else could go wrong today?

She needed a minute before facing reality, so she stomped up the dirt road to the top of the levee, part of the system that protected Belle Terre from the unpredictable waters of the Atchafalaya. Here the river was fed by Cormorant Lake which nibbled on dozens of smaller tributaries further north which finally nursed on the Mississippi.

That was the problem — melting snows and heavy storms in other parts of the country and dumped their problems down to the basin. Everything rolled downhill and Harley and Belle Terre were there to greet it.

She crossed the open gates through to the calmness of the other side. Like magic, the rush of passing cars dissipated, leaving only the occasional call of a whooping crane or whistling duck as a reminder that life went on. The damp earth with its musty perfume of algae and decay, unpleasant to many, were a balm to Harley. They were the smells of a legacy of life that had been there long before today arrived.

Most loved the lake, the rough water giving skiers a good ride while not being too much to sit and enjoy an afternoon of fishing. But for Harley, the choppy whitecaps ruined the spell and the wide-open space let everyone know where you were and what you were doing.

She preferred the bayou; calm dark waters hid a myriad of challenges and the endless channels provided solitude and privacy. The land, what there was of it anyway, was thick with cypress and oak but enough solid ground could be found to plop a one or two room cabin. She'd spent time with her granddaddy and daddy on the waters, fishing, trapping, running trout lines. They were some of her best memories.

"Harley?"

The deep bass filtered in through her subconscious and she dragged her eyes up as the town's newly elected sheriff crested the small rise to the top of the levee.

"Sheriff Guidry," Harley acknowledged with a nod, mentally pouring some steel into her spine to mimic a confidence she had to fake. She had less than six weeks before her family voted on whether to sell the distillery. Her bargaining chip - the only pallet of Fortune's Brew *Lucky Lady* - now watered the weeds along the highway behind them.

"Congratulations on the election last month." Not everyone's future was as uncertain as hers, she admitted, and jerked the green-eyed monster into submission. "I heard it was a landslide victory."

Unlike her, Jackson Guidry was a transplant to Belle Terre, arriving almost a year ago while passing through to somewhere else. Fate had stepped into his life, delivering true love and a new job, and not for the first time, Harley wondered what she'd done to piss off the universe. She didn't expect true love or a perfect life, but a few less knocks would be nice.

"Thanks, Harley."

Sheriff Guidry matched her posture, his weight resting on one leg while he scratched a line in the ground with the toe of his boots. "I need your signature for the wrecker to hook up to the truck."

Harley took a mental snapshot of the peaceful waters then headed back with the sheriff to the scene of the accident. Their feet scraped against the dirt as they descended the small hill, and the roar of traffic enveloped them as they neared the road.

"Do you think it's a total loss?" He gestured absently to the broken pallet of boxes in the middle of the road, the boxes a darker brown at the bottom where the cardboard was drunk on her whiskey. But even the boxes on top had the telltale markings. So much for her plan to salvage.

The words knifed her gut and a huff of pain escaped before she could stop it. "The Fortune luck holds true."

He grimaced, like he'd known the answer but asked anyway out of politeness or a false sense of hope. "Will you still be able to meet the entry requirements for Crescent City?"

Of course he knew, Harley reasoned. People in town knew what was at stake. You couldn't hide much in a small town, even when you lived twenty miles outside its borders.

The Crescent City MicroLiquor Spirits Competition was being held in New Orleans in a little over two months. It was the biggest for the smallest, those looking to break into the market. It was the first time in fifteen years Fortune's Brew would be represented.

The wave of nausea swamped Harley's senses and she locked her knees to keep from falling to them. "I put my entry application and application fee in the mail this morning."

It was the very last of her money. She'd hit the point where she'd promised to stop if they hadn't made it yet. Going further put everything in jeopardy: the house, the property. Everything her family had worked for generations to acquire.

"But I'm not sure if we'll qualify. The final bottles to meet the ten-thousand-unit quota are perfuming the air as we speak." The heady aroma of moonshine mixed with the mulberries and dewberries ready to blossom as the weather started to warm. The next words strangled on her pride. "Uncle Everett wants to meet at lunch."

The sheriff watched her, waiting, then prompted, "Did he say why he wanted to meet?"

"'*To discuss the future of the company and what was best for all concerned.*'" She repeated the words as Uncle Everett had delivered them that morning when he dropped by, though she doubted they'd tasted as bitter on his tongue.

Probably more *suggestions* to change their operation so they tasted like every other whiskey out there. Cheaper corn. Shorter distillation run. *No thanks*, Harley had told him. *We've used the same recipe for two hundred years. There's nothing wrong with our product.*

She didn't let herself think too long about whether or not the problem was her.

She loved him but Uncle Everett didn't have a vision for Fortune's Brew. He had a vision for himself and his husband retiring on the proceeds from the sale. Not that really needed the money. Uncle Vic had done well with his gallery in the French Quarter, combining his love for classic art with the quirky styles only New Orleans could birth.

Ready to change the subject, Harley inclined her head toward the accident and she and Sheriff Guidry walked down. She pointed to the man sitting in the back of the ambulance, wrapped in a blanket not even winter in Louisiana required. She stuffed back a length of hair that escaped the ball cap on her head. "Is Dean ok?"

The sheriff waited for the roar from a passing semi to die down, then scrubbed a hand across his jaw. "His vision and reflexes are just fine based on the rate of his texting and posting to social media. You have insurance, right?"

"Liability." The word came out sharper than Harley intended, so she cleared the attitude from her throat.

It was all they were required to carry by state law. It wasn't Sheriff Guidry's fault she'd cancelled the collision part of the policy to try and save a little money. Money she'd needed to pay their suppliers so they could ramp up production. Production, she noted with a pained looked, currently getting this part of the highway sloshed.

If there was a wrong way to go, Harley would find it. Her last name had become an oxymoron. Or maybe *she* was the oxymoron.

She sighed, sucked in a breath, let it out slowly. "Sorry. That came out —" but the sheriff waved her off with a sad smile.

"Dean's going to be a problem for you."

Her eyes snapped to follow the slight incline of the sheriff's head. "He's been a problem since we broke up last year." Then at the man's worried quirk of a brow, Harley quickly clarified, "Nothing extreme but my grandmother was right. You shouldn't fish off the company pier."

Sheriff Guidry gave a short burst of laughter empty of

humor. "If Dean tries to bait your hook with his worm, let me know."

"I appreciate that," Harley shoulder bumped him, though her shoulder barely reached his upper arm. "Dean's not a bad guy."

"Are you trying to convince me or yourself?" His tone challenged but remained respectful.

"Myself probably. I wounded his manly pride." That was not all she wounded when he wouldn't take no for an answer, but their families had been friends and business partners for decades. She was trying to make allowances. "I couldn't fire him on top of that."

She'd also forgiven him for cheating on her, but she'd not been willing to wait around for a repeat performance. Some things didn't deserve a second chance. Harley tried not to wallow in the past although her entire life seemed to be centered around fixing it. Her parents. The distillery. Dean.

They stood in silence while a few more cars passed the accident, the vibration of tires on pavement dancing up her calves. The sun was high enough in the sky to be noticeable, the weather warmer as the Mardi Gras season wrapped up later than usual.

A nails-against-chalkboard screech of metal against cement brought her upright as the pickup truck was hauled back onto the road, the front wheel's rim bare of rubber.

When the truck rested quietly on the road, Sheriff Guidry turned to Harley, face grim. "Dean is saying another vehicle, a gold sports car, swerved into his lane and caused the accident."

Gold sports car? "I saw a car like that when I pulled up." Hope flared in Harley, at least until she glimpsed the sheriff's furrowed brow. "But?" she prompted, knowing there was a but coming. There was always a *but*.

Sheriff Guidry shifted his weight and crossed his arms. "The skid marks don't start until the shoulder and they're in a straight line. Like the vehicle was drifting and the driver realized it when the front tire went off the road then slammed on the brakes. If the driver had swerved to avoid another vehicle, the skid marks would likely swerve. Of course, there are no cameras out here, nothing to contradict Dean's statement. Unless a witness comes forward, I really have nothing to either support or refute Dean."

The sheriff pushed off the back of the Mercedes. "Sorry to deliver more bad news," he added then went to manage the accident scene, leaving Harley with thoughts she'd rather not think.

Her heart raced with a mixture of anger and adrenaline as she stalked toward Dean and the ambulance. Dean was a screw up; always had been but like so many other things at Fortune's Brew, he came with the property. He'd been working summers for the family since they'd been in junior high school. His family owned the farm where Fortune's Brew grew their special corn. Not even his dad would hire him though. That should have told her something.

"Glad you're —" Harley breathed deeply as Dean flashed the palm of his hand at her then texted one handed faster than she could with two. She shoved the tips of her fingers in the front pockets of her jeans so she wouldn't rip the ever-present phone from Dean's hands. As much as she hated the contraption - she could barely keep up with hers - Dean was rarely without it. When he finally looked up at her, his expression was bored.

"Yeah. What is it, Harley?" The blank expression slipped slightly, eyes Harley once looked into with affection were now narrow and hard. The flush of anger deepened his breathing and darkened the walnut tone of his skin. Dean's attention shifted almost immediately over Harley's shoulder and she had to resist following the gaze.

"You just totaled our only truck and destroyed three weeks' worth of work. Perhaps you could..." She opened her mouth to continue, but snapped it closed. It wouldn't do any good.

"Wasn't my fault." Dean lifted the oxygen mask draped over his lap and took a hit.

"It's never your fault, Dean." The muscles in her arms tightened at the shoulders until her upper body was a tense line. "It wasn't your fault when you forgot to clean out the malting barn and we had to replace the floor because of mold. It wasn't your fault when you missed cutting the head from that last batch and ruined the run. And it wasn't your fault when you hooked up the propane tank incorrectly and nearly destroyed the still house." Even now her lungs burned from the smoke inhalation from trying to put out the fire. "It's never your fault."

Dean drew the blanket tighter around his shoulders. "I can't help it if you won't provide adequate resources. I'm the only one out there and can't be expected to be everywhere at once."

The sheer arrogance of his words punched Harley in the throat and this time she held up her palm to stop Dean. She swallowed twice to tamp down the words biting at the back of her throat looking for air. "You're the only one out there." It wasn't a question. Harley knew in his delusion, what he said was true. With effort, she kept her voice steady. "Lautaro and I work eighteen-hour days while we're lucky if you show up for six. Tomorrow, don't bother showing up. You're fired."

Harley spun on her heels, knowing she'd just made a huge mistake. *Another one*, her inner critic amended. She stalked back to the car, feeling the watchful eyes of the sheriff on her front and Dean on her back.

"I'll be talking to you later, Harley," Dean shouted as she retreated to her car. "We have to discuss compensation for my injuries."

"Then I suggest you get a sponge because our only assets are leaking onto the asphalt while you suck up more oxygen."

Chapter Two

By the time she cranked the engine, the sheriff had stopped traffic and waved her back into the steady flow returning to town.

"This is not happening," Harley informed the universe and anyone else that happened to be listening.

She practiced some breathing techniques Laurtaro went on about in his Zen Mexican-accented voice. *In through the nose. Out through the mouth.* She got to the count of three before her scream slapped against the interior of the Mercedes.

Not feeling better in the slightest, she focused her energy on getting through town without running anyone over accidentally. Harley made a quick detour to downtown Belle Terre, wanting to grab a coffee before hitting the long stretch of nothingness that made up Highway 1 after she crossed the river. Granny didn't believe in coffee. How the two of them were related meant the universe had a wicked sense of humor in Harley's mind. Coffee was life. Actually, coffee was life for those unlucky enough to be around

Harley, whose day began when sunrise hadn't yet tickled the horizon.

Harley slowed to a crawl on Front Street, hemmed in by one of the LCB Construction trucks in the front and a tailgating van full of post-Mardi Gras revelers twirling beads from the windows. The river walk area was crowded for a Monday morning. The waning Mardi Gras celebration had people floating upriver looking for distraction and Belle Terre had craft beer and the best supply of crawfish and blue crab this side of heaven.

If Harley could get things together at Fortune's Brew, south Louisiana could boast one of the best small distilleries for moonshine - and only the second one owned by a woman - in the nation as well. It would also preserve the legacy of her family, the very thing her mom and dad had died while trying to accomplish. She owed them that.

It was her fault they were dead.

The truck turned off and disappeared behind the fence to the new AmeriMart outdoor mall coming to life at one end of the Main Street boardwalk. The tailgating van dropped back, the passengers hanging out of a window to yell at others on the street. She zipped to the other end of the busy shopping area, squeezing her car into the last available spot across from The Book Nook.

The owner, Lara Caldwell, had opened a second business next door called Beans and Bubbles, a coffee house-slash-laundromat. Between the coffee, the state-of-the-art washers, and the bookstore, she had the market cornered on ways to kill time while the spin cycle did a number on your delicates.

Harley pocketed her keys as she took the two steps up to the boardwalk, the weight of seven generations of expectations dragging her feet. She stopped to take in the overflowing flower boxes along the walkway filled with red tulips and red anemone. Not even the world crumbling around her could make her ignore the color red. It was her mother's favorite color, the color her memory associated with love, with family, with security.

She sucked in a breath tinged with the bite of fresh brewed coffee laced with fabric softener. The tailgating van reappeared, squealing around the corner to draw Harley's attention. Around the side of the building, she spotted a gold fender, the sun dancing on the custom paint job that faded from a fiery sunset at the base to a warm honey on the hood. Harley knew this car, and she remembered the sheriff saying Dean claimed a gold sports car had forced him off the road.

"Hope you have insurance," Harley muttered but she took a picture of the license plate, which was also custom: CSANDAU.

Curiosity as much as coffee pulled her through the doors etched with the business logo: an oversized mug of coffee with steam rising, the letters for Beans and Bubbles filling in the bubbles. A QR code sticker sat on the saucer, the newest addition to the business' online presence.

Fortune's Brew had no online presence. They barely had an in-person presence. They needed a website. A logo. Something people would recognize and associate with their business. Maybe a black cat looking in a broken mirror while standing under a ladder.

Stop whining, Harley, she reminded herself as she pushed through the doors. *Granny hasn't decided how to vote and she's the deciding factor.* Even if her aunt and uncle voted against her, Harley's forty-nine percent ownership beat their forty-eight percent. Granny's three percent was the deciding factor. All Harley had to do was convince her grandmother.

Then again, the same was true for Uncle Everett and Aunt Elsbeth.

Whoever won Granny's vote, won Fortune's Brew's future.

Her eyes adjusted slowly to the dim interior, the hum of washers and dryers in the background as a steady ripple of customers moved between the coffee counter and the bookstore.

"Hey Harley." Lara Caldwell breezed in from the bookstore. Though barely four months pregnant, the growing baby bump made it through the door first.

"Lara." Harley smiled but her attention was on the customers, looking for the owner of the golden chariot outside. He wasn't hard to find among the tourists and locals. Even when she'd met him out on the highway, he'd looked like neither. She gave him a once over. Then did it again because once wasn't enough.

He'd found the suit coat she'd suspected he owned, the color matching the grey slacks. It was tailored to look like he'd washed it on a hot water cycle, snugly fitted around his excellent build. She'd read that was a trend somewhere, though in her world the jeans and the untucked button down she wore was trendy enough. He'd at least tried to tone down the businessman's aura with the black V-neck tee bringing Harley's mind back to his washboard abs.

Lara followed Harley's line of vision and joined her at the front of the store, an appreciative smile quirking one end of her mouth. "You look extra focused, Harley. Is there a problem or are you just admiring the view?"

Blushing, Harley tore her gaze away. "You're happily... happily, Lara," she teased, gesturing to Lara's midsection. "Why are you noticing the view?"

But Harley had to admit, the view was pretty nice. Six-foot plus of lean muscle packaged in a swimmer's body - broad shoulders tapering to a narrower waist and long legs - filled out the designer suit. Now that the sun wasn't in her eyes and the distraction of her ruined life perfuming the air, she could pay attention to other things.

Purposefully, perfectly mussed hair the color of a perfectly brewed chicory coffee with a matching scruff darkened the sharply edged jaw and high slash of cheekbones. Everything about him screamed *ego*.

Harley had gotten dressed without turning on the lights, like she did most mornings. Thinking back, she couldn't remember if she'd combed her hair before putting on the ball cap.

"I am happily-happily," Lara said and nodded, her hand absently going to the aforementioned measure of happiness pushing against the red apron with a matching logo in white. "I'm not dead. You should definitely go for it though."

"Are you suggesting I ask him if he wants to see my Berber carpet?"

Rumor had it more than the new Berber carpet had been laid in the house where Lara first rekindled her relationship with her current significant other, Will.

She rolled her eyes and patted her protruding belly. "Taking the first step is the only way you'll get what you really want."

"My first steps tend to take me over the cliff," Harley countered.

"Then make sure you fall for the right guy and he's there to catch you at the bottom."

A frantic-looking man waved at Lara from the area of the washer and dryers and Lara started in that direction. "Tell your cousin Piper I said thanks for the idea about the laundromat. It's doubled our business in the bookstore. And customers love using our app to call in their orders. It's just what I wanted."

Harley gave her a nod and wondered briefly what she would want if she wasn't wrapped up in trying to revive her dad's business. Even after fifteen years, it was still her dad's business, no matter what the lawyers said.

Her attention returned to Mr. Helpful. She moved slowly to stand behind the man just as his turn came at the counter.

"You're going to be my favorite new friend today, Julie." His tone, low and sultry, still managed to be masculine but said he was used to being indulged when he used that voice.

Julie's eyes dipped down while Harley rolled hers, the young girl's shoulders rising slightly as the redness bloomed upward from beneath the collar of her white t-shirt. She absently looked to the name tag to make sure her name was Julie, and the demi-god was talking to her. He'd won her over with one sentence.

"How can I help you today, sir?" The teen barista flashed an eager look, a black marker twined in her fingers as her hand hovered over the three stacks of cups. The bright red apron matched her cheeks and practically swallowed her thin frame.

The man angled his hands into the pockets of tailored pants without disturbing the crisp line of the pleat, the sharp cuffs over shoes so shiny they reflected the grain of the hardwood floors. Miss Perla would be impressed with both the floors and the pleats.

"I'd like a Grande triple half-caf breve, half half-and-half, half soy, no foam latte, extra hot with a whip and double shot of caramel, upside down."

The smile wobbled on the teen's face. She snatched her

hand back from the Grande tower like it was an aggravated cottonmouth. "Uhhh...what?"

The look of calm on a face free of worry never fluctuated. He tilted his head down a hair to look over the rim of the sunglasses Harley recognized from earlier. She read the brand on the stem. Yep. Expensive. "Grande triple half-caf breve, half half-and-half, half soy, no foam latte, extra hot with a whip and a double shot of caramel, upside down."

"You want your coffee upside down?" The young girl looked to Harley for help and Mr. Helpful's eyes followed then widened as he took in Harley's presence. "Won't it spill?"

Mr. Helpful leaned toward Julie conspiratorially, his laugh easy and practiced. His eyes never left Harley, however. "Not if we do it right."

Gooseflesh pebbled down Harley's arms. She cleared her throat, drawing the attention of the baffled barista. "He just means he wants the espresso poured in last."

He rested his arm on the waist high counter and leaned his weight, then pushed the shades up to the crown of his head.

"Hello again." Amusement crinkled the corner of his eyes. Eyes which Harley realized now were not light brown but amber. Honest to god amber, like the sunlight had been tanned to a warm gold then splashed with wisps of chocolate swirls. "Must be my lucky day."

More flirting, but Harley didn't take it to heart. Flirt seemed to be a steady state with this guy based on her two interactions with him. She ran a finger along the brim of the ball cap sitting on her scalp, resisting the urge to tug it lower and hide beneath the brim. "Just a coincidence. If you want coffee in this town that doesn't taste like it was blended with diesel this is where you go."

He cocked his head to the side, his brows arching in disbelief. "This might qualify as a coincidence, but my dad told me there was no such thing as a coincidence."

"And your dad would never lie to you?"

"Not when it involves women or whiskey."

The eyes never left hers, Harley noted reluctantly; didn't do the quick head-to-toe she was used to seeing from men who wanted to assess her place in their hierarchy of females: friend, fling, fleeting, or forever.

She thought of the gold car outside and her totaled truck being hauled to the old truck graveyard. "Then your dad was right this time. It's not a coincidence."

"Definitely my lucky day." He leaned a little closer, his posture relaxed. He scrubbed a hand over his ear. "Tell me you followed me from the highway, or saw my car and stopped hoping to get to know me better."

While she hadn't felt small standing next to him out on the highway, Harley calculated the difference in their height and had to stop herself from stretching up to her tiptoes. "Something like that."

"Uh, Harley, he wants his coffee extra hot," Julie interrupted, probably missing the death rays shooting from Harley's eyes to melt the golden-eyed outsider. "What does that even mean?" Julie's eyebrows were starting to draw together, creating a deepening ridge on a forehead still too young for wrinkles and worry. "Isn't all coffee hot? Unless it's iced and he didn't say he wanted it iced. Did you?" Julie deflated a little more. "I sort of lost track."

Harley moved closer to the counter, which put her too close for comfort with Mr. Helpful. The smoky, nutty scent of cardamom and something spicy tickled her nose. She ignored the masculine aroma even as she breathed deeply. "Heat the dairy to one-eighty. Lara keeps a thermometer near the machine if you're not comfortable doing it by touch." Harley pointed to a drawer.

Julie's blank look morphed into something more fearful, the whites of her eyes taking over her narrow face. "Lara!" Julie sprinted from the counter, the wake of her departure causing the cup tower to teeter.

Harley whistled slow and low, reaching over the counter just in time to halt the tumble of cups. "Holy cow, I think you broke the barista."

"I have Triple A," he shot back and winked, his head tilted at the absolute ideal angle to catch the single ray of sun filtering in through the blinds. The light played in the darker flecks of an amber iris. "I'm sure we can get her up and running again."

She had to shake her head to break the spell, enthralled by Mr. Helpful's eyes. "I'm sure you're good at jump-starting things."

"Only when invited." There was power behind the grin when he turned it on, the perfect amount of straight white teeth behind a crooked smile. "Otherwise, I never touch a woman's battery."

The low pull in Harely's gut set off warning bells in her head. He scrubbed a hand through his hair, every strand falling perfectly back into place. *Of course it did*, Harley admitted. He had to be an alien. Or supernatural. Or a Mississippi State fan.

Turning her attention to the counter, Harley smiled as another young barista took Julie's place.

"Hey, Harley," BeckyLyn Kenner lifted her chin in greeting, her body posture a little stiffer than the smile she forced. "I don't see anything from you on the board. Did you order from the app?"

"No," Harley blushed at the admission. "Not today."

The teen barista's mouth quirked up at the edge. "Did you lose your phone again?"

"You promised not to ask me that question anymore, Bex."

Bex mouthed *OK* and rolled her eyes. "You want your usual?"

Harley nodded, pulling the brim of her ball cap a little lower, feeling the weight of the stare from the man pushed into her personal space by the rack of pre-packaged coffee at his back. "Please. Make it a tall today."

Mr. Helpful straightened, his broad shoulders now even with Harley's eyes. "I'll have —"

"Yours is coming," Bex interrupted without looking his way then returned to her station at the espresso machine.

He settled back to leaning on the counter, the relaxed posture putting him more at Harley's eye level. "You know your coffee."

The proximity was tempting, making her want to lean in closer, smell the cologne, check out the eyes. *He's like the Loch Ness Monster*, she consoled herself. Once it pops its head out you want to look closer, unsure if your eyes are playing tricks on you. "The doc checks my caffeine level whenever she does bloodwork."

"You can tell a lot about a person by the coffee they drink."

"I guess that makes you complicated and hard to understand." The words were out but she'd not meant to say them out loud. There was just something about the guy that made her want to take him down a notch or two. Or twenty. Get his clothes dirty. Muss his hair.

"No, I'm exactly what you see. I never try to be something I'm not."

But Harley saw the doubt behind the statement, if only for a second.

Bex appeared from nowhere and slid Harley's reason-for-living across the counter, breathing out, "Tall drip black," as she whirled in a single motion and disappeared back behind the counter.

"Plain black coffee for Harley." Mr. Helpful repeated, her name rolling off his tongue. "Unusual name. No nonsense coffee. Independent. Straight forward. Resistant to change. Probably hiding a secret love for..."

This time his eyes did roam her body, but Harley could tell it was her clothes that drew the focus of his attention. What did he see? Ripped jeans. Wrinkled button down. Her dad's favorite ball cap. She spent eighteen-hour days trying to turn corn into world-class hooch. She reached forward to snag her coffee, but he finished his thought.

"...a raspberry chocolate dream Frappuccino."

She hesitated, and his smile tilted to a knowing grin. She loved a raspberry chocolate dream Frappuccino. Had taught Bex and Lara both how to make hers. She just didn't indulge that often, cursing the genetics that had let her top out a hair over five foot two while her ass wanted to be six foot one. The junk in her trunk did put a nice wiggle in her walk, or so she'd been told. Not that she'd been told anything about her trunk or any other parts in quite some time. And no one had ever checked under her hood. She was a classic or an out-of-place relic depending on who you asked.

Mr. Helpful's knowing look was back as Harley's mind had slipped into private territory and she yanked her thoughts to more public-appropriate musings.

"You like things a certain way. Your way. But you're very sweet about it so people don't mind."

His voice — rich, like him, smooth, also like him — coated her in warmth, made her want to snuggle in.

Harley mostly ignored the warmth and snuggling. He looked at her as if expecting peals of laughter, a feminine *oh-you're-so-funny* perhaps with a light slap on the arm. He even flexed his respectable bicep in preparation, Harley realized as he leaned forward so she didn't have to reach too far.

She knew how to rumple Mr. Helpful's air of perfection. "Would that Triple A be for the expensive gold sports car outside?"

His eyes widened, a hint of panic dimming the sparkle.

Bingo, Harley chimed inwardly, triumphant.

"My car?" Coffee forgotten, he walked toward the front door, peering sideways through the front window. "Is there a problem?"

"Your car is fine. The driver from that accident this morning said a gold sports car forced him off the road. I'm wondering where your car was about earlier this morning."

The well arched brows — Harley wondered if they were plucked for that level of arc — knitted together over hooded eyes.

He pulled a cell phone from his pocket and effortlessly swiped to wake up the screen. Harley ignored how much she hated him for that alone. Her phone rebelled at her touch.

"It was with me." The voice came off as pleasant, the look more cautious as his fingers danced across the screen, reminding Harley a little too much of Dean's callous disregard earlier.

Her chuckle was forced, a huff of air as she tried for relaxed, but tension electrified the atmosphere. "You sure it didn't go off on its own? Maybe run that truck off the road out on Lake Opelousas Drive, then come back into town for a coffee order that should be illegal?"

The relaxed smile returned but didn't reach his eyes this time and he reached over to open the door for a woman toting an overstuffed hamper. She chirped "Thanks" and shuffled toward the washers and dryers in the back. "My coffee order is the result of years of research and experimentation to get the perfect blend of hipster chic and tattooed badass."

Her curiosity reared its nosy self. Did he have any tattoos? Where? Of what? *Focus!*

He headed back to the coffee counter and Bex watched him approach under the brim of her red Beans and Bubbles cap. She didn't look pleased.

Harley didn't either, and followed in his shiny loafered footsteps. The uppity tourist wasn't taking her seriously and after the day she'd had, not to mention the news from her uncle about the pending family meeting, putting up with the runaround wasn't high on her list. "Then enjoy your coffee. You're going to pay for what you did. I have your license plate and I'm going to deliver it to the sheriff."

"Please do," he said, leaning his back against the counter on his elbows and crossing one ankle casually over the other. "I didn't run anyone off the road. I came upon the accident and stopped to help, called the sheriff. And if I caused it, I can afford to fix it. I don't need to run from my problems."

The relaxed posture was gone, however, replaced with something a little more determined, a little more dangerous. He wasn't used to being wrong. Harley would bet on it.

Bex delivered the man's coffee and Mr. Helpful pulled a leather wallet from his back pocket. He fished a twenty from a well-padded line of fifties and turned enough to hand it to Bex. "Hers is on me."

Harley bristled. She couldn't be bought, and certainly not for the price of a large coffee. "Hers in on her own tab, please, Bex."

"Keep the change," he added brightly, nodding to Bex before redirecting his charm back to Harley. "I take care of my responsibilities."

"I doubt you've been responsible for anything in your entire life. You have no idea what it's like to be left behind, having to clean up after the carelessness of others." She was projecting. Harley knew it. But the frustration of her day soured like over-heated milk in her stomach.

He pushed from the counter and grabbed his coffee. Walking past her, he added in a low rumble, "That's quite literally what I do for a living, Harley. I left a business card in the fishbowl. Look me up."

He didn't wait for an answer and disappeared beneath the jingling bell over the door, his stance relaxed again as if her accusation hadn't bothered him.

Harley fumed, her problems swirling in her head like hurricane force winds. The lost product. The contest. Money. Her family circling like vultures waiting on her to fail.

She sipped her coffee, nearly choking as the piping hot liquid burned her tongue.

"*Thit*," she lisped and left the store to confront her life, certain the day couldn't get much worse.

Chapter Three

Chance Gold pulled the door to the sheriff's office closed behind him and stepped back onto the covered walkway along Main Street, satisfaction replacing the anger goading him after his confrontation at the coffee shop. It hadn't taken long to find the office and although the man himself wasn't in, the very efficient front desk clerk Connie quickly gathered his name and information.

When Chance offered a download of his GPS history to prove the timeline of his whereabouts since leaving his apartment in New Orleans before dawn, she'd provided an email address as well. The logger app let him track his mileage for billing purposes and today it would not only earn him money, but apparently save him a ton as well. Once people discovered his identity — more accurately once they discovered his parents' identity — they tended to see dollar signs.

He'd learned early on that everything — and everyone — had a price. The currency and cost may change, but everything was for sale. For example, today he'd played good Samaritan, not just once, when he stopped after seeing the loaded pickup truck skid into the ditch after the driver over corrected the drifting vehicle, but twice when he'd tried to make sure that Harley woman was not going to pass out on the side of the highway. It had cost him an hour of his time, not to mention a slice of his resolve to be the gentleman his father taught him to be, even when the alternative was tempting.

He stalked right to return to his car, eating up the boardwalk with long strides to burn off some of the frustration. That woman's assumption he was guilty pushed a few of his buttons. Like most people he didn't like being accused of something he didn't do. But it was her jab about being left behind to clean up a mess he didn't make that really irked him.

The insecurity needled him more.

A man darted out from the savings and loan as Chance rushed by the door, the two nearly clipping one another in their haste. Chance and the man circled like prize-fighters before recognition erased the tension on their faces.

"Mr. Gold." Everett Fortune drawled out the name more than necessary, punching his right arm forward for a handshake. "I wasn't expecting you in town for a few more days."

Chance accepted the man's hand, stiffening as Everett pumped his arm with more force than necessary. "Please, Mr. Fortune," he said, contained. "For business purposes I use CJ Diamond. Keeps my business interests separate from my family's and I prefer it that way."

The people who came to Chance for his consulting services hardly ever knew his real name. Working under the alias his entire career kept the connection to the Gold name as distant as possible.

Most couldn't decipher his personalized license plate – CSANDAU – diamonds and gold. It was a reminder and a talisman to the duality of his life: public and private closely entwined but carefully hidden.

How Everett Fortune had learned his true identity was not yet clear to Chance but he'd find out eventually.

Everett winked conspiratorially and Chance winced inwardly. He thought back to the same gesture he'd offered Harley in the coffee shop, not to mention the flirting on the side of the highway. He normally liked that people saw him as charming. Today it made him feel slimy. No wonder she hated him even before accusing him of fleeing the scene of an accident.

"Of course, Mr. Diamond." Everett guided Chance to an out-of-the-way space of the boardwalk with a hand to his elbow. A stream of shoppers and construction workers passed by them, their voices mixing with the low rumble of the train passing around the corner.

The noise settled into a steady hum and Everett jumped back into their conversation.

"As I said you're earlier than expected. I'm not sure they're, uh, ready out at the property for your arrival." The man pulled at a cuff nervously.

Working his jaw back and forth, Chance glanced to the steady traffic inching along Main Street, clearing his throat. What else did Everett Fortune want to hide? Chance didn't know if it was just the man's unease about the operation at Fortune's Brew, or if there was more going on. Unwavering instinct told Chance where to put his money, however.

"That's why I'm here early. I find I get a better sense of the operation if you haven't had too much time to plan, put the lipstick on the pig as they say. I can't offer sound advice if I don't know the scope of the issue."

"A very solid approach, planning ahead for all contingencies. You've obviously had good role models in your father and mother."

The words scraped along Chance's spine. And his pride. He knew his father wouldn't betray Chance's confidence. Did his mother have something to do with Everett's insider knowledge of Chance's identity? If Chance worked hard to keep himself separate from his father's name, a name well respected in the industry, he worked doubly hard to keep his connection to *that* woman a national secret. Even if she made it impossible with her choice of brand name: The Gold Standard.

Your father couldn't make his dreams come true, Chance. What makes you think he can help with yours?

How she made her dreams come true was not well known but Chance did not have the blinders most sons wore for their mothers. If he was being polite, she was an unrepentant industry spy and gold-digger. When he wasn't being so nice, the words would make a drunk Marine sound tame.

Chance's jaw clenched. "I didn't know you and my parents were acquainted."

Everett made a back-and-forth gesture with his head. "It's a small circle. Did Sondra mention she and I had a meeting recently where she floated the idea of a merger between our labels?" Everett's tone softened, his words edging out slower and slower.

Chance's attention snapped back to the conversation at the mention of his mother. Her label currently reigned supreme for small batch whiskey in the US and was rapidly gaining traction in Europe.

Merger? Chase pushed the word around his brain. His mother likely wanted to acquire Fortune's Brew as part of her own distillery brand, if not crush it outright. Fifteen years ago, Fortune's Brew delivered The Gold Standard's only defeat at the Crescent City MicroLiquor Spirits Competition and Sondra Gold did not believe in second place. They likely would have continued to dominate the market had Elias and Vivianne Fortune not died on the way home that very afternoon.

"That's news to me, Mr. Fortune. My mother is not one to share so a merger doesn't sound like something she'd willingly do."

The fifty-something man squared his shoulders, tucked his chin against the finely ribbed neckline of the cashmere turtleneck. He tugged at the hem of the skinny jacket; his frame too bulky for the narrow cut. Chance recognized the brands. He had a few himself but was now seriously considering a change in his taste of clothing. He'd always dressed for success, not dressed to be an ass.

Non-plussed at the correction, Everett let the gator-wide smile slide across his face. "Negotiation always starts someplace as I'm sure you're aware. A favorable report from you will surely improve our standing on the market when we sell."

Not *if* we sell, *when* we sell. Everett had no intention of making Fortune's Brew a winner. That soured things for Chance. He liked winning. He wasn't here to put a pretty bow on a bargain for his mother to snatch up.

"And you've hired me to evaluate your operation, not negotiate the sale."

"There's more than just a potential sale on the line, Mr. Diamond," Everett added, the cadence of his speech slowing. "She's agreed to nominate me for a position on the board of The Gold Standard. I'm sure you understand what that could mean in our business."

Not if you're selling out your company, Chance reasoned internally. "I see. Have you mentioned this to the family?"

"Not yet, which is why the NDA you have is with me and not with the business entity. I expect you to honor the confidentiality of this information."

Chance had to unclench his jaw to respond. "I always honor my agreements, Mr. Fortune. How you and my mother conduct business in not my concern. I'm not connected to her company and," *more importantly*, Chance added silently, "she's not connected to mine."

Despite his efforts to remain separate, Chance knew his instinct was correct about Everett's knowledge of his identity when they'd signed the contract for his consulting services a few days ago. How he knew this, Chance didn't know. Usually, he asked better questions, ferreting out any details a client was trying to keep hidden. Hearing about his mother's interest in Fortune's Brew put a new twist on his arrival.

Chance thought of backing out right there and then. He'd worked very hard to maintain a respectable distance between The Gold Standard Brewing and Diamond Spirits Consulting. It had taken him the last nine years to build a name on his own as a whiskey sommelier. While his dad was CEO of the number two label in the US, Isaac Gold was well respected in the industry. He didn't want his dad's reputation to open any doors for him; and Chance wanted help from his mother even less. He'd not needed her since she'd walked out when he was eight.

"Come to think about it, this is a pretty sizeable conflict of interest for me, Mr. Fortune. I don't think I'm the right person to work with you on this."

Everett's thick eyebrows bunched together. "You're being hasty, Mr. Diamond. I expect nothing from you except your expertise about our label." His lips parted in what Chance suspected passed for a reassuring smile. "You know the market and that is all I want; to know where Fortune's Brew sits on the food chain."

He considered his options. More importantly, he considered his current situation. He'd already spent the last few days researching what he could find about Fortune's Brew's distillation process. Not that much existed. Not even Everett had the recipe apparently.

Walking out now rankled his sense of pride in the job he did. He'd walked away once in the past year to protect his sense of integrity. Chance hoped he wouldn't regret not walking away today. But he had a reputation to protect and a business to run.

He could stay impartial, even if Everett Fortune wanted him to do otherwise. "Good enough. Just remember I'm not here to grease the wheels with what happens between you and my mother."

"I understand, Mr. Diamond." Relief flowed out of Everett Fortune. "I've not shared the details of the offer yet with my niece and ask that you keep it confidential for now as well."

Chance bristled at the deception, but he was under obligation to Everett, not Charlotte Fortune or Fortune's Brew. Of course, he was using an alias for business purposes, so his high road was limited. Still, he wasn't pretending to be anything he wasn't. CJ Diamond had a reputation for knowing whiskey and whiskey distillation. Everett was paying his fee, and Everett could divulge the details of their arrangement as he saw fit. Whatever his final report to Everett said, it would be based on Chance's unbiased opinion of the brand's potential. What Everett Fortune did with that information was not Chance's responsibility.

But it rankled his pride. He could make Fortune's Brew

a top contender. He'd done it with other distilleries with less promise. Everett kept his gaze narrow, obviously seeing short term profit over long term growth and sustainability.

"Will I see you or your sister at the distillery?" Chance was eager to be on his way and start work. Everett and his sister, Elsbeth, controlled forty-eight percent of Fortune's Brew stock. Not enough on their own to force a sale.

"My husband and I have a short vacation planned and my sister has very little to do with the business."

Yet she'd gone on national television and promoted another brand over her own. Interesting, Chance noted to himself.

"Then we'll talk soon, Mr. Fortune."

Chance continued down the walkway, his dress shoes making a hard *thump* against the wooden walkway in rhythm to the *thump* of his heart against his rib cage. Chance didn't like someone thinking they had the upper hand. That was his play, and he did it well.

Everett followed at a clipped pace; arms clasped behind his back as if in serious thought. "Again, about my niece..."

Eager to get on with his day, Chance tempered his disappointment. "What you decide to tell your niece is your concern, Mr. Fortune. The trust gives you the authority to have a third-party evaluation done prior to the assets being distributed to the beneficiaries. Your mother is still the sole trustee, correct? And her three percent is needed to put you and your sister's votes over the necessary fifty percent to gain control."

Everett stopped short, then rushed to catch up as Chance descended the first set of boardwalk buildings and crossed the street to the second set. The luscious aroma of apple pie floated out from the River City Cafe, luring in customers and making Chance's stomach grumble in protest as he passed without stopping.

Everett came even with Chance once again, grabbing his coat's cuff and stopping their forward motion. "I'm surprised you know that Mr. Diamond."

Chance pulled his sleeve from Everett's grasp. "I requested a copy of the trust deed from your attorney, as stated in my contract. I have to know the legal restrictions and ramifications before I go into a situation such as yours. You and your sister only have voting authority to sell if," Chance lifted his chin, looking over Everett's shoulder, and repeated the document verbatim, "*the primary beneficiary, Charlotte Vivianne Fortune, doesn't have the business operating with the high likelihood of profit in the estimation of the trustee by the time she turns twenty-five.*"

The man fussed with lapels of his jacket, his expression sour. "I don't know that I like that you've pried into our business affairs as such, Mr. Diamond."

Chance went statue-still and narrowed his focus. "Then fire me, Mr. Fortune."

Chance played a mean game of chicken. Like everything else, he didn't lose. The ultimatum was a calculated risk. Chance was not just his name but what he liked to take. He'd not built a name for himself playing it safe. He'd never been wrong so far.

Everett hesitated but Chance read the decision when the pucker disappeared from the tight line of the man's mouth. "That's not what I meant. Just please remember your contract is with me personally, not with Fortune's Brew. Our non-disclosure is very specific."

"Yes, it is, Mr. Fortune." Chance narrowed his gaze. "And it works both ways. Your contract is with CJ Diamond, not Chance Gold. I hope you'll remember that."

Crossing the final length of the boardwalk, Chance retrieved his keys from his pocket, the familiar rush of adrenaline as he opened the car door and settled against the leather seat of the classic Eldorado. True, his career was made through change and advancing techniques used for generations but behind that he held a great respect for the old ways.

"I'm going to finish up my tour of the local eateries and bars. I'll be out to the distillery in a few hours, Mr. Fortune."

Everett hesitated, the telling pucker back.

"Have you even told her you've hired me?"

Everett studied Chance beneath hooded eyes. "She'll be informed today." Short, clipped words.

And likely would not be too pleased about his arrival, Chance added internally. His brain flashed back to the feisty coffee connoisseur that morning. He was on a roll for pissing off women today. Why should Charlotte Fortune be any different?

"Lautaro Sanchez is our master distiller. You'll likely find him in the still house. There's an office toward the back. I'll let him know you're arriving today. Shall we say around six? They're usually wrapping up things around then."

"Thank you, Mr. Fortune, but please don't notify him." Chance knew he would anyway, but at least he'd done what he could. "I prefer to see the operation as real world as possible."

"Very well, Mr. Diamond."

Chance started the engine, the rumble a soothing white noise, and backed away from the building under the scrutiny of Everett Fortune. The man yanked his cell phone from a jacket pocket before Chance even made it down the street.

The lunch hour was just beginning, and Chance wanted

to make a quick circuit of some restaurants he'd tagged online. They all served alcohol and he wanted to understand the place Fortune's Brew held for the locals. He'd only found two restaurants in New Orleans that served the brand, and a half dozen more up the highway in Lafayette. Not strong market placement for a local brand that once took top honors at Crescent City, the penultimate competition in North America for small distilleries. He didn't know what kind of businesswoman Charlotte Fortune professed to be, but he intended to find out.

Then tell her where she'd gone wrong.

Chapter Four

C hance eased up on the gas as he took yet another bend in a road as unforgiving as the waterway it mimicked. The GPS map showed him on single slash of yellow in a puddle of blue. The thick trees only hinted at a sliver of the full river now and again. Mother nature wanted some things to be kept a secret.

Without warning, his thoughts returned to the raspberry chocolate dream Frappuccino in the coffee shop. Chance had an ego. He knew it. He usually kept it in check, but that woman had not seen one thing about him she'd liked from the moment they'd met.

Normally it wouldn't bother him. He'd learned long ago not to base his own self-image on the actions of others. Years of therapy as a kid had reinforced the idea. If you weren't good enough to make your own mother stick around, what hope was there for others?

His personal line buzzed on the phone and he swiped open the FaceMeet app, silencing the classic rock playlist - and his own insecurities. "Hey Leo."

Leo Quinn, his longtime friend and potential business

partner, adjusted the camera angle, leaning in. His square face filled the screen, the dark skin and darker eyes almost lost in the dim lighting. "Weston declined our meeting."

The weight of failure thrummed across Chance's shoulders. Weston Ventures was their last hope for A Shot and a Beer, the whiskey and craft brewery Chance and Leo planned to develop in the French Quarter. They had the building all lined up at a prime corner location. A top New Orleans chef ready to jump ship and bring her rising star to their kitchen. Vendors waiting in droves to stock their shelves.

They just needed money to build the shelves and stock the kitchen.

The partnership agreement was sitting in Chance's office waiting for his final signature. He didn't think about why he hadn't signed it yet, instead blaming the demands of his work on the delay.

"Did he give a reason?"

A female hand skimmed over Leo's shoulder, a slip of a purple silk robe visible, the flash of a turquoise and pearl necklace, but the face remained out of the camera's range. A female voice mumbled in the background; the words unintelligible, but it didn't remind Chance of Leo's high maintenance girlfriend. He'd not met that woman either, come to think of it. Leo liked to play the field.

"Soon, sweetheart." Leo crooned over his shoulder. An impatient huff as the click-clack of heels faded against the tile. Leo's attention followed the woman, though Chance couldn't see her, and didn't return until a very loud slam to a door echoed across the phone.

When Leo spoke again, his voice dropped an octave. "Diamond Investments and Lazy River are unknown to him." Leo cleared his throat, looking off camera. "His secretary's second assistant said the risk wasn't something he was willing to carry."

Chance could mouth the next words out of Leo's mouth, seeing the man's obsidian eyes peer at him like a drunken frat brother trying to convince the chapter's scholarship officer that failing organic chemistry wouldn't impact his desire to become a master whiskey distiller before he turned 30. "If we ask your mother Weston would back us. Why won't you ask her?"

So many reasons pinballed through his head. Sondra Gold walked out on her family when Chance was eight. While she'd not disappeared, she'd made no attempt to be a part of her son's life. Chance had no desire to be a part of hers now.

"You know the answer to that, Leo."

Chance wanted to build something, but he wanted to do it on his own. It was why he liked consulting. Everything he did was in the background. He had the opportunity to go in and create a strong foundation the owners could make successful. It gave him a sense of success without the question of whether his parentage or his skills had played a part.

An ugly twist of Leo's mouth sharpened the razor's edge of his cheekbones. His pupils constricted to pinpricks of ebony. "I know your relationship with your mother is —"

He cut off Leo with tight, clipped words. "I don't have a relationship with her, Leo."

"Fine, then your father could at least open doors for us. He's respected in the industry and you still like him. Damn he's the CEO of the number two label. That counts for something. Not using your parents' connections was fine and noble when we thought we could get the money on our own. But we're at the point where a Shot and a Beer is about to be filed in the *has been* category before it gets off the ground." Leo's phone dinged at a series of incoming text messages and he snatched up the device and silenced it, slamming it against the desk. "You're the golden Gold, Chance. Why not use it?"

"Last time I used my name to your benefit I had to walk away from my job with the distiller's association." The first hint of anger edged Chance's voice. He had to will his foot back from the accelerator, loosen his grip on the steering wheel.

"They were never going to let an underdog like me have a shot if I played fair."

Leo finally had the good sense stay quiet while Chance digested the regret at having to choose between friendship and business. He'd chosen friendship and until now, hadn't doubted the decision.

"You run your business your way and let me run my business my way, Leo. I will not ride the coattails of my parents."

His friend huffed back in his chair, waving his hand dismissively at Chance's point. "I won't have a business much longer at this rate. The orders we got after that reality couple called us out on *Pareja Feliz* didn't turn into long term sales like I hoped."

Product placement will get you noticed, but you need a quality product to get a customer. Leo had trouble with the second part. Chance kept that little piece of consulting advice to himself.

He again felt the prickle of doubt scratch at his instinct. How Leo had ended up on the Costa Rican reality show starring Everett Fortune's sister bothered him. He didn't believe in coincidence. He should cancel this job with Fortune's Brew but since walking away from his gig as a judge for the distillers' association, business had fallen off.

Apparently, having integrity could hurt your reputation.

He had a feeling it was the other judge he'd gone up against, however, using the power of her national platform to sink him. Professionalism at its finest. It's why he had rules for his work, and he didn't break the rules.

Leo did a little side to side motion with his head, a swatch of inky hair falling over one eye. Chance always wondered if he'd practiced the maneuver. "I need to do well at Crescent City. I don't have a pedigree like yours. You're proof the Gold DNA is truly golden. They'd never let you fail."

Chance was good at what he did. His track record proved it. But without the pseudonym he'd never know if the people hiring him were legitimately interested in his skills or, like Everett Fortune, were trying to curry favor. His dad wouldn't play games behind the scenes - hell his dad wouldn't even give him an internship during college. Chance had found his own and appreciated standing on his own two feet. But his mother...well she thrived on manipulation.

It wasn't easy but Chance had managed to create his alter ego and keep it separate. He'd chosen the name intentionally. Diamond to his mother's gold. It was his father's name, but she'd made it a household name.

"*In a quarter mile, make a right,*" Mick Jagger announced from the GPS. "*What the hell is a quarter mile, mate?*"

It was Chance's turn to sigh. "I'm on the road Leo. Let me think on it and get back to you. We'll do this. We've been planning it since college. A Shot and a Beer is going to happen."

Leo stared blankly, the contempt showing a split second before the call disconnected. Chance made the turn, angling his car into a parking spot in the last row at *Gastineaux's de Louisiane.*

Had his chest not heaved beneath the struggle to contain his anger at the last few moments, Chance might have been more awed at the sight before him. Gastineaux's occupied a massive two-story structure, the intricate iron-work on the one-hundred-foot veranda leading visitors from the parking lot to the shaded sitting area beneath the porch. Floor to ceiling windows occupied the front of the building and the grand entrance boasted a massive stained glass magnolia tree over the double doors.

He shut off the engine and pinched the bridge of his nose, trying to massage away the spike of stress piercing behind his eyeballs.

His work. His connections. His name had to be enough.

He had to be enough.

As a kid, he'd gotten caught up in the belief that his mother had left because of him. That somehow, his love and presence hadn't been enough to keep her around. Even at eight, Chance understood how a marriage could fail; most of his friends had divorced parents.

But their parents had never disappeared like his mother. Therefore, there must have been something wrong with him. It had taken a few years for him to understand the fault was with her, not him. Still, the crack was there. Chance harbored self-reliance like a talisman.

Pushing that all aside he exited the car, sweeping his gaze around the property. The building was shaded beneath a canopy of cypress and oak trees, the wide trunks twisted and split, the branches sweeping the ground like the hem of a woman's hoop skirt.

Smaller outbuildings dotted the back of the property and jutted out over the water where men and women perched along the wharf, in lawn chairs, on coolers, and on the deck with their feet draped over the sides, fishing poles in hand.

His research indicated this was the most popular restaurant in thirty miles. If Fortune's Brew hoped to entice customers across the nation, they needed to win over the hometown first. Mostly pickups filled the parking lot, an indication of a mostly male clientele, but the lot was packed. It usually meant good things about the food.

Chance pushed through the large double doors into a small foyer. Concrete *faux-bois* benches sat snug against the wall beneath a Baccarat crystal chandelier. A group of several well-dressed women waited at the hostess station. The two twenty-somethings, chic, a matching softness to their features and coloring, waited with bored expressions. They wore identical teal scarves, but beyond that, they appeared night and day.

One clicked her phone incessantly, phubbing her companions, not even bothering to look up. "That man of mine is working my last nerve, Pips," she muttered.

"That man of yours is a cheating asshole." Pips responded with a roll of her shoulders to match the roll of her dark brown eyes.

Phubber sighed dramatically. "We were on. A. Break."

"Not even my degree in marketing could spin a trip to visit your parents as a relationship break," Pips whispered, crinkling her nose slightly. The young woman turned and smiled apologetically at Chance, the change in her immediate and profound, lifting the tension from her shoulders and erasing it from her eyes. "Sorry about that."

Chance waved away her apology. "No need," he whispered back. "Cheating assholes should be called out."

The young woman laughed behind her hand; her rich

brown eyes framed by a long fringe of lash. The older woman turned, silver-haired, elegant in her casual slacks and silk blouse, her face showing the passage of time with deep creases at the eyes and mouth. She still had a peaches and cream complexion touched by only a swipe of lipstick.

"Yes, they should," she joined in their private joke. "But not in public."

"Sorry, not sorry," huffed the phubber, still not taking her eyes off the phone.

"Have either of you heard from Charlotte?"

Chance's attention sharpened.

The phubber scoffed. "Not if it requires her to use a phone. She's the only twenty-something on the planet that can't use a smart phone."

Pips, however, nodded. "It either said she's on her way or she's put on weight. That girl cannot text to save her life."

The older woman's eyes lifted as the door behind them opened. Chance stepped back and Everett Fortune filled the gap, bending his head to kiss the older woman on the cheek. "Sorry I'm late, mom. The bank took longer than expected this morning."

When Everett's attention pulled out, his mouth puckered at the sight of Chance, but the hostess came forward to save the moment from turning awkward.

"Afternoon Ms. Fortune, Everett. We have your tables all set up in the back. Y'all can follow me."

The foursome disappeared into the restaurant, but they gave him an indication of what he'd be working with on this job. Charlotte Fortune would likely be a somewhat prissy prima donna looking for a distraction from her boring life. She may have spent the last five years trying to make Fortune's Brew a success, but he doubted she'd tried really hard.

Oh, and she apparently couldn't text to save her life.

While he waited, Chance let his attention wander to the drawings and pictures of the restaurant dotting the entranceway that showed the history of the place, including a planned construction of a bed and breakfast and meeting venue upstairs. A "Pardon our Dust" placard near the door announced some ongoing construction and an array of architectural renderings promised a new and upgraded dining room by the end of the summer as well.

The hostess returned; a grumpy baby now shelved on her hip. She greeted Chance with a genuine smile reaching kind eyes the color of brandy. "Welcome to Gastineaux's. It'll be about ten minutes for a table, or you can sit at the bar." The baby boy grabbed a handful of her straight brown hair, pulling it toward his drooling mouth as she gathered up a menu and set of silverware. When she freed her hair, he went for the nametag. Miranda, it read.

"The bar is fine, Miranda. Thanks."

Her face brightened at the use of her name. "Right this way."

Chance fell into step behind Miranda, the baby's eyes lasering in with an uncomfortable intensity. He'd never considered having a family and had no brothers or sisters with which to practice being the cool uncle to nieces and nephews. After his parents' divorce his father remarried quickly but Evie, as much as Chance cared for her, was not mother material. Neither was his mom, apparently. Or she wouldn't have left for 21 years.

They weaved through a narrow aisle between the cable spool tables still ladened with dirty dishes. Wait staff dashed between the dining room and the kitchen, loaded trays spilling the tantalizing aromas of boiled shrimp and fried catfish into the dining room. "Your reputation smells justified."

"You'll have to tell me after you eat if the taste lives up to the smell." She glanced part way over her shoulder. "Is this your first time here?"

"Yes." His eyes found the path the Fortunes had taken but could see nothing beyond the main dining room. "In town for business. My secret sources tell me this is the place for seafood."

Miranda slid the menu and silverware at an empty spot at the bar and nodded toward the bartender. "Your secret sources didn't lie. Bar's full service." She waved at the bartender. "Hudson there will take your order when you're ready." As she stepped back, the baby boy waved and blew spit bubbles.

Chance laughed and waved back as he propped his hip on the stool. "You have a future host in your arms, Miranda. He's tops at customer service already."

Miranda hiked the baby a little higher. "Yes, he is. Unless you're serving vegetables then he's not so much a happy boy."

"I can't really blame him on that."

Miranda bobbed her head. "Enjoy your lunch."

Chance sat back, crossing an ankle over his knee and turning his stool to look out over the crowd. The place was comfortably busy. Most lunch service was done by one or one-thirty, with only tourists and executives hanging out past that. The dining room, and what he could see of the back-room tables, was filled with a mix of tourists, office staff, and blue collar workers. The inside of the house wasn't much more refined than the outer but that didn't seem to matter. The food must be good.

The swinging doors separating the main dining room

MAGGIE PRESTON

from the back of the restaurant swished open and a waiter hurried to the point of order system used by the staff. As he punched at the screen Everett Fortune pushed from the back, his eyes zeroing in on Chance in a single heartbeat.

The older man's posture stiffened, leaving Chance again with the impression he was hiding something. Beside the offer from The Gold Standard, that is. Why Everett would want to hide that puzzled Chance. If the other family had to vote on the continuation of the business, wouldn't knowing their options be beneficial?

Unless Everett didn't intend to share the proceeds from the sale.

"Welcome to Gastineaux's."

Chase turned to find a man a few years younger than himself setting a napkin on the bar, adding a one-two shake of salt before placing a glass of water within arm's reach. Condensation already beaded the exterior but when Chance picked it up the glass didn't stick to the napkin.

"Not many bartenders know that trick anymore, Hudson." Chance raised his glass in salute before taking a sip, the cold water washing away some of his tension.

"You hang out in too many bars if you do," the bartender laughed, picking up a blue rag to wipe down the unoccupied space between Chance and the wall.

"Hazard of the job." Chance motioned to the back of the bar where an army of backlit bottles filled glass shelves, the prism of light shifting the rainbows reflected across the mirror's surface. "What would you recommend?"

"That depends on the drinker. Are you adventurous or status quo?" The man abandoned the rag and stepped closer to the promised land of half-filled bottles from color-less to a golden hickory. "We've got it all from a nice chardonnay to granddaddy's secret recipe whiskey."

"Whiskey, definitely." Chance wanted to get to a recommendation without leading. If Fortune's Brew could stand up, maybe it had a chance.

Hudson's hands rested on two bottles and the labels seemed similar enough they probably came from the same distillery. "Do you want something smooth or maybe a little sharper?"

"Let's go with smooth before two in the afternoon. Besides, I need to be somewhere for a meeting in a few hours and I'm going to need to be at full court press for this one."

The bartender plucked a bottle from the battalion on the shelves. "Good choice." In practiced motions, Hudson grabbed a shot glass, returned to the bar, and poured a small draught. He looked down the counter as another customer waved for his attention. "This is technically moonshine according to the distillery but if you want smooth, there's nothing better. Taste first, then we'll figure out how you want it fashioned. I'll be right back."

Chance lifted the glass and held it toward the natural light filtering in from the front windows, a near colorless, clear liquid to the eye. He inhaled gently, the fragrances of vanilla and mint filling his senses and prodding memories from the recesses of his brain. How his Gran's inviting kitchen could produce such a god-awful fruitcake at Christmas amazed him and his dad, but they ate it dutifully, dumping the remains far from her home at the end of the day.

Finally, Chance tasted a small sip then a larger one, the buttery warmth sliding over his tongue to hover for a second then ease down his throat, the final spicy fruitiness lingering on his lips and palate.

Damn, that was good.

He finished the shot, slid it back across the bar with a satisfied exhale. He'd purposefully not looked at the label, wanting an unbiased opinion of whatever he tasted. Now that he had, he reached over and spun the bottle.

"Fortune's Brew. Where good fortune meets good whiskey."

Charlotte Fortune had a gold mine just waiting to be discovered.

If she could keep her product in the bottle rather than on the highway.

The grin tipped up the corners of Chance's mouth as the spreading warmth of the liquor kicked up his adrenaline a notch. When he showed up early for his six o'clock meeting this evening, he'd find out more about what was behind making this kickass whiskey.

"What did you think of Lucky Lady?" Hudson returned to his spot at the bar.

Chance leaned back with exaggerated slowness, his feet finding the foot rail with ease. "I've had very expensive liquors that didn't taste that good."

"It's the best we have. I'm going to miss the brand when I leave town in a few months." Hudson held up the bottle in an unspoken *want another*?

Chance nodded. "An old fashioned, please," he answered the unspoken question and opened his menu then realized he'd left his glasses in the car. The accessory was new to him, a birthday present from his ophthalmologist for his thirtieth.

When the hell did I get to be thirty?

He shook his head, wanting to distract his thoughts from the tick-tick-tick of the clock in his head. Time was running out to get things in motion with Leo for A Shot and a Beer. They were going to lose the conditional lease Labor Day weekend if they couldn't start the renovations on the property. The owner wasn't willing to let it sit empty any longer.

He pushed the deadline aside, bringing his attention back to the present. The future was too uncertain to see much. "I'd better get some food to go with this. What's good?"

Hudson pulled a clean glass from beneath the bar and tipped the bottle generously. "Everything." He looked up at Chance from beneath hooded eyes, his complexion swallowing the low light and dusky shadows that always hung around a bar. "I know you'll think I'm saying that because I work here but the owner can cook. I wouldn't want to hang out with the guy on your side of the bar, but he knows how to set the heat without watering the eyes."

"Then pick something for me, please." Chance closed the menu. "Dealer's choice. Appetizer. Main. Dessert."

"You are adventurous. OK, one surprise lunch coming up." Hudson reclaimed the menu and tipped his head before retreating through the doors to the kitchen.

Chance settled back with his drink, savoring the warmth and subtle notes of the moonshine. There was little difference between whiskey and moonshine unless you were talking to the distiller. Some liked the illegal connotations of the word moonshine. Others thought whiskey was more refined. Chance didn't care what you called it – it was the taste that counted.

And Fortune's Brew had what counted.

The liquor smoothed out the tension thrumming through his muscles, but the conversations with Everett then Leo would not be silenced even beneath the muting effect of a good drink.

Leo reminded himself that Chance meant well, not that good intentions helped. But he was right, Chance admitted reluctantly. Without the financing of an investor like Steve Weston, A Shot and a Beer was a shot in the dark.

Hudson returned and slid a red food basket lined with paper toward Chance, four fried round balls centered with a ramekin of sauce. Chance lifted a brow in question, but Hudson zipped his lips, so Chance picked up one of the appetizers and dipped it in the sauce. Bravely he took a bite, his mouth watering as Hudson predicted as the spicy mix of meat, rice, and mustard bathed his taste buds. He groaned appreciatively, taking another bite without saying a word.

"I know, right?" Hudson gestured to the rapidly disappearing starter. "Boudin balls."

Chance swallowed, licking the mustard from his fingers. "Boudin balls. Is that the Louisiana version of a Rocky Mountain oyster? Is some gator going to track me down because you cut off his reason for living?"

Hudson laughed loudly, swiping the basket back from Chance as the last crumb disappeared. "Nah, man. Boudin is a Cajun sausage. The chef makes ours fresh. Sweetest mix of pork, rice, and the holy trinity you'll find."

The basket disappeared beneath the bar and Hudson dealt with a group of customers at the other end while Chance again watched the crowd. He liked the small town feel of Belle Terre and had spent his early days in a town not very different. When his dad had relocated their family to Memphis, small town life went away. He wasn't sure if he missed it some days. Chance turned back from his walk down memory as Hudson delivered his main.

"Today's special. Spicy crawfish-tasso hollandaise served over eggs benedict with a parmesan cornmeal waffle and asparagus."

The server disappeared before the first bite and again, Chance resisted the urge to lick the plate. The subtle bite of the cayenne didn't overpower either the eggs or the asparagus. The waffle, so light and fluffy, held up against the hollandaise. It was almost a shame to cover it with anything but butter.

Just as Chance forked the last bite into his mouth, a reflection in the mirror over the bar caught his attention and he looked up in time to see an older Hispanic man spirited through the dining room by the hostess, his shoulders rigid. The man paused outside the double doors, his attention going back to the main entrance. Lautaro Sanchez. Chance recognized the master distiller at Fortune's Brew. He had been with the family for more than forty years. Chance wanted to meet the man who'd beaten his mother all those years ago.

Chance catalogued the people waiting in the room when Lautaro looked over the swinging doors but remained outside. The older woman had to be the matriarch, Trudy Fortune. Holding only a very small piece of the overall business, she had all the power as sole trustee. Everett's younger sister, Elsbeth, was an equal partner with him but she'd married and moved to Costa Rica with her husband many years ago and spent her time making a reality tv show. The two younger women were likely cousins, the daughters of Elsbeth Fortune.

He was about to wave Hudson over to cancel dessert when Ms. Raspberry Chocolate Dream Cappuccino trotted into Gastineaux's, her shoulders tight, her grim face focused straight ahead as she made a beeline for Lautaro.

Something tightened in Chance's gut, but it wasn't the anger or frustration, or even indignation he expected after their earlier encounters. It was interest. She was short - he couldn't help but notice her lack of height out on the side of the highway as she'd tried to crane her neck over the circle of spectators. He'd noticed it again inside the coffee shop, which was why he leaned on the counter, wanting to be more eye level with the woman. He topped out at over six four and women in the past said it made him intimidating.

Add to her height the rumpled look - torn jeans he doubted she'd bought intentionally torn, and an untucked and wrinkled yellow button down she tugged to smooth self-consciously. The ball cap was gone, the angled cut of loose waves swinging just beneath her chin at the front.

Sturdy was the word that came to mind, but it wasn't an insult. The woman was full of curves, though he doubted she saw it that way. Women never did see their assets and boy did that untucked shirt skim one of her assets. Chance dragged his focus back, not needing a hard-on in the middle of a busy restaurant. Olive-toned skin deepened beneath the interior lighting of the restaurant, but Chance remembered it in the sun, the pale gold undertones both sharper and softer in the natural light.

She reached her target, Lautaro Sanchez, who handed her something he couldn't see. The young woman took it and stuffed it in her back pocket. They hunched together, whispering, her expression tight and angry, his relaxed and soothing. Lautaro looked up and noticed Chance's gaze and pulled the other woman into the back room. The doors flapped shut.

Chance fell back against the bar, arms crossed.

Just who the hell was she?

Chapter Five

The road wound along the Lower Atchafalaya River until it skirted Bayou Cane then ribboned like a worn piece of black velvet through the hackberry and peppervine fighting for the last dredge of sunlight with the oaks and elms. Harley's own self-image reminded her of a tangle of kudzu and poison ivy.

She'd been fighting for Fortune's Brew the last five years, playing a combination of Rachel Ray and mad scientist with the family's moonshine recipe. When she started, youth and arrogance told her she had all the time in the world. Her parents' Will gave her full control - under Granny's guardianship of course - until she was twenty-five. Now that birthday loomed just six weeks away. Time slipped faster than panty hose on Miss Perla's freshly waxed floors in the main house.

Not that Harley was likely to be wearing panty hose, but Mama always made sure the floors were as shiny as a new penny. She'd said, *This house may be older than dirt but that doesn't mean it has to look it.* Daddy would laugh and tell her she was going to shine a hole through the floor and mama would reply, *That's ok. It'll be a well-polished hole.*

The memory caught Harley between breaths, a twisting heaviness that squeezed her heart. They'd been hurrying home after winning top honors at the Crescent City Micro-Liquor Spirits Competition to make her piano recital. She'd made them promise to make it, not wanting to face the nasty wrath of Miss Doylene alone when she missed a note or screwed up the arpeggio she'd struggled to master.

She'd been crushed when their faces were missing from the audience even though everyone else - Granny, Miss Perla and Mr. Shaw, her uncles, even her aunt and cousins - had been there watching. When the state troopers showed up at the end, they'd brought the news. Harley didn't touch a piano for years.

Restoring Fortune's Brew to what her mom and dad had built became her dream. It had been his dream after inheriting from his father, a dream her mom had shared with the same amount of passion she had for her husband.

Granny, on the other hand, wanted more these days. She'd sacrificed a husband and a son to the whiskey gods. She'd had enough. When Uncle Everett and Aunt Elsbeth voted to sell, she'd throw in with them and call it good. The Fortune family recipe, a legend for more than seven generations in the history of southern Louisiana, would be packed away, or worse, sold to someone who'd want to change it.

That was the news she expected to hear at Uncle Everett's family lunch meeting but no, it was worse. He'd hired a consultant to come in and evaluate the business. More to the point, evaluate her.

Someone knowledgeable of the market and market trends who can assess Fortune's Brew's probability for long term success.

Uncle Everett's words reverberated in her head, the

bitterness biting her tongue even as the words swamped her brain. CJ Diamond arrived at six tonight, which didn't give her much time. She'd show him professional. She'd show him success.

She didn't have a clue how she'd show some overweight know-it-all wanting to change their operation, so it tasted like every other whiskey out there that she and Lautaro knew what they were doing.

That Lautaro, at least, knew what he was doing. Other than her, he was the only one with the receipt to Fortune's Brew. And that was how it would stay as long as she controlled things.

Go home, Mr. Know-it-all. We've had the same recipe and distillation process for two hundred years and are doing just fine by ourselves.

If you ignored all the failures. If you ignored the crap Dean had pulled and the pressure from the family to sell and the dwindling bank account needing CPR to keep breathing.

If you ignored the five grand she'd stuck in the mail that morning. Crescent City required either annual sales of ten thousand units or two top-tier finishes in qualifying events. Two very long months and three tough competitions stood between her and Crescent City in May. Miss that, and her five grand was gone, along with Fortune's Brew. She didn't have the money to continue beyond May.

Maybe that wouldn't be such a bad thing. The thought came unwelcome, and guilt pushed it back into the dark spaces of Harley's consciousness. No. This was what she was raised to do. Daddy had said Fortune's Brew was their legacy, their mark on the world. She was a part of that legacy. The only one still fighting to keep it.

She groaned, a low rumble that itched her lungs and dented her soul.

Harley turned right off the highway as the sun completed its escape beneath the horizon, the Mercedes swaying on the dips and ruts of the dirt road connecting the Fortunes to the rest of the world. On cue, she passed the massive oak that had once guarded the entrance to the property, cut down in the early twentieth century by hurricane winds.

As was the tradition taught by her grandfather, she waved at the drunk skunk carved into the trunk, the gesture always bringing a smile no matter what else was on her mind. The Fortunes were built on traditions and legacies, the ghosts of her predecessors hovering everywhere on the property.

She doubted the road had changed much since her namesake, Charlie Fortune, won the land in a poker game a few years after the Louisiana Purchase. Fresh off the boat from Ireland, he'd thought he'd struck it rich with that deed in his hands. He hitched a ride with a group of Chitimacha Indians traveling to the area and when they left him at the river, he sat down and cried. The only thing this swampy piece of mess was good for was growing mosquitoes and heartbreak.

He'd been right on both accounts.

It didn't take him long to hobble together a still like his daddy's granddaddy had run in the home country and Fortune's Brew was born.

Harley guided the ancient Mercedes through the fence her own granddaddy had built as a kid to the still house her daddy had built as a teen. History held this place together like a corset on a buxom brunette - tight enough to keep things from moving but showing enough to keep things interesting.

She killed the engine when Lautaro poked his head out of the still house, illuminated in the cone of light from the overhead spot. His weathered face showed signs of a squall, his gaze leading hers toward the main house.

Harley's indigestion spiked at the familiar gold sports car in the driveway.

She pushed open the door with the toe of her shoe and jumped from the belly of the car. "What the hell is he doing here?" Harley forced the words from between clenched teeth, the spike of adrenaline tensing her jaw. "How'd he find us?"

"The consultant?" Lautaro met her before she stormed inside, his palms on her shoulders to bring her body to a halt. "I imagine your uncle gave him our address. Have you met him?"

Harley let Lautaro push her back to the car. "I think so." She explained about Dean's claims regarding the accident and how she'd confronted the guy at the coffee shop. "He's not supposed to be here for another few hours."

"Then he's early." Lautaro's accent was never stronger than when he tried to calm her down. "He arrived with me after the lunch. He's been here since."

He'd been there for at least a couple of hours then. Harley's mind raced. Maybe this guy would hold a grudge over her accusation about the accident. He could royally screw her over. She mentally slapped herself. She'd done it again. Even when she hadn't intended to do anything but protect her business.

"This has got to be some kind of conflict of interest then. If he was involved in the accident that —"

Her friend and surrogate father gave her *the look* and

Harley withered beneath the common sense poured into the steady gaze. Her shoulders drooped. "Dean."

The one word was all she needed to remind her Dean was not exactly reliable. Not as a boyfriend. Not as a worker. Worse yet, she'd let herself forget how he liked to manipulate the truth and now she was at a disadvantage with the consultant. While being at a disadvantage was familiar territory, she didn't like starting out that way with someone who had the power to shut down Fortune's Brew.

How could she fix this? There had to be something - apologize, beg, bargain. "What's he doing?"

"He's looking at our inventory."

Harley's stomach knotted. She hadn't updated the files last night before going to bed. She usually did that on Fridays but last Friday she'd been dealing with a mix up on an order for their primary client in Lafayette. The frantic list of things she hadn't taken the time to fix or file flitted through her mind like moths around a flame.

"Breathe, Harley." Lautaro gave her a little shake. "It is what it is. Our product is what counts. Not our files and checking little boxes." He checked a box in the air to drive home the point. "Fortune's Brew can stand up to any outsider."

She dragged in a frenzied breath, nodded her head once to Lautaro. "I know that. But he's here to find our weaknesses, not our strengths. And he'll exploit those weaknesses to give Uncle Everett and Aunt Elsbeth and —" the next words stabbed her heart "—even Granny the little bit of a reason they need to vote to sell this place in six weeks."

In an action born of things worse than being out of a job, Lautaro shrugged. "If his truth is for sale, there isn't anything we can do to change his mind."

The cold reality of that statement was enough to slow

Harley's pounding heart and release the tremble from her fingers.

Lautaro sucked in a deep, steady breath. *In through the nose* his familiar action reminded her.

His voice always quieted her, even if it was only in her head, the solid bass a foundation when she faltered. She exhaled loudly and finished the thought. "Out through the mouth."

The familiar welcoming smile stretched across the landscape of his face, a roadway guiding her to calm from chaos.

"Introduce me to the jackass."

"Harley." Lautaro warned gently, putting a hand at the center of her shoulders as they crossed beneath the weathered barn doors.

"You're right. Mr. Jackass. Granny told me to respect everyone, even when they didn't deserve respect."

The temperature change beneath the solid cedar timbers as well as the scent of the wood always brought Harley home and her skin pebbled. Beneath that, the bite of vinegar used to clean the distillation tanks permeated the air.

It reminded her of the Saturdays before Easter and dyeing eggs with her cousins and grandparents out on the small dock platform. Even Lautaro, Miss Perla, and Mr. Shaw would get caught up in the activity. When she was growing up, before her parents had died, this had been her favorite place in the entire world. Now, sadness crowded the happy memories.

Lautaro interrupted her thoughts. "He's not what you were expecting?"

When Uncle Everett had told her about the consultant, Harley pictured a cheap suit and combover. Not hair she wanted to finger comb and high fashion designs her first cousins could probably name from fifty yards.

"No. He's likely worse. Probably likes change for the sake of change. Doesn't see why anyone would want to do things the old way when a new way will be cheaper, faster, and almost as good."

They skirted the still safe just inside the door, the gleaming aluminum box reflecting the overhead lights. The tapered cap on the primary copper distillation pot was open and Harley stopped, pointed to it in an unspoken *Why?*

Lautaro gestured absently to the thumper, the secondary container where the product went to double before hitting the condenser. "I was spider-legging a bit of the next batch to see if reducing the temperature a notch would reduce the tail. We're losing too much at the end of distillation and I want to know why."

"I didn't think the next batch would be ready for another couple of days." It usually took five to seven days for a batch to stop *passing gas* after they added the sugar and yeast to the mash, a sign the fermentation was done and ready for distillation.

Lautaro grimaced and Harley steeled herself for whatever bad news came next. "The thermostat was set on 76."

Her eyes jumped to the vats of mash fermenting against the north wall of the still house. They kept the place cool at 68F because of those vats. Whiskey making was as much about science as it was about feel. The wrong temperature and the fermentation process changed. If they didn't start distillation when it was ready, they risked the batch coming out too sharp on the tongue.

"Dean." The name soured on her tongue. "I fired him, by the way. It's just us."

Lautaro quirked one eyebrow at her. "It always was."

They continued past the propane set up jacketed by bricks used to build the first house on the property. Fortune's Brew was about legacy, from the recipe to the very timbers of the buildings - every bit of it led back to building on what Charlie Fortune had started over two hundred years ago.

Harley shook free the weight of that albatross as she rounded the corner past the proofing tank and into the modest lab taking up space at the back of the still house. They'd already started labeling bottles for the next batch and the boxes sat stacked in silent anticipation waiting for her success or failure.

The office took up the back corner and as she approached it she saw Mr. Helpful bent low over her desk, long fingers twined around a pen while he flipped pages of the inventory.

He'd shucked the suit coat from earlier but had traded the t-shirt for a crisp black oxford shirt buttoned to the top, a pale, yellow tie the only relief to the dark grey suit. A pair of glasses rested on the slope of his nose, the frames, like his hair, a swirl of browns and golds.

He pressed a phone to one ear, his voice low but the angry grumble filtering out the door.

"Don't call me again." The sharp words exhaled on a rush of air. He slapped the phone against the desk, sliding his thumb and forefinger under the eyeglasses to pinch the bridge of his nose.

Their presence must have weighted the air because he looked up, the already familiar charm erasing the tension from his face as he flowed to his feet in a move both powerful and filled with grace. He removed the glasses, folding them and tucking them in the coat pocket. "I'm sorry, Mr. Sanchez. I was distracted by a personal phone call." His amused gaze went to Harley, held hers for a few uncomfortable seconds. "Third time's a charm?"

Harley leaned against the door jam, tucked her chin and crossed her arms. "In baseball it's the final strike."

HIs face twitched in an irritating way, lifting a corner of his mouth and bringing a glint to those light brown eyes. "Guess that's why I prefer soccer." His attention seamlessly shifted to Lautaro. "You said the owner was arriving? I'm very eager to sit down with Charlotte and discuss Fortune's Brew."

Seeing her disadvantage go *poof*, Harley stepped into the office before Lautaro could respond, extending her hand over the edge of the desk. That subtle fragrance she already associated with him - sweet and woodsy - hung in the air. "I'm Harley. The junior distiller."

"CJ Diamond. Diamond Spirits Consulting." He accepted her handshake, wrapping her smaller hand in his, long fingers nearly meeting around the back of her hand. His thumb fell to the small indentation where her hand and wrist married, rubbing absently. "Everyone calls me Chance."

His brows shot up, as if he'd surprised himself with something.

Harley pulled back; the warmth of his skin lingering. She stuffed the hand in the back pocket of her jeans, blaming the tingle on nerves. "Everyone calls me Harley." She cut her eyes to Lautaro in a silent plea for his support. "The owner sends her apologies. She's been called away unexpectedly. You're stuck with just us for now."

Chance's face fell but he quickly recovered, steeling a look of confidence over the wariness. "That's disappointing. I was told she would be here on the property during my work. To provide the most comprehensive look at Fortune's

Brew and its sustainability for profit and growth, I really need to meet with the entire management team."

Harley motioned to Lautaro, his dark brown eyes hooded, his face blank, and a split second of hesitation crossed her mind. She knew she was starting off on the wrong foot, knew it would probably be a mistake she'd come to regret later.

Inside, however, she was doing a little dance.

For once, she had the upper hand. She could get to know Chance's take on things before he reported to Uncle Everett and the family. "You've met the team. Lautaro has Charlotte's full trust and authority. I do whatever Lautaro says and we get the information back to Charlotte when needed."

He shuffled the inventory pages with sharp, precise motions, stuffed the papers back in the folder marked 'to file later' in her own blocky script. "I was led to believe that she was more involved in the day-to-day operation. I should discuss this with Mr. Fortune before I go any further."

The golden opportunity was slipping away, and Harley didn't want to have to face another consultant sure to be hired by Uncle Everett, or worse, the possibility they would just decide to sell in six weeks with or without justification. "Mr. Fortune was headed out of town earlier in the day. I think he and his husband were going on a cruise so they may be unavailable the rest of this week."

Harley shifted her weight and nudged Lautaro when Chance's attention went to his leather satchel propped against the printer.

"Uh, Miss Fortune is involved in the decision making," Lautaro fumbled, then scratched his head. "It's just right now she is, how you say, shifting her focus to marketing while me and Harley make the production for our customers. There is no deciding in the production for now and she will be back very soon." He nudged Harley right back. "Won't she Harley?"

"Very soon, Lautaro." Hope wiggled its way into her face in the form of a strained smile. She considered Chance, who should look out of place in her ramshackle office with his suit and tie and shiny loafers, but who looked as comfortable there as he had in the coffee shop and on the side of the highway this morning. "I can show you the set up, get you up to speed with whatever information you need to see how we operate. When she returns, you'll be all set."

Chance lifted the strap of the satchel and looped it over his shoulder, leaning against the weight of it. An easy charm flowed from the one shoulder shrug. "Then we'll see how it goes. I'd like to see everything but that's probably easier in the daylight." He motioned to the darkening square of light showing through the window. "What's on the agenda for tomorrow?"

Harley opened her mouth, then remembered she was just the junior employee, so followed Chance's gaze to Lautaro who looked startled at being the center of attention.

"We've got a batch that will be ready for distillation in the morning. We'll start there. About eight I think."

Chance nodded and hoisted the overstuffed satchel higher. "I'd like to take a look at your recipe, to compare against your inventory and calculate the yield quantities. See if there are places you could optimize the process."

"No way." Harley's voice sharpened on the edge of her distrust. It was bad enough she had to have this outsider in her still house, watching her work, taking over her office. There was no way she would share the two century-old recipes with him.

Suspicion darkened behind his light brown eyes and

Harley remembered she was supposed to be a junior employee. "Charlotte would never allow that."

"I have a signed non-disclosure with Mr. Fortune, Harley. The information will be well guarded, I assure you."

"I don't care if you stamp Fort Knox on your —"

"Harley!" Lautaro barked, eyes narrowing as he crossed his arms.

"Forehead," she quickly amended, sparing a quick glance to Lautaro, feeling the heat rise to her cheeks. "No one but Charlotte can release that kind of proprietary information."

Chance remained silent but kept his eyes on Harley. She remained still beneath his steady gaze, knowing she could play chicken with the best of them. She'd faced down tougher obstacles than CJ Diamond.

"Very well. I can discuss this with the owner if needed. I'll be here about seven, just to observe your set up. Will that be alright?"

"Do we have a choice?" Harley asked bitterly and raised a hand to rub at her throat when Lautaro turned and muttered beneath his breath.

"Everything is a choice, Harley. You can choose to work with me, or you can choose to work against me. Doesn't mean I'll leave any sooner."

"As long as you leave." At more grumbling from Lautaro, Harley acquiesced as much as she could. "Seven will be fine. I'm usually the first one here."

Chance leaned forward and met Harley's eyes, the smile crinkling the corners of his eyes. "I'll bring coffee. Good night, Harley. Mr. Sanchez. Thank you for everything today."

"*De nada,* Mr. Diamond." Lautaro and Harley backed up

as Chance came around the desk. At the last minute, Lautaro added, "Harley will walk you out to your car."

"I will?" Harley said before thinking, then hastily repeated the words with less doubt. "I will."

Lautaro disappeared without catching Harley's eye, leaving her with Chance. Up close — they were sharing the doorway though he had to stand sideways to accomplish it — she found her attention jumping between the shifting coppery hints of his chocolate-colored hair and the snug fit of the grey coat over shoulders that looked wider than she remembered. Since her eyes barely reached his shoulders, she got a good look.

She didn't like feeling small next to people and generally kept them out of her personal space. Chance made her feel petite, not helpless. Her throat struggled to swallow the lump of discomfort but for the life of her, she couldn't make her muscles move to put distance between them.

"I know you don't want me here," he said.

The husky tone of his voice brushed over her skin, which warmed everywhere at once. "This isn't one of the major labels you're used to dealing with Mr. Diamond, where some cold board of directors makes decisions and sends them in an email. Fortune's Brew isn't just a family business. It's *family*. It means everything to —" The words were the cold shower she needed, snapping her head back. Her gaze locked on his. *I'm just a junior distiller,* she reminded herself and quickly continued beneath his curious expression. "Charlotte."

He nodded, the movement slight but the taut line of his mouth said he understood what it was like to have all you ever wanted at the whim of someone else. "I get it. It's more than just a business for her, I'm sure. But not all of the major labels are the cold corporations you seem to think. Many of them started as family operations. They've just grown beyond the one- or two-person operation, and they've done it with smart decisions. I can help Charlotte do that."

That spark of hope in Harley got a little bigger. Maybe she could make him understand what was at stake. Throwing a hand out, she motioned to the still house and beyond the open dock door, to the malting barn and supply shed. "She's worked for years to get the place up and running again. I'd hate to see all that hard work come to nothing because the family just wants to wash their hands of the place."

Chance dropped his gaze from hers, shifting the satchel to his other shoulder. "We're a long way from that right now."

They shifted back into motion, his stride matching hers as they returned to the main section of the still house.

"I have to ask," he grinned, and pointed to the slab of oak over the main door etched with the words *The Tipsy Turtle*. A dazed looking turtle tilted precariously beneath the words. "And at the turn off from the highway you have *The Drunk Skunk*. There has to be a story there."

Harley laughed, her shoulders dropping a little as the tension eased from her body. "Legend has it that during prohibition my great-great-great," she counted off the greats on her fingers, "Grandmother would store the moonshine in the hidey hole at the bottom of the trunk of that oak. Customers would come by, leave their money, and take a pint jar. The liquor wasn't technically on the property so the revenuers wouldn't bother them much. One day a customer came up to the house and complained he couldn't get near the stump because a skunk had managed to break one of the jars and proceeded to get – "

"Drunk as a skunk," she and Chance finished together.

The shared laugh between them was comfortable, and Harley's mind flashed to his kindness out on the highway, and the mischievous sparkle in his eye at the coffee shop when he'd flustered the young barista. Was the charm a weapon he turned on and off at will, or a natural part of his personality?

Harley cleared her head with a mental slap. She was not a teenager to be gobsmacked by a cute face and hot body. "That sort of started it."

They'd passed through the door and stood outside, a few moths flittering around the gold circle of light. She was too aware of his body - where he stood, the line of his shoulders beneath the jacket - so she took a step back and motioned to the outer buildings and continued across the yard.

"The malting barn became The Boozy Bear, the shed is The Smashed Squirrel and the main house is The Sloppy Possum."

They were standing at the end of the driveway now, the night thick with dill, ginger, and feverfew from Miss Perla's herb garden hot house in the back of the house. "Although Miss Perla was quite put out about that name when she hired on. She said nothing about her house is sloppy."

Even in the dim light from the front porch bulb, Harley recognized the amused tilt to Chance's mouth. Amazing how she already knew this look in the few hours they'd been acquainted.

Enemy, her brain shouted.

Harley tensed, again taking a step back and crossing her arms across her chest. "That's the grand tour." Her voice, gruff and tinged with regret, filled the short distance between them but as Chance's face lost its amused look she knew the message had been delivered.

Chance shifted between his loafered feet and dropped

the satchel to his hand to dig out his keys. "I appreciate the tour."

His gaze darted to the house, the interior lights slipping between the cracks in the curtains on the front windows. He opened the door to his car, tossing the satchel across the driver's seat to clunk against the passenger door.

He scratched a through his hair before turning his attention back to her. Hesitation made his eyes jump between her and the night sky. "If you talk to Charlotte, please tell her I hope to speak with her soon. I'm only going to be here for a week at the most and there's a lot to discuss before I write up my report for her uncle."

Harley nodded, his jaw clenched. "I'll do that."

"Good night Harley." Chance stood on one leg, the other resting inside the car, as if he couldn't make himself fully commit to leaving. "I'll see you bright and early."

"Don't forget the coffee," she added as he slipped behind the steering wheel, and the jolt of pleasure when the amused tilt to his mouth returned warmed her.

"I'll try not to break the barista."

The car door slammed shut, cutting him off from her, and Harley stepped out of the way as he cranked the engine to life and backed out of the drive. Chance nodded at her once through the window before following the twin beams of his headlights down the pitch-black road back to the highway.

Tomorrow.

Excitement and dread mixed in the pit of her belly, and she wasn't sure which emotion went with the promise of his return and which she should assign to the challenge of saving Fortune's Brew.

. . .

The only thing heavier than Harley's legs as she dragged her exhausted body up the front steps to the house were the emotions condensing through her body to a single, concentrated thought: *I'm going to lose Fortune's Brew.*

After that Chance guy had left, she and Lautaro had checked the remaining batches of mash to see if the temp change in the still house had any serious effect. Luckily it was only the one batch. Still, that pushed up their production by a few days. Tomorrow they'd have to get the distillation batch running so they didn't lose the product.

Harley had emptied the bank account to pay the entrance fee; there was nothing left for supplies if the batch was lost. They had enough to finish their current orders and produce enough for the competitions they'd need to enter to qualify for Crescent City. If anything went wrong...

The weight of that thought carried her into the darkened house, the door clicking shut behind her. As Harley's eyes adjusted, her head snapped to attention. Wait, not a darkened house. Everyone was generally asleep by the time she trudged into the house from work each night. Miss Perla and Mr. Shaw had the run of the second floor. She and Granny T kept rooms on the main floor.

But not tonight. Tonight, a puddle of light spilled from the kitchen and once Harley pulled her mind from her own thoughts, she could hear the familiar scraping of a spoon against Granny T's jelly pot.

That sound was her first lullaby as a baby. Tonight, it played a sadder tune.

Harley let the light lead her into the kitchen, stopping short at the picture framed beneath the doorway. Granny stood over the stove, peering into the jelly pot through the bifocals perched on the tip of her nose. How those glasses never ended up in the pot, Harley didn't know. She managed to drop her phone from her back pocket into a vat of brewer's beer at least twice a year.

"The jars are ready," Trudy Fortune announced without looking up from the pot, and Harley was in motion before the words registered fully on her brain.

She inhaled deeply as she scooted behind her grandmother and grabbed the jar puller from the counter, then started lifting the Ball jars from the pots of still-steaming water. "Peach and... ginger?"

"With a touch of honey," Granny said, pushing herself back from the stove as the first bubbles hugged the edge of the thick brew of sugar and fruit. "You always had the best nose."

"It's early in the season for peaches."

"Shaw put some in the green house last year to see if we could get a year-round crop. Perla loves fresh peaches."

Harley ignored the lump in her throat, blaming it on being tired and worried about the business rather than a longing for what Miss Perla and Mr. Shaw shared. She imagined the only thing worse than never having such a grand love, was to have it as her grandmother and grandfather had shared, then lose it. Granny had been a widow for more than twenty years now. "He'd move the moon if he thought Miss Perla wanted it done."

"That's what love does to you, sweetheart." The older woman leaned her shoulder against Harley's, their heights nearly identical, and pressed a kiss to her temple. "Makes you want to do the impossible."

Harley thought about her grandmother's words:

Did love make you want to do something even if it was impossible? And was that a bad thing? Love should make you want to climb mountains or keep the family business going, even if no one else thought it wise.

They worked in silence, straining and filling the jars, setting the lids. There should be tension between them, Harley reasoned. They were on opposite sides right now. Sure, it had happened before.

After the deaths of her parents, Harley refused to touch the grand piano in the living room, her mother's pride and joy. Granny rationalized, reasoned, coaxed, cajoled, bribed, and threatened Harley to play again. Still, Harley refused so Granny resigned herself. When Harley shadowed Lautaro, Granny was opposed. When Harley got her GED and didn't go to college, Granny was livid.

Harley couldn't quite decipher Granny's mood. The overhead kitchen light haloed in the silver hair now pushed back with the frame of the glasses Granny had pushed up onto the crown of her head. Her eyes focused on the job at hand, lips set in a firm line but not firm enough to deepen the creases at the corner of her mouth.

Still, Harley recognized the shadows beneath her eyes. She'd noticed them earlier at lunch along with the reluctant smile creasing Granny's face. For a woman who loved to laugh, Granny T wasn't doing much laughing lately.

"Are we going to talk?" Harley couldn't take it any longer. She'd rather face the wrath than fear the silence.

Trudy Fortune grabbed two spoons from the drawer, scraped a bit of leftover jam from the pot and handed one to Harley. They both tasted, *hmmm-ing* in harmony. "Do you need me to say anything?" She dropped her spoon in the dirtied pot and moved it to the farmhouse sink.

Harley grabbed the damp sponge and scraped the pile of peels into the trash can. "I'm guessing Connie called you." The sheriff's front desk clerk was one of Granny's Canasta partners. Granny T usually knew about crime in Belle Terre before the sheriff.

"Only so I wouldn't worry that you were driving when I heard about the crash." She added a squirt of detergent to the pot and flipped on the hot water, her attention focused on the rising suds. "Dean's such a...a..." She harrumphed in frustration, hitting the pot with her scrubber. "I don't know how such fine people as Wylie and Joanie Blanchard birthed such a...a... turdmuffin."

Harley grinned at what passed for cussing for her grandmother. She didn't think she'd ever heard Granny say anything harsher than *hellfire and damnation*. Unless it involved Dean Blanchard. Granny had provided her subtle guidance on the matter of dating Dean two years ago. *I'd rather welcome an Old Miss fan into the family than see you with that boy.*

Harley sobered then as Trudy's words of warning about Dean floated in her thoughts. "I know you're disappointed in me. And about more than just my relationship with Dean."

Trudy pivoted with bright eyes, punching a fist against her waist, cocking a hip to the left. "Don't be a drama queen, Charlotte Vivienne Fortune. You've never given me a reason to be disappointed, even when I disagree with what you're doing." Granny turned to finish washing the pot and tip it to drain in the dish holder.

Something like relief mixed with the smile twitching on Harley's mouth. She closed the garbage bag and tied the draw string, the heavy aroma of peach wafting up. They had an orchard behind the malting barn, some of the sweetest fruit you could find thanks to the warm Louisiana weather and damp soil, a mixture of orange, peach, and apple trees that kept their jelly and jam pots rattling throughout the seasons. Random berries filled in the months and added to the collection of Granny T's heavenly spreads.

"But you think I made the wrong decision about Crescent City. And in trying to get the distillery going again. But I'm going to make it successful. I'm going to do everything that dad wanted without selling out to one of those corporate labels. I just need —"

"Time." Trudy Fortune's voice cracked on the word. She braced her hands on the counter, contemplating the darkness out the window over the sink. "Time is a wicked mistress, Harley. She steals everything." Trudy reached out to Harley, grasping her hand over the counter. "She steals our youth. She steals our hopes. But mostly she steals our memories."

Trudy's eyes clouded over with tears and Harley pulled her grandmother forward, wrapping her arms around the older woman and burying her face in the space where her shoulder curved into her neck.

Trudy sighed heavily. "I'm losing him. Losing your father's voice. I can still hear your grandfather clear as a bell; we had thirty years together. But Elias...I can only hear him as a little boy now. I'm afraid I'll forget him. How does a mother forget her son's voice? I don't want the same thing to happen to you. I don't want you to lose yourself trying to chase after ghosts. I can't lose anything else to this business."

Harley sat back, wiping first her grandmother's tears then her own. "I won't let that happen. I promise, Granny. I have Lautaro and we'll hire someone to help. I'll even go back to playing the piano if you want."

"I know you play now when I'm out of the house." Trudy brushed back a swatch of Harley's hair and cupped her chin.

"You're just like him. You won't trust anyone else with the work." Her mouth thinned into a grim line.

"You're voting with Uncle Everett and Aunt Elsbeth." The admission drained what little energy Harley had left from the day. The accident. The confrontation with Dean. The arrival of the consultant. "Uncle Everett probably hired that consultant so he could convince one of the big labels we were perfect for absorption into their own brand."

Venom stung her words. Harley hated the thought of losing her identity to one of the major labels. Sure, they were successful, but they had no heart.

We only sell the heart, Harley, her father had explained when teaching her about distillation. *It's the purest part of the batch. It's how you know which brands are in it for the money, and which are in it for the whiskey.*

Trudy held open the back door as Harley dropped the trash bag into the larger bin off the porch. "I'm *listening*, Harley. *Listening* to the proposal and the sale they've put together. Just like I listen to you. I've also voted in your favor the past five years, so don't forget that."

They each grabbed a dish towel, Trudy drying the cooling jars of peach jam while Harley wiped down the jelly pot.

"I haven't forgotten." Harley folded the dish towel and hung the jelly pot back in its traditional spot over the stove. The collection of skillets and pans *clanked* together softly with the swaying of the rack as the jelly pot found its home, reminiscent of how Harley's family sounded when they were together.

Still, she was home.

They were her family. She loved them all, even her vapid first cousin who couldn't be bothered to learn anything more than the latest fashion trend or the name of the hottest new actor in Hollyweird. At least Piper, also her first cousin, tried to be fair and helpful by staying out of the way.

Trudy pulled two tumblers down from the cabinet, sliced two healthy wedges of peach from the leftovers and dropped one into each glass with a curl of ginger and a dollop of honey. She poured a splash of Lucky Lady and slid one toward Harley. "Pretty as a picture, don't you think?"

Harley fumbled in her back pocket to retrieve her phone. "I should take a picture of these for the website." She punched at the menu, trying to pull up the camera to take a picture of the drink. Damn, she hated this thing. She lost it twice a day, using relying on Lautaro to find it in the oddest places, and could never get the apps to work.

After a few minutes of no success, her grandmother took the phone from her fingers, nimbly opened the camera and snapped a picture.

"You have a website?" She returned the phone to Harley.

"Not yet. But I know we need one. Most distilleries have one." Even to Harley, the words came out rushed and unplanned. She'd not thought of a website until that morning entering the coffee shop.

"Connie met the consultant Everett hired."

Harley had guessed he'd run right down to the sheriff's office after their own meeting at the coffee shop. But after meeting him at the still house, she'd started to revise her opinion. He wasn't the sleazy con man she'd expected. But maybe all that charm was just a cloak to a sleazy heart. Goodness knows her judgment of men was not the best. She'd dated Dean after all.

Harley lifted the tumbler to her nose, letting the aroma peach and whiskey calm her frazzled mind as she sipped. "Was he waving around his lawyer's card or his daddy's money or both?"

"Neither." Trudy exited the spacious kitchen and tucked into the cushioned window bench that looked out over the back yard. She sipped at the drink in her hand, closing her eyes briefly. "She said he was helpful and polite and cuter than a baby possum."

Harley laughed before she could help herself, thinking of the Good Samaritan she'd met on the side of the road, then the outrageous flirt in the coffee shop. He had been nothing but helpful and polite during those two occasions. Until the gloves came off.

Then he'd been nothing but business.

As Harley joined her grandmother in the window seat, she could see only the pitch blackness of night on the bayou when a moon didn't intrude. She knew beyond the spacious yard was the orchard with its rows of trees, and beyond that, the murky waters of Bayou Cane.

While she knew what lay beyond the trees as well as she knew the layout of her own bedroom, Harley didn't miss the symbolism of the darkness. It clouded things, made the path a little riskier. The future was out there whether she chose to accept it or not. She could keep moving forward trying to save the business or she could walk away, take a safer route. Or even a different route.

She didn't know which way her heart was leading, however. The last five years had been dedicated to saving the distillery. If she wasn't doing that, she was walking into the dark. What would she do?

And now CJ "Everyone calls me Chance" Diamond had been brought in to shine a light on the business. On her. Harley hated being in the spotlight. Chance came across as someone who enjoyed being the center of attention. Harley doubted he did much work. Consultants liked to point at the things that needed attention.

They didn't get their hands dirty by actually doing any work.

Maybe she could use that to keep him distracted. Keep him focused on giving her advice while she and Lautaro worked behind the scenes to get ready for the upcoming competitions that would earn them a late entry to the Crescent City competition roster.

Harley knew her business. She may not always make the best business decisions, but she knew whiskey on an instinctual basis. No one could question that.

Chance Diamond was an idiot if he thought Harley would give an inch where her whiskey was concerned.

Chapter Six

"You're an idiot," Chance repeated, and not for the first time since returning to his hotel. He'd been flirting with Harley all day, even when he hadn't known who she was exactly. Like a fifteen-year-old just introduced to his older sister's college roommate, as if he had a shot.

Flirting.

But he couldn't help himself. He settled into the hotel's uncomfortable desk chair at the small corner table, pushing away the remnants of his dinner. He tried to focus on the research he'd gathered on the Fortune family, the market projections, a new trend analysis indicating the dismal numbers of the industry's female demographic.

Which brought him right back to Harley.

When he'd seen her on the side of the road that morning, looking as if her life had puddled at her feet, he'd been drawn to her and it wasn't his good Samaritan nature she tugged at. It was something less noble. And so completely opposite of everything he normally valued in his life.

Neat. Defined.

Even times like now, when things weren't going exactly

as he wanted, he knew they would eventually work out in the end. They always did. People like Leo claimed Chance had a golden touch but in reality, he worked damn hard to be where he was without relying on his dad's name or reputation.

He loved his old man. Respected him just as much. But Chance needed to do things on his own, if only to prove to himself he could. No one else seemed to have any doubt as to his powers of persuasion, charm, and ability to turn lemons into a well-balanced whiskey sour.

Harley was anything but neat and defined. She practically accused him of a crime in the coffee shop, and when he'd seen her out at the distillery, his respect for her went up a notch, attributing the confrontation by the lake to a protective streak. That he could understand. He protected his own as well.

Her triangular face reminded him of the statues he'd seen in Athens, classic, carved in soft determination. Free from any hint of make-up. She looked like she'd rolled out of bed five minutes before jumping in her car, wrinkled, rumpled, her hair stuffed under an old ball cap, the brim shading suspicious, sad eyes.

Maybe that was the fixation, he rationalized.

She went against the norm. *His* norm. He was looking to upend his world by branching out from consulting into ownership. Was she just another way to break away? Stacking the takeout containers, Chance carried them to the trash and dumped them unceremoniously into the bin, then grumbled when they missed the plastic bag lining the bin and bent down to clean up after himself. No sense making more work for someone else. Since he was something of a cleaner himself, he appreciated those who had to deal with the mess others left behind.

Hands sticky with black bean sauce he stomped into the bathroom and gave his hands a quick rinse. Seeing his shirt dotted with the stuff as well, he unbuttoned the shirt with sharp, jerky motions. Chance cranked the shower knob to volcanic, stripped, and stepped into the shower to let the steam cloud envelope his body. He planted his hands against the cool tile wall, the contrast welcome against the sting of the water as he dipped his head beneath the hot spray.

Even here, however, he couldn't escape the image of olive skin and blue-green eyes or the rumpled tail of a button down bouncing against --

"Dammit!"

Chance squirted the combination shampoo-body wash into his palm and lathered himself from head to toe, reducing the water temp when the erection turning his balls blue wouldn't subside on its own. Giving up, he let the image of Harley fill his head and release his body from its torment.

Her hand, not his.

The heat of her body, not the cool tile beneath his fingers.

Her breath, her groans mixing with his, not the grunt of his solo voice in the hotel shower as he crashed over the edge faster than a horny fifteen-year-old.

It was as if every professional rule he'd ever made went out the window.

Stepping from the shower he scrubbed the towel over his head before wrapping it around his waist.

"Remember the rules," he told the fogged reflection staring back at him in recrimination, then recited the mantra as he finished toweling off.

"Rule one. Play the game." He pointed at his reflection

with his toothbrush. "You're a ringer. Nothing more. Win the game for the client." Which quite easily led to rule number two.

"Give the glory," he mumbled around a mouth full of toothpaste. "It's not about you."

Chance loved to win, and he could put a check in that column when his clients exceeded their goals by listening to his advice. As he rinsed his mouth and doused the sink, he counted off the clients - every single one, as a matter of fact - that had seen production costs decrease and sales increase when following the plan Chance developed.

Of course, he mostly fixed stupid mistakes and knocked egos out of the equation. People, Chance discovered, were usually blind when it came to their own best interests.

This rule also worked because Chance liked being in the background, not front and center. It was also why he'd been using an alias the past nine years. It kept the focus where it belonged: the work.

Finally, the most important rule, and he turned to look at the shower and remember the thoughts that had steamed the glass walls more than the hot water.

"Never think with your dick."

Maybe that wasn't exactly a professional rule, he admitted, but it was still the most important rule. Thinking with the wrong head was almost as deadly as thinking with the heart when it came to business. His dad had learned this one the hard way and made sure Chance benefited from the lesson.

As Chance yanked a clean t-shirt over his head, he already knew he would fail miserably.

~

Sunrise was still a promise in the night sky when Chance angled the Eldorado behind Harley's old Mercedes and killed the engine, the soft chill of the early morning spring air whirling into the window. The *tick, tick, tick* of the cooling engine faded slowly, leaving nothing but crickets and the steady slap of water against the pier in the distance. Chance grabbed the coffee, stacked it on top of his overstuff satchel, and carefully balanced the load as he pushed from the car.

He wasn't surprised to see Harley already here. The light from inside the still house sluiced out of the doors and small windows and guided his path across the darkened yard, his sneakers crunching across the gravel. He'd suspected she'd be here earlier than seven when they spoke last night.

He'd also suspected her identity wasn't as simple as junior distiller and a quick search of social media last night after his shower had confirmed his suspicions. Or at least confirmed she wasn't a junior distiller. That left only one person unaccounted for in the Fortune family dynamic. Harley was Charlotte Fortune.

He could find nothing about Charlotte online. No social media. No criminal record. No marriage certificates or graduation photos for the local high school. She was a ghost in a world that made anonymity difficult but not impossible.

So why was she hiding her identity?

Why was he?

He raised his hand to knock on the opened still house door before entering, the fluorescent lights harsh in the pre-dawn darkness but stopped short. Harley's sharp, angry voice bounced beneath the cedar planked roof.

"I know I locked up last night. He must have stolen a key."

Chance scooted sideways between the door frame and the door to see Harley and Lautaro leaning over the top of the large copper distillation tank, their faces scrunched in anger and concern. They shared the top rung of a step ladder, but Harley hopped down, surprise raising the corners of her mouth before she remembered to tighten it down to a grim expression.

At least he wasn't the only one confused by their interactions yesterday.

"Good morning." Chance took the coffee carrier with his free hand and dropped the remainder of his belongings by the door, curious as to what could have gone wrong so early in the day. He held out the peace offering, deciding to take it slow. "Coffee?"

"Blessed virgin," Lautaro breathed, and the wrinkles in his brow smoothed out. He clunked down the ladder, his gait stiff-legged as he propped one booted foot on the brick retaining wall surrounding the distillation set up. Holding out his hand, he added unceremoniously, "An uncaffeinated Harley is an unpleasant thing this early in the morning, Mr. Diamond."

Chance handed over one of the coffees, suppressing a grin. "It's too early for formalities. Just Chance will do."

"*Buenes dias*, Chance." Lautaro breathed deeply from the cup, relief easing the creases from his face. "I am Lautaro to my friends."

Harley scoffed but her eyes were all for the raspberry chocolate dream Frappuccino sharing space with his own plain espresso in the paper carrying tray. He'd put in his order online last night and had been waiting this morning before they opened the doors, Barista Bex eyeing him cautiously as she whipped up the beverages without comment.

He took his own cup, setting the tray down on top of the spirit safe with Harley's drink still unclaimed. "Sounds like there's a problem. Anything I can help with?" He edged closer to the distillation tank, stepping over the retaining wall. A pungent odor slapped at Chance, what he would only call death. "Is that... bleach?"

"And turpentine." Bitterness weighed down Harley's words and sharpened her gesture as she pointed to the two empty containers set on the retaining wall. Bleach and turpentine. The bottles were not new, but judging from Lautaro's and Harley's expressions they were not from the cleaning supplies on site.

She plucked the Frappuccino from the tray, pulling the paper off the straw and stuffing it in the pocket of her jeans. She turned her back on the scene, the twitch of her carotid pulsing beneath her clenched jaw.

Chance cursed under his breath, his eyes pinging from Lautaro back to Harley. She wasn't wearing the ball cap today, the waves of soft brown hair stuffed behind her ears instead.

"I'm guessing Dean." Chance turned his back on the ruined vessel, remembering the driver from the accident yesterday. The instant burn of hatred soured the coffee in his stomach, and he returned the cup to the tray almost untouched.

"Probably." Harley reached for the ball cap that wasn't there and her eyes cut left. Chance followed her gaze to find a silky piece of material draped over a nearby chair. He remembered seeing it earlier on Pips and her matching companion at the restaurant.

Battling owners and staff over cooking times or the ideal ratio of corn to barley was one thing, Chance reasoned.

Sabotage was not something he'd encountered since his own mother—

He stopped the train of thought, snapping his attention to the present, not the past. Chance closed the distance between him and Harley, the tension prickling the air between them like a live current. Everything in him pushed him to reach out, to pull her into his arms and tell her he would make it better. "Have you called the police?"

Harley cleared her throat, her Frappuccino mostly untouched. She met his gaze. "The desk clerk gets in at nine. I'll give her a call then, not that it will do any good. We can't prove anything, and we can't wait for them to arrive."

"You should take pictures regardless."

She took out her phone but Lautaro held out his hand with a knowing look passing between them. Harley handed it over without a word.

Defeat cast shadows behind eyes the color of the Mediterranean. Her pupils were dilated, leaving only the turquoise rim visible. "I don't know if we can salvage the tank and even if we can we'll need 24 hours to clean it properly. Not that it matters."

"We are not finished, Harley," Lautaro challenged, determination stiffening his spine as he recorded the damage on the phone. "I am not finished yet. There is the smaller tank on the dock. It was wrapped before storage so only needs to be rinsed. We can still make batches to send to our customers. We will not be too late with the orders."

Harley plowed her fingers through her hair, the ends flaring out as she turned too quickly. "That's a hundred-gallon copper tank, not steel." She waved in the general direction of the fermentation vats; fingers splayed as if she could hold back the tides of time. "We have fifteen hundred gallons of mash to distil over the next five days before it over ferments. There's not enough hours in the days between now and Saturday." Her body deflated, her breath leaking out in a ragged stream. "We needed that order this morning to make our quota."

"Our quota?" Lautaro rolled his head back on his shoulders and huffed. "Tell me you did not do this."

Harley nodded. "The crash yesterday was our qualifying batch for Crescent City. Without that we need two top tier finishes in regionals or..."

She cut her eyes to Lautaro whose eyes widened before a sigh dragged down the line of his shoulders.

Tugging at the leather bolo tie at this throat, he finished Harley's thought. "You sent in the money for the entrance fee."

The five grand entrance fee for Crescent City was the steepest of the competitions and, Chance knew, completely non-refundable. He started calculating distillation times in his head.

Harley kicked at the brick retaining wall, posture stiff. "Today is the deadline. The batch was on the road. I thought... Charlotte thought we'd be ok."

"You mentioned Saturday. The Houston Craft Distillers Regional Competition?" Chance headed for the spoiled tank to examine the set up. "You need less than five gallons for judging and vendor tasting. That should be easy enough."

The first light of hope dimmed the shadows of defeat behind her eyes. "But it won't be our normal process. I'd have to check the rules."

Harley hurried to the office and returned carrying a stack of papers. She scanned the papers, then looked up to meet his and Lautaro's waiting expressions. He already knew the answer, but she needed to find the solution and make the decision. Chance wanted to guide, not dictate. It didn't do any good if he left a client unable to think critically about their business. He wouldn't always be around.

A cautious grin tugged at the corners of her mouth. "There's no requirement for regionals or Crescent City that you enter the same product in all the competitions. As long as it's good enough to place, it's good enough to count."

Chance squatted at the edge of the tank, tracing the propane lines that fed the jacketing. He turned, Harley already beside him, hunched down to see what he was doing.

"What do you want to do?"

Her eyes widened; brows lifted in surprise at his question. Did she expect him to tell her what to do? Probably, which might account for her resistance and reluctance around his presence. It wasn't his way.

After a moment, she responded. "We can spider leg enough product to for our entry in Houston. The rest can go to the customer as planned. We can clean the bigger tank while that distills." Harley disconnected the propane tank from the steel jacket in preparation to move the bigger tank. "Let's get that other tank in place."

He pushed to his feet, approaching the three five-hundred-gallon mash vats waiting against the south wall of the still house. Chance lifted the edge of one of the vat covers, the fragrant whiff of distiller's beer greeting him and tugging a smile to his face.

"Smells good, doesn't it?" Harley joined him, drawing a deep lungful of the aroma swirling from the vat.

"My dad would come home from work smelling like this." The nostalgia hit Chance from out of the blue. "We had one of those stay-away-from-drugs-and-alcohol lectures in health class and I was convinced he was an alcoholic. I waited up for him one night, then staged an intervention based on what we'd seen in a film during the lecture."

Lautaro joined them at the edge of the vats, resting his arms on the large vessel. "You cared about your father. It is natural to worry about those we care about."

Harley shifted uncomfortably. "Was he mad?"

Chance shook his head. "No, just the opposite. It's like Lautaro said, he knew I cared." He turned his head enough to study Harley's profile, the small nose, the determined set of her jaw. "He took me into the office the next day, showed me the distillation set up, the vats waiting for fermentation. I've been hooked ever since."

Chapter Seven

Harley let herself get tugged into the memory with Chance, forgetting for that slice of time that he was the enemy. Someone sent by Uncle Everett to undermine her and Fortune's Brew and push her toward selling.

She shoved herself away from the fermentation vat as harshly as she shoved at the nostalgia, reaching for the brim of the baseball cap before remembering it wasn't there. She didn't think over long on why she hadn't stuck it on her head that morning. Or the fact she'd combed her hair. Twice.

"This is the only office I've ever known." Harley gestured with sharp, jerky motions of her hand, wanting to carve out the emotion that softened her toward Chance. He'd exchanged the stuffy suit for a simple oxford, the tails untucked over a pair of faded jeans. Tennis shoes replaced the shiny loafers. Though Harley tried to ignore it, the slow burn of interest kindled in her stomach. And lower.

She lifted the lid off another of the fermentation vats, wafting the aroma of distiller's beer toward her nose. The earthy mix of grains and corn was sexier than any bottle of expensive French perfume according to her dad. Mom had laughed and responded, *"Don't think I'm putting that behind my ears when you come to bed."*

"Granny said I would cry up a storm when mom brought me to the house but get quiet as a mouse when in here. It was my nursery, my playroom, and my first school. Dad taught me about percentages and yield and calculating proofs before I started kindergarten."

"Your mom worked here along with your dad and Mr. Fortune?" Chance's finely arched brow lifted in question and Harley realized her mistake.

"She would visit dad and Mr. Fortune."

Not technically a lie, Harley consoled herself as she dropped the lid back on the vat and stomped over to the storage room. Her dad was there, and her uncle was another Mr. Fortune. Lifting a hand to yank open the storage room door, she found Chance already there, putting his back into shifting the massive set of doors.

His muscles bunched and flexed beneath the fabric of the shirt, temptation rippling along Harley's frazzled nerves. The cuffs of the shirt were rolled to the elbow, tight around the upper forearm, revealing defined muscles and skin darkened by something other than a tanning booth. The CJ Diamond she'd met on the side of the highway and in the coffee shop had charm and privilege oozing from his pores. This guy, Chance, had two feet on the ground and his head on business.

The heavy door rattled along the overhead rail, setting into the pocket of the wall with a familiar thud. Chance stepped back, arms crossing over the breadth of his chest as he studied the contents of the small storage room. Harley pulled her attention from the man and focused on the machines. Or at least on the kettles the machines needed to operate.

Lautaro shimmied between the crates of bottles and labels waiting for purpose, craning his neck. "The wrapping is intact from what I can see." His voice filled the space and Harley couldn't separate a memory in this place from the man. He'd was as much a part of Fortune's Brew as the recipe or their hybrid corn. Without it, she'd be lost.

"Then let's get it out here." Harley swung the dolly into place and started loading crates, not surprised this time when Chance went to work right next to her. "Whiskey and women wait for no man."

Chance laughed, a full-throated sound that skimmed along her skin like soft denim. "That sounds like some age-old wisdom passed down through the generations."

She hefted the doily back on its wheels, catching the top box with her shoulder as it slid to the right. Chance was there before she blinked, settling it back into place. She nodded her thanks, unable to let the moment pass unacknowledged.

Without thinking, she shared a story from her past. "One of the granddaddies joined up with a political group up near Shreveport during the Civil War. Said he didn't want to fight for a cause he couldn't support, but neither would he begrudge another man the same right to choose." Harley settled the crates against a back wall in the dock area then returned to the storage room. "So, he became more of an activist. When he left, he told his wife and children - all daughters - to mind the house but leave the stilling to him for when he returned. And his wife told him —"

"Whiskey and women wait for no man." As Harley prepared to slide the dolly under another stack of crates, Chance was there to lend his support, helping her maneuver the boxes smoothly into place. "Apparently the tradition of women leading the Fortune dynasty into the future hasn't been lost over the generations. Charlotte Fortune will be the first female COO on record for Fortune's Brew. That must make you proud."

Harley bristled beneath her deception, never comfortable with subterfuge. She was doing it to save her family's legacy, she reminded herself, even if it meant saving it from her family.

From the corner of her eye, she could see Lautaro giving her the once over as he unwrapped the copper piping for the smaller tank. She struggled to tilt the dolly, the front heavy weight more than double her own.

"It's an uphill battle right now," she grunted out the words and moved the load slowly, careful to keep it balanced. "I'm not sure how smart it is to swim upstream in a fast-moving current."

"The best things are made with patience and pressure."

As she arranged the last of the crates on the dock, turning the dolly back toward the storage room she looked at Chance, his face flushed but with excitement, not exertion. She, on the other hand, probably looked like she'd gone three rounds in a pit fight. "Why do you do this?"

Those light brown eyes narrowed but mischief constricted the pupil. "Move crates? It's easier to move them than the dock."

Harley smiled, trying to swallow back the laugh. "No, this." She gestured to the still house, to the 100-gallon tank now sitting in the middle of the floor as Lautaro disconnected the ruined tank from the condenser.

She rested her shoulders against the stack of crates, crossing one ankle over the other. "You've been hired to assess this place for sale, yet here you are at the butt crack of dawn trying to help us do something that could save it."

"I've been hired to assess the business. Whether or not that means it's for sale is up to the owners, not me. I give an honest appraisal of the strengths and weaknesses. What the owners do with that information is out of my hands."

Harley let that swirl around her brain as the sounds of their labors crested beneath the timbers of the cedar roof as they guided the dolly and new tank into place. Lautaro dropped to his haunches to begin connecting the new piping.

Chance sprinkled in questions about Harley's life in Belle Terre and Harley answered, blaming the distraction of their work for her loose tongue. Wanting to keep the playing field even, she peppered him with questions about his life as a consultant and the regional competitions.

She handed Lautaro the tools he needed before he asked, her mind returning to why Chance was there. His interest in their work went beyond the cursory details of how much corn they used or the yields each batch provided.

Chance was as curious about the people, about Charlotte, as he was the business. She recognized the protective instinct in him not only to make sure the right decisions were being made, but that she — or Charlotte — could say they were doing their best for the business.

"How does helping us save this batch play into your goal of assessing the business though? Shouldn't this go into the 'they don't know what they're doing' section of your report?"

He shifted his gaze from the copper piping Lautaro was connecting to the still house in general, his eyes roaming over the condenser and spirit safe then higher to the cedar beams overhead.

Chance shook his head, pulling his attention back to

her. "I've only seen the beginning of your business. Your inventory system is basically manual and that needs to be updated if you want to expand beyond your current customer base and go national but it's accurate and appropriate for your production levels at this time. You need a marketing plan and someone who can put it into action."

"I don't know many people willing to work for free."

"Have you asked?" he challenged.

"Asked who? I don't see how a marketing plan or computerized inventory will matter if we'll be out of business in a few weeks.

Chance shrugged. "I think Piper has marketing experience. Start there. And I don't know many owners or distillers that could plan for sabotage but you're handling it. I'm sure Charlotte is concerned about what happens after the family votes but she and Lautaro are thinking beyond that which is good business."

Her expression must have mirrored the surprised jolt in her belly at the compliment because he added, "You're a problem solver and you make a damn fine whiskey."

"Uncle Everett is only interested in unloading Fortune's Brew. And even Aunt Elsbeth chose to promote another distillery, Lazy River Whiskey, over us. It doesn't matter how good the whiskey is, the family doesn't support it."

"Why do you think that is?" Chance looked away and Harley wondered if he knew more about Everett's plans than he was letting on.

It was Harley's turn to shrug. She'd thought about this a lot. "Uncle Everett and Aunt Elsbeth aren't hurting for money. Both went into other businesses when the distillery went dark after..."

She had to pause over the memory of her parents'

deaths. Her grief had become manageable over the years, but it could rise and swallow her whole on some days.

"Even if they were in need of money, the sale of Fortune's Brew was not going to set up anyone for a life of luxury."

While Lautaro finished with the final connections of piping to the new tank, Harley grabbed the ladder, but Chance took hold of it at the same time. "Capper?" He motioned to the top of the bigger tank that would need to be changed out and switched over for the smaller.

A flash of *I-can-do-it-myself* burned in Harley's gut and her fingers white-knuckled on the legs of the ladder. It'd just been her and Lautaro for so long, even when Dean bothered to show up for work, she'd developed a rhythm for her movements while they worked.

CJ Diamond was cutting in.

She didn't mind, although Harley didn't think on the reasons for that overly long. He fit, she realized, seeing him standing there with the ladder, the tank's piping waiting like a child holding out a hand to cross the street.

A shuddery tingle zipped across her flesh and the short length of space between them didn't feel far enough. His arms were extended, holding the ladder, the line of his shoulders straining against the fabric of his shirt, pulling the hem taut at the waistband of his jeans. She got to thinking about his abs again before she could stop herself. The earthy aromas of coffee and cardamon swirled around him, but beneath that was something else.

"I know you can do it, Harley," Chance's voice broke into her derailing thoughts. "I'm just offering to help do this while you set up the pumps."

He hadn't moved while her brain worked its way through the mud of her insecurity and curiosity. Hadn't pulled the ladder away. Hadn't fussed at her to do something else. He'd either guessed at her thoughts or the consultant in him was stronger than the man that needed to be in charge.

Harley released the ladder, taking a step back. "Thanks. I'll..." She pointed to the food grade pumps they'd use to move the mash into the tanks, but the words weren't making it to her tongue which suddenly sat thick and useless. Much like her brain.

As she backed away, letting Chance move the ladder to the bigger tank, Harley glanced down at a too-silent Lautaro. The barely contained grin filled in the parentheses of wrinkles around his mouth. She mouthed *shut up* at him then spun on her heels to get to work, stumbling over her own two feet in the process.

Harley stopped, inhaled, clenched her fists at her sides to refocus the thoughts ricocheting around her head like moths flitting beneath the light outside. Logic warred with emotion as she walked, slower now, over to the pumps and began the task of setting up the transfer to the copper tank.

Luckily, her fingers could move on their own to match the fittings, line up the vat with the tank because her brain was all on Chance Diamond.

What a fake name, she said to herself, ignoring the niggle of guilt over her own deception. She'd heard of Diamond Consulting, knew of CJ Diamond and his nose for perfection and his taste for winners. Anyone in her business knew the major players. Diamond was a major player.

If Uncle Everett had hired him, either he had a deal in the making and needed a gold star recommendation from someone like Diamond, or he had something else in the works. Either way, a good word from Diamond was likely to mean the end of Fortune's Brew. A bad word from Diamond could also mean the end of Fortune's Brew. Bookends of waiting disaster.

Lautaro eased over to her side, his presence calming as always. At least it would be if he'd wipe that know-it-all smirk off his face. "Chance knows his way around, sí? It can be good to have an outsider's perspective."

She cut a quick look to Chance as he maneuvered the cap from one tank to another, brow furrowed in concentration as he checked the fit, as if he had anything to gain or lose by making sure it was right. "He's here to pull us apart layer by layer, Lautaro. His only perspective is a paycheck at the end of the day."

Lautaro shook his head as he blew on his coffee. "I do not think so." The older man sipped his drink, watching Harley as she finalized the settings on the pump. "He has nothing to gain and everything to lose if he is dishonest in his appraisal. He has a reputation to protect. We are small potatoes in his garden so I do not think he would risk damaging his name on our behalf. I think it is your Uncle Everett we must watch."

Her instinct sided with Lautaro and she trusted him as much as she trusted her grandmother. "I agree. I just can't figure out what Everett wants. It would be easy enough to sell Fortune's Brew. What does hiring this consultant get him?"

Lautaro leaned in, cocking his head to the side. "That is what we must dig up."

Chapter Eight

S hortly after noon, Chance huddled next to Lautaro and Harley around the spirit safe. Lautaro had set up the spiderleg and they waited like anxious fathers for the first milliliters of clear liquid to be birthed into the collection vessel.

"You pulled off too much for the head," Harley griped yet again, eyeing the ten gallons of liquid Chance had insisted they discard at the front part of the run. It was normal to discard the first 10-15% but Chance had pulled out almost twenty. He had his reasons, not that Harley didn't debate each and every one. The woman was stubborn, but she knew her stuff. Chance could respect that.

She continued, nervously swiping at the hair brushing the tops of her eyebrows. "We're only going to see a 15-17% yield normally as it is and because of the smaller tank that will likely drop."

Chance smiled patiently, rolling the flask between his fingers as the heart of the batch continued to dribble into the flask. It had a slightly pale straw tint, likely from the copper tank. But the clarity was near perfect.

"I know it's hard to trust me, Harley," Chance cut off the nozzle to redirect the remainder of the heart into the spirit safe. "But Lautaro backed me up." He looked up to see the older man returning from the office with three glasses.

Lautaro set the glasses down on the crates of empty bottles waiting to be filled. "The copper heats differently than steel. Let us see how this run goes. We can adjust with the next batch if needed, Harley. It is better not to risk the heart if we don't have to."

Chance nodded at the wisdom, reading more between the lines than what the elder man probably meant. It had been a tough morning trying to keep his attention on the work. Harley wasn't just a whirlwind; she was intuitive in every aspect of the business. She'd worked off feel alone to determine the temp of the batch and because regulations required them to have a thermometer installed, Chance had checked. She'd been right on the mark.

Chance poured them each a half shot of the first few ounces of the heart. In choreographed movements, they swirled the liquid around the short tumblers, then lifted it to inhale in quick in-out movements. Chance watched Lautaro's and Harley's faces as the first hints of barley hit his own nose. Subtle.

He held it up to the light, though what filled the still house was too weak for his purpose. Regardless, what was in his glass was clear enough to read the sign over the still house door. Then the taste, letting it roll over his tongue and around his mouth. He swallowed, the flavor lingering for a few seconds, evolving along the notes of the barley and corn until it faded, the warmth carried to his stomach and outward to the extremities.

Damn, he thought. They had something here.

Lautaro and Harley were silent, their glasses empty.

When Lautaro put his glass down on the box, he studied it, his brows relaxed beneath his thoughts. He started nodding, slowly at first but it picked up speed. "That gives me, how do you say, pimples on the goose."

"Goosebumps," Harley and Chance answered together.

Harley's head swiveled to him. Her look said she was caught off guard by the moment.

"What do you think?" Chance motioned with his empty glass, then set his to join Lautaro's on the crate.

"We've only ever used the steel. I hadn't considered the difference copper would have on the flavor." Her eyes were wide, the fan of her lashes darker half-moons against the honeyed wheat of her skin.

She tipped her empty glass to the side, studied the bottom of the tumbler. Finally, a grin. A shit-eating grin if Chance had to label it. "That's good stuff. That may be the best stuff to ever come out of this place."

Lautaro's face suddenly sported a matching grin and Harley launched herself into the older man's arms. He spun her and when the master distiller set Harley on her feet, she wobbled a little then wrapped her arms around Chance's neck and buried her face against his shoulder.

A little taken back by the act, his arms encircled her waist, surprised at how small she was, at how easily she fit against his body. The aroma of distiller's beer and peach blossoms mingled beneath his nose. He nuzzled into the curve of her body, his chin brushing against her temple and he tightened his arms around her waist to pull her in closer, hold her their longer.

She held her breath, he could feel the stillness of her body against his because his own breath lay trapped in his chest. He let her slide until her toes brushed the ground, putting her face at chin level where he could look down into her eyes, see the constriction of her pupils, the flare of her nostrils as her breath finally returned in short, quick shudders. Her lips parted and Chance was lost in the thoughts of kissing her mouth, sliding his tongue along the seam, tasting the whiskey on her breath.

Harley pulled back from the hug, her face ten shades of red and Chance reluctantly released her. She tugged nervously at the hem of her shirt while Lautaro cleared his throat, mumbling something about checking inventory as he grabbed up the empty glasses and hurried toward the back of the still house.

"I didn't mean to do that." Harley avoided looking at him, but Chance found his eyes wanted to be nowhere else. He liked seeing her like that - unsure, vulnerable. Not because it gave him an advantage but because so far he'd found Harley to be a *what you see is what you get* kind of person. You knew where you stood with her. Chance liked that. He liked knowing where he stood with someone. No games.

"It's ok. Next time you can mean it." Chance sidled away from her, finding himself suddenly feeling awkward when her eyes shot to his face.

It was his turn to look anywhere but at her. He checked the thumper then the pump settings, his own pulse thudding throughout his body for reasons he didn't want to think about too long.

"Do you think it's good enough?"

Harley stood behind him now, their shadows mixing on the floor, one on top of the other. He had to swallow past the lump cutting off his oxygen. Since when did he get flustered being next to a woman?

"You're up against some heavy hitters, even at the regional level." His mother among them, Chance thought to himself. "But I've not tasted anything that good in all my years of consulting. I think you've got a shot, Harley."

She bounced a little on her toes, sucking her lower lip between her teeth, her eyes shining like two copper pennies. "We won't have any time to let it sit and age." Harley made some quick calculations on her phone – it only took her three tries to get the app to open - writing out the rough estimates for proof times, resting, and bottling on the whiteboard beside the spirit safe. "At this rate we'll be bottling Friday night. It'll be straight from there to the competition in Houston on Saturday."

Chance leaned against the wall, crossing one ankle over the other. "It doesn't matter when it's made, only that it gets there on time." After a brief pause, he added, "Do you know if Charlotte will be at the competition?"

Of all the things he expected to come out of his mouth, that had been the last. Pushing Harley now was a bad idea. But if she wasn't going to go all in with Fortune's Brew he needed to know now. He had other clients he could work with. Clients that would bend over backwards to have Diamond Consulting, to have *him* help them. That wasn't arrogance. That was just the truth. He was good. Everyone but his mother seemed to know it. Well, everyone except Charlotte "Harley" Fortune.

Harley crossed her arms, the simple gesture telling. Lautaro had come back into the room, his attention on the pump and the next vats of mash that needed to be processed. She slid a look at him which he avoided. "I'm not sure yet. She's still... away."

He needed Harley to trust him. She was sitting on a gold mine, he thought, ignoring the irony in the words. He thought for a moment. It might be an opportunity for him to get an idea about Everett's plan for Fortune's Brew, understand what the man was cooking up with Chance's mother.

"What about Everett or Mrs. Fortune?"

"I'm sure Lautaro will tell them. He's in charge."

Lautaro's mouth thinned into a grim line. He finished examining the last of the vats and let the cover slam shut but he didn't contradict Harley.

"I'd like to go with you to the competition."

Suspicion hooded Harley's eyes and Chance could almost hear the walls slam shut to cut off the momentary elation he'd just witnessed at her success with the distillation. "Why? Don't you think Lautaro and I can handle it?"

Chance angled his body toward Harley, keeping his hands by his side. "Not at all," he quickly assured but disbelief lasered from the sparks in Harley's eyes. "Usually, I spend a few days observing the operations. What happens at regionals on Saturday will play a large part in my recommendation. It might also be an opportunity for me to get an idea of why Everett is so anxious to sell."

"Why would you want to help me? Us? Charlotte?" Harley quickly corrected. Her shoulders tightened and crawled up around her ears and she had to visibly shake her body to make her muscles relax.

He closed the distance between them, wanting to reach out and put a comforting hand on her shoulder, hold her hand, hold her close again and erase the worry darkening the shadows in her eyes. But he couldn't.

Rule number three, he reminded himself.

"I'm good at what I do, Harley. I don't say that to be arrogant. I don't like the idea of being used and it feels like Everett is withholding information, not only from me but from the family. But it doesn't look like Charlotte cares about Fortune's Brew."

Fiery splotches exploded on Harley's cheeks, setting off the fire in her eyes as well. He could hear her back molars grind together. "This place is all that *Charlotte* cares about."

"Then where is she?" If he was going to make this work, he needed Charlotte on his side. He didn't think too long on why this place mattered to him so much. He could smell his mother's machinations in the supposed deal with Everett Fortune. He didn't know what that meant but he wouldn't let Harley be caught in the middle. Harley needed him, whether she knew it or not. "With everything on the line why isn't she here?"

Harley cut her eyes to Lautaro who refused to meet her gaze.

Chance saw something in this woman, someone who needed him but was still independent enough to challenge him. He just needed to convince her he could help without selling her out.

She gave a slight shake of her head, the hair tucked behind her ear falling forward. Harley looked down at the floor.

"Fortune's Brew is a winner." Chance pushed, then decided it was time to reveal his trump card. "The question is do you, Charlotte Vivienne Fortune, want to be the one to introduce it to the world or do you want to let someone else do it?"

Chapter Nine

Harley sucked in a breath, the air heavy and hot in her lungs. She spun on her heels and marched to the spirit safe, snatching up what remained of the liquor in the collection vessel and downing it in a single gulp. She would have liked for it to burn going down, to cloud her vision with tears so she couldn't see the look of disappointment on Lautaro's face or the look of suspicion on Chance's. But damn if the whiskey didn't go down smoother than a politician's promise before election day. She already knew what she was going to name the batch.

"I didn't intend to lie to you."

Which was true, Harley acknowledged to herself. After everything that happened with the qualification for the Crescent City and Dean, she needed to catch a break. She turned back around, feeling the weight of everyone's expectations pushing down on her.

"I didn't know you were coming until lunch yesterday and assumed you were going to be a mouthpiece for Uncle Everett and Aunt Elsbeth and sign off on a sale no matter what you saw. I thought if you didn't meet Charlotte—" she air quoted her name "—right away I might convince you that Fortune's Brew was salvageable."

That I hadn't screwed it up too much. The unspoken words clogged in her throat.

There was more to it than that, of course. Harley wanted to bring Fortune's Brew back to life to remember her parents, to make sure they weren't forgotten. Because, god help her, she was losing the last vestiges of their memory. Her grandmother was right. They were slipping away, and it ripped something inside of her to lose even the tiniest bits of memory.

Harley watched Chance swallow, then look to Lautaro first then back to her. He shrugged and scrubbed a hand across his dark brown hair, small wisps of it curling up over his ears. "I don't need to be convinced, Harley. Fortune's Brew could be something big." A huff of breath accompanied a huge grin. "I mean it. Everett would be a fool to sell this place, but I don't know that he'll listen. If we have something to back it up with..."

The heady rush of hope hit Harley harder than any liquor as she picked up on Chance's train of thought. Harley leaned forward, studying his face. "Like a win in Houston."

Chance nodded. He crossed his arms which pulled the shirt tight across broad shoulders and well-toned biceps. "A top three finish would definitely add some weight to my recommendation."

"What recommendation is that, Mr. Diamond?"

Harley snapped her head around at the nasally drawl of her cousin, suspicion an acidic burn in her stomach as the young woman cast a disdainful glance around the room.

Paisley stood in the door; her body angled slightly away while she looked down her slender nose at the three of them. Piper came in behind her, arms stiff at her side. She glanced around the still house, eyes widening for a moment.

"Paisley. What are you doing here?" *Looking for the scarf*, Harley thought bitterly.

She'd recognized the scarf worn by both Paisley and Piper at lunch yesterday. Harley and Piper weren't close, but Harley didn't think her first cousin had a vindictive bone in her body. The same couldn't be said for Paisley, who'd been jealous of Harley since she'd come to live with Granny T after her parents had died. How someone could be jealous in that situation still baffled Harley.

"I thought I'd come visit with Grandmother. She looked upset at lunch given all the nastiness with Dean. Dean's been a family friend for years and your treatment of him is embarrassing for the family, Harley."

Dean had wasted no time calling Trudy Fortune to lay out his grounds for not only a civil lawsuit, but criminal charges over the poor condition of the company truck. The Fortune matriarch wasn't one to be cowed, however, as Dean had learned.

Apparently, he'd found a new champion in Paisley.

Paisley could have been the one to let Dean into the still house last night. She might even be the one to have convinced her parents to promote another whiskey over Fortune's Brew. The question was why. Why sabotage Fortune's Brew? To Harley's knowledge, she'd never cared one bit about the operation. Or Dean for that matter.

"You're not the only granddaughter, Har," Paisley droned on, "even if everyone pretends you are."

Paisley's pinched expression gave her fish lips and Harley wanted to snag her with a hook and drag her outside. But she held back, the effort burning in her chest.

"I'm family and it's a family business, Harley."

A sharp spike of pain radiated into Harley's temple and she worked her jaw back and forth. "I guess that's why you've been around so much since we started operations back up."

"Some of us have lives, Harley. Boyfriends. Real careers."

"You post on social media for your parent's tv show."

Paisley ignored Harley's retort and pushed off an invisible wall, back stiff, and propelled herself forward. Her bottomless eyes were all for Chance and she stalked him like a cougar who'd eyed a tasty morsel.

She extended a hand. "My uncle told me you'd be out here today. I've read a lot about you, CJ. I'm Paisley Pallares."

Chance took the hand as it was presented - as if he were to kiss it - but he merely grasped the fingertips and smiled politely. "Nice to see you again, Ms. Pallares."

Paisley tipped her head to the side, the surprise registering in the slight rise of one well-crafted eyebrow. "Such a gentleman, CJ, but please call me Paisley. We haven't met, however. I would remember you."

Jealousy warred inside Harley with a need to protect Chance as stepped back when Paisley went to drag a blood red nail down the front of his shirt. The edge of his smile tightened into something forced and uncomfortable. "Your sister and I shared a laugh over cheating assholes at Gastineaux's."

Harley had to swallow a laugh at the flush darkening her cousin's cheeks. Paisley was not used to being denied or being at a disadvantage. Although she and her sister, Piper, were less than a year apart, they were as different in personality as they were identical in looks.

"That was you behind us." Paisley raked her eyes over the body her fingers were not allowed to touch. "I'll have to pay more attention next time."

"I'll try and be more noteworthy next time."

"Granny T is in town today, Paisley. She volunteers at the elementary school on Tuesdays."

Paisley pouted, the moue of her mouth sharpening the angle of her cheeks. "That's too bad." She strutted to the makeshift distillation setup, eyeing the piping that led to the condenser and doubler. She motioned to the smaller copper pot. "If you're trying to make up for the losses yesterday, why not just use the bigger pot? That would make more sense."

Chance stepped between the two women. "Your uncle has hired me to evaluate the operation. My work requires adjustments to the normal process so I can assess what works best."

Paisley dragged her eyes from Harley to Chance. "You're always stepping up for the underdog, CJ. Be careful. You could be bitten again."

Chance swallowed, the long column of his neck working slowly, patiently. He tilted his head slightly, considering Paisley's statement. "I stand where I'm needed, Ms. Pallares, regardless of the dogs snapping at my heels."

Harley bit back the bitter words swimming on her tongue at Chance stepping in to rescue her even though she knew he was trying to help. She could understand Dean breaking in last night and sabotaging the operation but not Paisley. What was her game? And what did she mean about Chance stepping up? Were he and Paisley acquainted?

Instead, Harley placed her hand close to the pipe leading from the tapered cap at the top of the copper pot to the condenser, confident the temp remained between 168F and 172F even as Lautaro fed the next batch of mash into the pump.

"We're trying a new recipe." Harley checked the thermometer the state regulators made them install, pleased it read 170F. "I want to have a good lineup for the summer release in May."

Paisley laughed, a trilling sound that grated on Harley's nerves with its practiced perfection. She pivoted around the room, reaching down to grab the scarf Harley had draped over a chair. "I wouldn't count on being around for the summer flavors, Har."

A shiver chased its tail around Harley's torso, settling around her heart. "I have six weeks left to convince the family I can make this place profitable." She risked a look at Chance, not sure if his added support would help or hurt her cause at this point. He'd moved to help Lautaro bring the transfer tank for the next phase of the process, checking the lines.

Paisley dragged her gaze from Chance. "After the family meeting yesterday, Mother gave her proxy to me since she's out of the country with daddy."

"When did this happen?" Piper demanded; the flush of anger high on her cheeks.

Paisley ignored her sister, tossing her hair back, watching Harley's face smugly beneath the fan of her lashes. "And after seeing how you've nearly bankrupted the business with one bad decision after another, I don't see how I can vote in your favor in good conscience. We have to think of Grandmother and what's good for her."

Harley stomped across the still house floor but Lautaro stepped into her path, his hands spread wide.

"Don't you mean what's good for you?" She spat the words around Lautaro's frame. "What's your game Paisley?" She flung out a hand to the scarf Paisley tried to hide at her side. "I know it was you and Dean in here last night."

Piper's jaw dropped even further but she remained silent

this time while Paisley flipped her hair and walked toward her sister and wrapped an arm around her shoulder.

"I don't know what you're talking about Harley. It's family property. You don't own it. Piper and I have every right to be here."

Harley tried to keep her heart from doing a nose-dive into her stomach. She didn't want to beg. But she couldn't lose this last piece of her parents. "Whatever you're doing, Paisley, don't. This place means everything to Granny T. Don't destroy it."

"I am looking out for it. At least if we sell the name will continue. If we let you continue to run things, you'll destroy the Fortune name and the family legacy along with it. This place is driving Grandmother to the grave but maybe you don't care about that as long as you get what you want."

The knife couldn't have been aimed any better had Paisley painted a bullseye on Harley's heart. All Harley cared about was family and saving the last pieces of her parents she had left. This was their legacy, and it was up to Harley to preserve it for them. But what if Paisley was right? Harley thought of her conversation with Granny T last night.

I don't want you to lose yourself trying to chase after ghosts. I can't lose anything else to this business.

Harley had been going full steam trying to get Fortune's Brew up and running, but she'd never really asked Granny T if that's what she wanted. Was Paisley right? Had Harley ignored everyone else to chase the dreams of a ghost?

Chapter Ten

C hance couldn't remember a time when he'd felt this lost around a woman. Watching Harley pour all her attention into measuring the proof of the new batch of Fortune's Brew the next morning left more bubbles inside of him than what currently resided in the hydrometer in her hands.

"We'll have to wait a few more hours for it to settle." He meant the distilled liquor but realized the words also applied to her. And him. His heart thudded and his palms were sweaty as if he were on his first job all over again and he wanted to impress the owners.

Her lips parted as if she were about to speak but Chance again got lost in heated thoughts about her mouth and how he wondered if the moonshine they'd distilled would taste sweeter coming off a kiss with Harley Fortune.

Rule Three!

Chance swallowed hard to give his brain something to do except think about kissing Harley.

"I know. I was just checking." Harley propped the

hydrometer against a mason jar but didn't look up. Instead, she scrubbed the heel of one hand across her eyes and stuffed the other in her back pocket and headed toward the dock.

They'd stayed until past midnight distilling two vats worth of mash. The sun hadn't broken through the pitch of night when he'd returned to the Tipsy Turtle that morning. Harley had been silent, she and Lautaro communicating through necessity and unspoken familiarity. He'd asked more questions about Fortune's Brew but when she made little attempt to answer, Lautaro filled him in on the operations that would take place today.

After settling, they'd measure the proof, dilute the mash, and bottle by hand. He'd already known the technical side of things; he'd wanted Harley to talk about the business, hoping that would remind her she loved it. He'd not seen an owner this passionate about their business in his career. He'd also never met an owner this stubborn about accepting help.

She'd been put out with him since he'd stood up for her with Paisley. He had his own reasons for being anxious. Paisley's comment hinted she knew about the incident in Chicago last year. The question was how.

He joined Harley on the storage dock, watching as she transferred cartons of bottles to the two-wheeled dolly in the center of the room. She moved with calculated precision, creating an assembly line when she couldn't get the dolly close enough. "I can help with that."

"I've got it."

A flash of resentment sparked in his gut. Chance was good at his job and those owners willing to listen to his advice always did better in the long run. That wasn't pride and arrogance. *OK, it's not only pride*, he rationalized, but practicality. Chance didn't reach for the stars without a ladder of the right height. He could help. If she'd only let him.

"I'm only trying to help, Harley. You don't have to do everything alone."

Behind him, Chance heard Lautaro issue a harsh 'Ha!' in response and he turned to watch the master distiller cleaning out the copper tank, mumbling words in Spanish Chance was probably glad he didn't understand. Obviously this was an old argument.

"I'm screwing it up."

Though her voice was barely above a whisper, her shoulders slumped beneath the weight of the admission. Hopelessness filled the space around her. She set the third carton of bottles on the dolly and slowly pulled the over sized work gloves from her hands.

"Paisley's right." She grimaced at the words then draped her arms across the handle, propping her chin on her forearm. "Everyone else wants to sell and I'm doing this—" she gestured at her surroundings with a tilt of her head— "out of some kind of selfish notion. I should sign over control to Granny T. She'll do what's right for Fortune's Brew."

Chance nodded, Harley's words touching his idealistic heart. Because he'd been there, questioning everything, listening to others who could only see failure on the horizon and pushing him to take a different path. Even when he knew he could succeed. Because Chance Gold didn't do failure. He trusted his judgment; right now, instinct told him Harley Fortune was a winner.

If he'd learned anything over the past few days, it was that Harley thought of everyone but herself. That didn't make her weak, but it made it easy for people like Everett and Paisley to manipulate. And just like that, Chance knew exactly what Harley needed.

He did a slow clap. "Pity party, table for one."

Harley snapped to attention; mouth open slightly. She white-knuckled the handle of the dolly then narrowed her eyes at him, her brows crinkling together. The flush of anger mottled her cheeks and Chance had to rein in the thoughts of how cute she was even if she was madder than the proverbial wet hen.

He twisted the knife a little more, hating to do it but knowing it was what she needed. "I was wrong. I'm going to recommend to the family that the brand be dissolved or sold."

It was risky, Chance knew. Sometimes a drowning man was so focused on not drowning he couldn't see a lifeline being thrown to him. But nothing would rile Harley up more than telling her Fortune's Brew couldn't be saved. This place was her heart and soul, and her instincts would be to protect it. Just like he wanted to protect her. He wasn't ready to decipher the reasoning behind that yet.

"While you stand here and enjoy the party, I'm going to pack up my stuff." He started the turn, hoping he was wrong. Hoping she wasn't too far underwater to see the lifeline. Chance couldn't do it on his own, but he damn sure could help.

Stop me, Harley. You can do this.

"Do you think this is funny?"

He whirled on her, anger and elation mixing in his chest as he claimed the few feet of space between them. Her hair was a tangle of curls and riotous wisps that refused to be tamed. Just like her. The scent of peach blossoms, wild, earth, kissed the air when got close. "There's nothing funny about this at all. You're giving up, Harley. No one will miss Fortune's Brew when it's gone."

Her eyes widened and she lifted a hand, finger pointed accusingly at him, but he cut off her words before she could speak.

"You've got a winner in there," he gestured sharply back to the still house, "but apparently bringing it to market is too much work for you. I misjudged your determination to make this place a winner."

The dock door was open, letting in the cooler March air to swirl with the scents of barley and corn and a sudden breeze ruffled Harley's hair, sending it in a silken wave to crash over her face. She scrubbed it back and with it, the look of hopelessness was replaced with irritation.

"Lautaro and I have been working for the last five years to get this place going, study the market, perfect our recipe. I've worked every part-time job this town has to offer to make money so I didn't have to live off the trust and could pour that money into this business and pay Lautaro a salary and keep up with payments to our vendors."

"But one little speech from your cousin has you doubting." He settled his hip on one of the oak barrels stored in the corner and looked at the inventory of bottles and labels around them. "Your grandmother doesn't impress me as the kind of woman who would do something foolish but if you don't believe —"

"Don't believe?" Her jaw clenched and he could see her throat working.

She was mad. Good, he thought. She was also ten kinds of beautiful when she was worked up, even with her wrinkled shirt and dirty jeans and a face going nuclear beneath its crankiness.

"You're the only one that cares about this place. Or at

least that's what I thought. You gave up going to college to stay here and work, or was that just out of a sense of guilt?"

"This place means everything to me." Idealization warred with a fierce protectiveness.

"It's just a business and sentimentality have no place in business."

"It's not just a business. It's the heart and soul of my parents. Maybe I can't bring them back, but I can sure as hell honor the memory of what they worked for. And If it's too much work for you, Chance," she yanked the dolly back, slapping her hand onto the cartons of bottles to keep them steady, "feel free to head back to the country club and have the maître d bring you a cocktail. I've poured every bit of myself into this place for five years and Lautaro and I are going to Houston this weekend and we're going to kick ass."

"I know that." Chance waited while the sureness behind his words sunk into her head. "I just needed you to remember it."

Her brows bunched together, wrinkled almost as badly as her shirt then she threw her work gloves at his head. A grin tugged up one side of her mouth. "Did you just reverse psychology me?"

He easily caught the gloves as they hit him mid-chest, but her smile hit him somewhere else. Somewhere he was reluctant to admit. Chance crossed the space between them, pulled by a need he couldn't resist to be close to Harley. Held back by a part of his brain reminding him about Rule Three and good business and a bunch of other things he wasn't sure he cared about anymore.

Because she called to him. Her toughness. Her independence. Her innocence. On a fundamental level a siren song that awakened instincts he thought he'd abandoned. He wanted to protect her, not that she'd let him, but it was the first time he was willing to try knowing failure was the most likely option.

He brought his thoughts back to business because his body was focused on anything but business. "All part of the Diamond Consulting services package."

She blinked rapidly as he neared, her eyes lingering on his mouth. "What else is part of the services package?"

The air suddenly seemed thinner; the breeze warmer. Chance eased the dolly from her grip and set it on the floor, the move putting him into the bubble of space around Harley. He could smell peach and cedar and beneath that the sharp familiar tang of whiskey on her breath. As strange as it was, the scent reminded him of home and family.

Her breathing got deeper, slower, and he lifted a hand to tilt her chin back before lowering his mouth to taste to her lips.

Neither moved for an eternity and Chance settled into the kiss by moving even closer, her breasts skimming his torso. Her touch was like that first shot of whiskey, pouring heat straight to his core. But still, she didn't move.

He kissed her gently, hesitantly, feeling the tension in her body as he waited for a signal he should stop. Her shoulders were a sharp protective barrier, and he traced a slow path up her arm with his free hand. Harley lifted her arms between them, fisted her hands against his chest, finally pushing up on her toes, melting against him.

She opened her mouth slightly and touched her tongue to his bottom lip. He angled his head so he could slant his mouth over hers more fully, taste her more deeply, palming the sides of her face before threading his fingers into her hair to draw her closer.

When his lungs threatened to strike if he didn't draw a breath, he pulled back from the kiss, brushing the corner of her mouth with the pad of his thumb. He rested his forehead against hers before taking a half step back.

"That was not part of a Diamond Consulting services package, in case you were wondering."

She wiped a hand across her brow, rolling her eyes. "Whew. I'm not sure I could afford the upgrade."

"Harley where are those—" Lautaro's voice boomed from behind as he ambled into the storeroom, skidding to a stop when he took in the scene.

Harley pivoted away, her cheeks flushed, fingers trembling as she grabbed the dolly. "Got the bottles right here, Lautaro."

She breezed past Chance, not sparing him a glance as she disappeared into the still house. Lautaro hung back, bouncing a knuckle against his pursed mouth.

"I cannot protect her from her family, Mr. Diamond." The older man's gaze followed the path Harley had disappeared. "But I can protect her from you. I hope I will not have to do this," he finished before he turned sharply and followed on Harley's heels.

Chance scrubbed a hand across his scalp, massaging the hard line of muscle at the back of his neck where tension seemed to find a home. So much for Rule Three, he berated himself but even knowing he'd broken the rules he couldn't regret the kiss. He'd been thinking about it nearly since the first moment he'd met Harley on the side of the road. She challenged everything about his ordered world and while his instinct was to swoop in and set things right for her, he knew that was the wrong approach.

Harley Fortune didn't want or need to be saved.

She was too strong for that and had come too far, mostly on her own, fighting her family, fighting an industry that didn't have many women, fighting her own sense of guilt over the death of her parents.

She wanted to shine on her own.

But maybe he could help point the light in the right direction.

Chapter Eleven

hance felt better sipping the strong coffee in his cup, letting the brew work its magic on his body and soul. The young barista Julie had gone catatonic when he and Harley walked into the Beans and Bubbles just as the door opened. By the time they'd reached the counter, however, Bex had their orders ready. Harley had sent the order online through the business app, she announced proudly. She didn't mention it had taken her two tries, which was one fewer than last time, and Chance wasn't going to bring it up.

They'd left with the sun, having packed up their entry for the Houston Craft Distillers Regional Competition in the trunk of Harley's car. Harley and Lautaro had labeled the bottles on their own, while he'd filled out the paperwork for today's competition. He'd left around nine to call it a night.

Chance had gone back to the hotel, but sleep was evasive, his mind continuously tumbling around the conflicting memories of that kiss with the inner voice in his head reminding him of Rule Three.

In the three days since they'd kissed, he and Harley had not spoken of the kiss after Lautaro had interrupted. Harley had kept the older man close to her side the remainder of the night, a buffer between them, and based on the energy she spent avoiding him it was clearly on her mind.

Chance had sensed an innocence in her kiss, a hesitancy in each touch, as if she were debating on the rightness of each move. True, that was a very Harley thing to do. She was a master planner in her work. But this was different, and he wondered if her experience was limited.

Not that he didn't understand her need for time and distance. He was drowning in a bit of confusion himself. She'd tasted of peaches and moonshine, sweet and sharp, the duality mirrored in her body language. Her hands pulled him closer. Her body built a wall.

He didn't know how to read the signals she was putting out, but he did know he needed to change the channel. This weekend would hopefully put them back on the right side of the client-consultant divide, and he could focus on what was important: getting his final report ready for Everett Fortune.

The man wouldn't likely listen to Chance's recommendation: give Harley and Lautaro the resources needed to make Fortune's Brew the national brand it would become in a few years. As a consultant, it wasn't his job to convince clients toward one path or the other. Just give them the information they needed to make a decision.

Fortune's Brew could be big, but the family would have to sink in the money for marketing and manufacturing capabilities. Fortune's Brew would blend into the scenery or it could stand out. The choice was theirs.

The scenery on Highway 90 was mostly cane fields broken occasionally by a patchwork of houses. Harley was driving, so Chance had taken the opportunity to review the list of entrants for weekend's competition available on the website. The Gold Standard topped the list as last year's winner. It didn't surprise him to see his mother's brand, nor did the momentary twist in his gut at seeing her name next to what have should been his legacy.

"Is that the competition?" Harley kept her eyes on the road but motioned to the paper in his hand with her cup of coffee, which she hadn't put down since they'd steered back onto the highway after leaving downtown Belle Terre.

"Yes. It's a good field. The list of newcomers is relatively small which is why I have you in the debut category."

"Does that put us in competition with Lazy River Whiskey?"

Chance looked up in time to see the tic in Harley's jaw as she grinded her teeth and he could hear the disdain in her voice. Her aunt's promotion of a competitor, especially one as new as Lazy River, had gotten under Harley's skin. Chance had begun to piece some puzzle pieces together and wondered if Paisley was somehow responsible. She'd hinted at knowledge of the incident in Chicago and her "cheating asshole boyfriend" description fit Leo perfectly.

His friendship with Leo was not relevant to his business interests, and their partnership was still only in the planning stages. Legally, he was covered. But it felt like he was playing with words not to let Harley know about the connection to Lazy River Whiskey.

"It does."

Harley thumped her fist against the steering wheel. "I still can't believe Aunt Elsbeth would promote Lazy River over us on her tv show. That could have really put us on the map."

Chance rolled his shoulders, stretching his legs as far as the front seat would allow. "And it might not have made a difference. From what I hear, Lazy River did not see a spike in sales after the episode aired. It was the wrong demographic, in my opinion. They attract a much younger audience than what typically purchases your price point. So it may not have been a good fit."

Lautaro, sitting behind Chance, leaned forward as best he could, held back by the seat belt Harley insisted he wear. "I expect we will see all the usual brands. The Gold Standard. What of Old Barrel? They do not show often but do well in the regional competitions."

The mention of his father's distillery raised a mix of pride and agitation. Pride over what his father had accomplished. Agitation that he'd had to do it twice thanks to the betrayal of Chance's mother. Still, he worried about Harley's blanket distrust of anything connected to a major label. Even though he maintained a separation, no one could question his connection to the top shelf brands.

"Old Barrel is not on the list, but they could be a late entry like us. The master distiller and the owner disagree on how many competitions it takes to stay relevant, so they usually only participate at the bigger events. This one in Houston is a mid-level competition but they always participate in Nashville."

"The bigger labels shouldn't be allowed to compete in craft shows like this." Harley looked to Lautaro in the rearview for support but didn't find it.

"We are competing on the shelves, *carina*. I do not see a difference if we compete here. This is a good competition for us, yes?" Lautaro asked from the back seat. "It is a newer addition to the North American Distillery Council."

Chance had been worried last night and this morning Lautaro would become an obstacle in his work after witnessing he and Harley kiss. The man obviously loved Harley like a daughter and would protect her as best he could. For the moment, he probably saw Chance as just another player in a game rigged against her.

"I believe so. They focus on quality around price point which means you won't necessarily be up against the more established brands."

Checking the primary category for debut brand on the entry form also meant that Fortune's Brew would be up against Leo's distillery, Lazy River. Leo was a businessman, Chance assured himself, and he knew Chance would do his job, but Chance had tasted Lazy River. They didn't compare to what Fortune's Brew was bringing to the table.

"Because we couldn't hold our own against the likes of The Gold Standard."

"Not at all." Chance pulled out the spreadsheet he had for Harley's income and expenses. "The bigger brands have more buying power which gives them wider margins and a lower price point even on the smaller batches. And on the larger batches, they can afford to age the product longer which gives it a smoother taste for the higher price."

Harley chewed her bottom lip between her teeth. "I hadn't considered that. I'd been trying to price competitively with them. No wonder I was losing money." She huffed angrily and shook her head.

"Your price point wasn't all that out of line," Chance reassured. "We can adjust the wholesale prices to better reflect your manufacturing costs. It's why this competition is good for you. Debut brands like Fortune's Brew are judged against other emerging brands so it puts you on a more level playing field."

"I am surprised that Old Barrel and The Gold Standard can still qualify for the regionals," Lautaro added from the back seat. "They are surely over the production maximum allowed by these smaller competitions."

"Old Barrel hasn't reached the case quantity yet. But The Gold Standard," Chance had to pause to swallow back the sour taste in his mouth, "they split into two corporations legally when they went international. The small batch side of the business means they qualify."

Lautaro harrumphed. "Now that does seem right, as Harley says."

Harley clenched the steering wheel in her hands, still worrying her lip between her teeth. "Since when has what's fair ever been a test for what happens? Everyone lies and cheats to get what they want. Doesn't matter who they run over in the process."

Chance knew the faces swimming in her head and fought the desire to reach over and touch her, to cup his hand behind her neck and hold her to him, to trace the firm line of her mouth with his thumb and erase the tension. Or, even better, kiss her until she melted against him. He could still feel the weight of her body pressed against his chest.

"Relax, Harley," Lautaro coached from the back seat. "Breathe in. Breathe out."

Shadows darkened the skin under the hollows beneath her eyes. "It's just that if we don't do well today, Uncle Everett and Aunt Elsbeth will vote to sell and I'm not sure Granny T will fight very hard to keep Fortune's Brew going if that happens."

"You can't think that way." Chance looked at the entrant's list, his eyes drawn to a single name. "That goal is too big to worry about right now. We don't need all the answers today. Starting is the hardest part usually. And there are several milestones we have to hit before anything else becomes important. Today, the goal is finishing in the top three."

Lautaro clapped Chance on the shoulder. "We will think

of today and let tomorrow's worries wait until then, eh, Chance?"

From the corner of his eye, he saw Harley nervously tug at the collar of her blazer then run her hand down the pencil skirt causing Chance to think way too much about the woman's legs. She had the single button on the blazer open, revealing the simple white tank beneath. The snug contours of the cotton and clean lines of the skirt had only confirmed what Chance suspected before: Harley was all softness and curves.

Back to business, he reminded himself. "What we do need to think about are the remaining regional competitions before Crescent City. There are a lot of people who'll be doing what we're doing, trying to make a showing to enter the contest without the production quota. We'll need to be strategic on where to enter Fortune's Brew and whether or not we enter the same product."

Harley huffed, the resignation lacing her voice palpable. "Then we need to find competitions where The Gold Standard is not participating. They win first place. Every. Single. Time." She punctuated the last words with a fist to the steering wheel. "They obviously have the production to enter Crescent City without the regional showings. So why are they at every competition?"

"Ego." Chance and Lautaro replied simultaneously.

Chance turned in his seat shocked by the sudden change in Lautaro's usually robust persona.

The older man kept his gaze out the window, his face a tight roadmap of hills and valleys. A muscle jumped in the hollow beneath his jaw and he swallowed hard before scrubbing a hand over his face. "There is always a price for ego. You just do not know who will pay the bill."

"Lautaro, don't." Harley's voice barely qualified as a

whisper, the choked words barely audible against the sound of the tires on the road.

"I must, Harley."

Chance sensed an old argument in the unspoken words. He remained silent, turning his attention back to his coffee and the road in front of them. He knew both the safety and danger in keeping things bottled up. His fingers traced a path over the line where The Gold Standard was printed, and next to that, the owner: Sondra Gold.

"Lazy River Whiskey has gotten some good press. Aunt Elsbeth called them out on her show a few weeks ago. I'm sure that has helped their sales."

Harley's voice brought Chance back from the inner wandering of his thoughts, but her topic was a touchy one and he debated on how much to reveal to her. He wasn't obligated to share the information, it wasn't a conflict for him to consult with other distilleries when his best friend owned one, even if they were in competition. But it wasn't as simple as that, and Chance knew it.

"Leo says it didn't." At her questioning gaze, he continued. "I actually know the owner. Leo Quinn and I went to school together."

Harley cocked her head to the side, as if the information was weighing down one side of her brain. He saw her glance in the rearview mirror and Chance heard Lautaro shift in the backseat.

"You have a full non-disclosure agreement with me, Harley." He resisted the urge to reach over and touch her arm, reassure her in some physical way.

When he was close to Harley the protective side of his nature was on full steam, not because she was weak. Anyone that thought Harley Fortune was weak was too stupid to be standing upright. He just couldn't stand manipulative people and Harley Fortune was surrounded by them. She'd held her own so far, though and Chance wanted to make sure she got the opportunity to show everyone what she'd accomplished so far.

"What happens at Fortune's Brew, stays at Fortune's Brew."

She cut her eyes to him and nodded once but he could see the internal debate war behind her eyes and in the white-knuckled grip on the steering wheel.

Hoping to distract her, he turned the conversation away from the upcoming competition and to her hometown. He'd not had much time to look around the city but had enjoyed what little he'd seen. He asked about the Main Street sea wall and she told him the story of the hurricane in the sixties that had delivered the Spirit of Belle Terre to the town center. She also explained why the boat was undergoing some major repairs after a mishap with a very large Christmas tree and a trio of thieving Grinches this past Christmas.

"The bartender at Gastineaux's is a fan of yours."

Harley laughed, an easy sound that hinted at the person beneath the stress and tension of her life. "Hudson's the best."

A spark of jealousy flared in Chance, not a familiar emotion for a man used to feeling like he was the best. He wanted to be the one to put the relaxed smile on Harley's face or draw that kind of genuine laugh from her.

But the spark didn't find tinder. Chance was glad that someone in Harley's life could make her smile.

Besides, he reminded himself, *Rule Three*. He needed to keep himself focused on business. Anything else would just interfere with his plans. He needed a way to get the money for his business plan with Leo, otherwise their dream of opening A Shot and A Beer was going down the drain before the first drink was served.

Lautaro joined in the laughter. "We are going to have to start paying him a commission on our sales, yes?"

"Or offer him a job. Now that Dean is gone, we'll need the help if we want to..."

She let the words trail off beneath the noise of the tires on the road but Chance could fill in the details. Harley wasn't confident there would be a future for Fortune's Brew. He wondered if she'd ever considered another line of work or, if like him, she'd never wanted to do anything else.

That had certainly gone over well during career day in third grade. He laughed, drawing Harley's attention.

She questioned him with a silent look, then prodded, "Don't keep the funny stuff to yourself."

"When I was in third grade we had our first 'what do you want to be when you grow up' essay, which we had to read aloud in front of the classroom. My essay started, 'I want to drink and make whiskey smoother than a baby's bottom like my dad because 'too much good whiskey is barely enough.'"

"Mark Twain said the last part," Harley added, a half-smile softening her features.

Chance sat tongue tied for a moment, his mind lost in thoughts of their kiss and the way her face had felt beneath his palms. The sun was just over the treetops in the sky behind them, the early morning light honeyed gold in the car's interior but it was that smile, even that half smile, that chased away the shadows and stole the words from his brain.

He shook himself mentally. "The teacher was not impressed with that little fact. They called my dad who by this time was number one on the school's speed dial list."

Harley gasped and thumped a fist against the steering

wheel, indignant on behalf of his eight-year-old self. "But you were telling the truth!"

If he hadn't been falling for her before that moment, he was certainly tipping head over heels for her after her quick defense. For Chance, the abandonment of his mother left him feeling unlovable. If the person who should love you more than anyone didn't love you, what did that say about your worth? Stir in the sense of confusion over his father's quick remarriage to a woman much younger than him, it had left Chance feeling alone.

"What did your father say to the principal?" Harley prompted at his silence.

He didn't want to share all of that with Harley, however, and edited the story playing out in his head. "My step-mother arrived." Chance tunneled his fingers through his hair. "I figured I was a goner. Little girls aren't the only ones who hear stories like Cinderella and associate *evil* with *stepmother*. Evie and I hadn't gotten to know one another yet; she and my father had only remarried a few weeks before this. I think she was as wary of me as I was of her."

Chance laughed again. "The principal was very confident. Private school. Mistress of her domain. She presented her reasoning for wanting to suspend me." He cleared his throat, stiffened his posture, looked down his nose and in a clipped, nasally voice said, 'We're studying Mark Twain in English this year. We can't introduce students to such things at this age. What would other parents think?'"

He lifted a hand to pause his story. "Now I have to give you some context here. Evie was a supermodel. I'm not talking ads for local papers or insurance company billboards, but a full fledged, walk the runway in Paris, face on the cover of Vogue and Cosmo, supermodel. She'd been working since she was twelve.

"Using what I would soon come to recognize as her you've-met-your-match voice, she asked, 'He's right, though, isn't he? About the quote and Mark Twain. Because if he's right he's not the one in trouble.'"

The three of them shared a laugh, and Chance relaxed back against the car's front seat, crossing his left ankle over his right knee. He'd never shared such a personal story with a client but couldn't find any regret for sharing it with Harley.

"You must have been feeling very alone." Harley's voice reached across the short distance between them and the emotion beneath her words seeped into his skin and warmed him. "If your dad had just remarried, I imagine that must have been very hard. Kids tend to think, no matter what, that their mom and dad will always be there so if your parents had divorced I would think bringing a new wife would end that fantasy for you."

Chance swallowed hard, emotion suddenly clogging in his throat. He felt like an idiot. Whatever insecurity he'd felt at his father's remarriage had to be nothing compared to what she'd felt at losing her parents at nearly the same age.

"I'm sorry, Harley. I wasn't thinking."

"No, don't say that." She reached over and laid her fingers over his hand where it rested on his thigh. "I don't have a corner on the market when it comes to sadness over losing a parent. I had my grandmother and Lautaro." She smiled into the rearview and he heard the love in the older man's voice when he whispered *Always*. Harley continued. "My aunt and uncles, cousins, a whole town standing with me when my parents died. It was hard losing them like that but I never felt alone or abandoned."

She squeezed his hand, and Chance took the opportunity to interlace their fingers. When she pulled back her hand, was it reluctance he felt? His own shields, his rationale behind Rule Three and keeping his identity a guarded secret, suddenly seem much less important.

Maybe tonight while they were driving back, he'd tell her everything, even the full story about his mother. Surely, she'd understand the need to protect himself and his father's business.

"Finish the story," Harley prodded. "Evie has rightly put the principal in her place. Was the teacher pissed when you came back to class?"

"Oh no, I got suspended for three days." At Harley's slack jawed expression, Chance explained. "It was my first lesson in that whole power corrupts rule. Evie was very well known. She'd gone to court to be emancipated so she could drop out of high school at fifteen and take the GED. The principal wasn't about to let some drop out get the better of her."

Harley was silent while the GPS directed them through Beaumont. Traffic was still light and moving easily for a weekend and it didn't take them long to navigate across town.

"What is it with people in power?" She finally asked when they were once again on open highway. "Not only do they have to keep the power, they also have to crush anyone else along the way."

"Fear." Lautaro's voice from the backseat was thick and raspy. "When you are in charge, no one can make you do what you do not wish to do. No one can take what you do not wish them to take. No one can hurt you. Or at least, that is the belief. There is always someone more powerful than you. You just have not met them yet."

"And of course there's usually a financial aspect," Chance added, thinking of Everett Fortune and their conversation over the future of Fortune's Brew. He wished he knew more about the backroom deal Everett and his mother were cooking. Did she want to absorb Fortune's Brew into her own brand, or crush it outright?

The smart thing may have been the absorb the existing labels. The batch they were entering today was some of the best Chance had ever encountered over the last eight years. Sondra Gold wasn't one to share, however, so the real question was what did Everett think he was getting. And why not share that with the family?

"Aunt Elsbeth is completely hands-off the business since she and Uncle Paolo went to live in Costa Rica for their tv show."

He watched as Harley checked the rearview mirror, adjusted the angle though she'd spent a good five minutes before they put the car into drive checking and rechecking the mirrors, the dashboard gauges, the tires. The hood had been raised when he'd first pulled onto the property while Harley checked the oil. Being in the car made her nervous, the reasons obvious. Her parents had died in a car accident. They'd died while returning from an event much like the one they were attending today.

Chance would do what he could to keep her distracted. He wanted her to see the business for its possibilities. Brands like hers started small but they didn't have to stay that way unless they wanted. There were plenty of opportunities for diversification. He could...

He let the thought trail off. His job would be done after today. He had what he needed to give his report. Fortune's Brew would live or die and there was little he could do about it. For the first time, Chance wanted to have more influence than his role as a consultant gave him. His job was to provide information, not solutions.

And his job didn't include falling for the client.

Lautaro's voice interrupted his thoughts and drew him back into the conversation.

"Everett is definitely focused on the dollar signs."

Harley nodded her agreement. "He and Uncle Vic have expensive tastes, but I've never seen anything that would make me think they're hurting for money. Even if they were, the sale of Fortune's Brew isn't going to make anyone independently wealthy."

"There must be something he thinks the sale will give him."

She sighed and drummed her fingers against the steering wheel. "Or he just wants out like Granny T." Her fingers stopped moving on the wheel. "Maybe it's time."

An unexpected dread tightened around his heart at the thought of Harley losing Fortune's Brew. He knew what it was like to lose the legacy you thought you were building. It had happened to him and his father when Sondra had walked away. It was hard enough having her leave, but she took The Gold Standard with her, something his father was on the brink of bringing to life.

"Let's not give up just yet. Today will give you an idea about Fortune's Brew standing in the market and after that, you can evaluate what's best."

He just hoped what was best for Fortune's Brew was also best for Harley.

Chapter Twelve

Harley took a step back so that yet another in a long series of people could come forward to greet Chance as they made their way to the registration table. Vendors. Competitors. Organizers. Restaurateurs. Mixologists. The men shook his hand, vigorously, clapped him on the back, praised his work and advice, thanked him for the guidance over some aspect of the business or trade. The women...

The women hugged him. Even those that didn't look like huggers couldn't wait to wrap their arms around him, drawn like magnets to lean in and brush cheeks and lips against his. Polite huggers, one arm huggers, full chested huggers, full frontal huggers.

The full frontal/shimmy huggers were Harley's favorite, however, and she had to hide the smile at Chance's pained expression as the overly made-up woman stuffed into the white silk sheath crushed her monumental breasts against Chance's chest.

She understood the appeal. There were parts of her that tingled for an hour after they'd kissed in the still house. It wasn't her first kiss, but it had been the first time she'd felt a kiss down to her toes. Not to mention other body parts.

Harley didn't have a ton of experience with men. Granny T had done her duty and taught her the birds and bees, but no one had been there to teach her the nuances of flirting or dating.

She'd done little of either in her life so far. High school made her feel awkward, but what was high school for, in reality? She'd played the piano and worked in the still house. Dean had been her first official boyfriend, and he'd not made anything tingle except her last nerve.

The shimmy hugger's pouty whine dragged Harley from her thoughts.

"You've been avoiding me, CJ." The woman pouted, her orange-red lips leaving a smudge on Chance's cheek as he avoided her kiss when she pulled back. She remained draped over Chance's torso like last year's sweatpants on an unused treadmill. "I think you left the judge's panel last year because you were afraid of being around me after our little *disagreement* in Chicago."

Chance pried her hands off his shoulders, maintaining a polite but neutral expression. Her pout deepened the crevices bracketing her lacquered lips. "We both know why I left, Kissy." He placed her hands together, giving them a gentle pat while taking a step back to regain some personal space.

Every nuance of his body language screamed discomfort, and Harley wondered at the history Chance shared with this woman. She also couldn't help but wonder how it would impact her. "I needed to focus on my work. Besides, it's good for the panels to see some turnover. I served for three years. They needed fresh blood."

The older woman's face morphed into a mix of oversexed cougar and melted wax doll. Kissy drew a finger over the hill of her breasts, then slid her hand around her side to cup her generous hip. "You had the freshest—"

"Kissy," Chance interrupted, opening his arm to bring Harley and Lautaro into the conversation. "Have you met Ms. Charlotte Fortune, owner of Fortune's Brew, and Mr. Lautaro Sanchez, their master distiller. May I present Kissy St. Germaine."

Nonplussed by Harley and Lautaro witnessing her display with Chance, Kissy waved in the general direction of a fussy looking man, a snide disdain widening the nostrils of a nose reddened by too much alcohol. "And may I introduce Mr. Glynn Bowers."

Mr. Bowers nodded his head but did not accept the handshake Chance extended.

"I've been showing him the ropes since you left, Chance. He has become quite the judge in demand since he joined our little family."

Harley recognized the names as two of the seven judges on the competition's panel. Kissy was also a leading food and wine critic. She was known to be harsh, almost cruel in her reviews and people courted her approval like the damned in hell wanted ice water. Not that it did any good. It was said she made chefs and distillers cry just to see if she could. However, a positive review from her was like being tapped by the gods; nothing could defeat you after that.

Lautaro extended his hand and Kissy nodded at both of them while accepting Lautaro's handshake with the tips of her fingers. "Mr. Sanchez. Ms. Fortune. Are you newcomers? I don't believe I've seen your label before. Then again," she waved her hand dismissively at the crowd gathered in the foyer of the ballroom where the judging would take place, "everyone that makes a bottle of something in a washbasin these days thinks they have what it takes for the market."

Harley swallowed, rapidly sorting through the list of acceptable responses that wouldn't alienate the judge or send Chance into fits. Although judging by the widening of his eyes, she wasn't sure if he was worried about her response or shocked at Kissy's little jab. She finally settled on something appropriate. "Hopefully, you can tell us if we're ready to move out of the washbasin and into the bathtub."

With a noncommittal *hmmm,* Kissy made air kissy noises at Chance. "You come see me later so we can resolve our little disagreement, or I'll be very put out with you CJ."

Chance smiled but it didn't reach his eyes. "I wouldn't want that, Kissy. But I'm working today so it will have to be another time." His voice was resigned, and Harley wondered what his little disagreement with Kissy had been about. "I'm going to take Harley and Lautaro over so they can get registered. I'll talk to you soon."

At the registration table, Harley signed in, her hands shaking as she handed over the registration form and fee, mentally calculating the dwindling balance in their business account, and accepted the packet of information and name badges for her and Lautaro. Chance remained quiet; his normal enthusiasm dismissed in the wake of Hurricane Kissy.

"Oh, Ms. Fortune," the woman behind the table held out the registration form, pointing to a blank space, "the label name isn't completed. We require that information for the judges."

Harley quickly jotted in the information, ignoring the jittery feeling in her stomach. Chance had filled in the registration form last night while she and Lautaro worked on bottling the new batch. She hadn't told him the label name and hoped he'd be pleased when he saw the bottles.

As they walked into the ballroom, she let Lautaro take the lead, hanging back to check in with Chance.

"You ok?"

Chance guided the dolly holding their three cases of Fortune's Brew, weaving through the crowds. Even as focused on him as she was, Harley couldn't help but notice the other displays lining the aisles and against the curtained walls of the grand ballroom.

Elaborate set ups showcased the competition's product, all with professionally printed signs, brochures, pamphlets, and business cards. Some offered food to pair with their spirits, fancy canapes and single bites lining silver trays offered by hosts and hostesses.

They were so out of their league Harley cringed at the thought of putting out their bottles on a bare table with a computer printed sign she'd made from her bedroom in the middle of the night.

He cleared his throat, shooting her a quick glance over his shoulder. "I'm good. I haven't been to Houston in two years so it's good to be back here."

The rote answer sounded like a soundbite someone would absently give to a pushy reporter. She was going to press the issue but saw Lautaro standing in the aisle, his heavy brows drawn together as he scratched his chin.

Oh no, Harley groaned inwardly. *We just got here. Has the Fortune luck found us already?* She needed a minor miracle to make the finals. Even with Chance's promising words on the quality of the product, Harley knew it wasn't likely they could beat out a hundred plus competitors their first time out of the gate. And seeing the other displays, they'd look like the washbasin amateurs Kissy St. Germaine detested.

Harley joined Lautaro and saw the reason for his perplexed look. A black canopy tent shaded their area and announced "Fortune's Brew: Where good fortune meets good whiskey" in silver script over a black matte background. The front table had several boxes stacked next to a few rough pine crates they could use to display their bottles. Several large arrangements of flowers – a delicate collection of orchids and gladioli – edged the display. Everything sat on custom tablecloths and table runners with their names in beautiful script.

She opened the smaller of the boxes, pulling out business cards that mirrored the overhead banner. Her name was printed in the corner next to the word "Owner." Harley had to run her fingers over the embossed silver lettering, then quickly ripped the tops off the other boxes to find brochures about Fortune's Brew. They even had a picture of the Drunk Skunk on the inside with another of the still house.

While she stood in muted shock, Lautaro started unpacking and setting up the display. Harley turned to Chance whose smile had finally reached his eyes.

"I know it was presumptuous. I had a friend in the area do up the sign."

Harley lunged at him, wrapping her arms around his neck, giving him the full frontal but holding back on the shimmy. But just like that her world tilted off its axis, the earth sliding out from beneath her feet to leave her suspended except where Chance's arms slid slowly around her torso.

"Thank you." She had to hold back on the kissing too because she wanted more than an air kiss from the man.

Chance's arms tightened around her waist, and he

nuzzled his mouth against the shell of her ear. "You're welcome."

Warm tendrils chased across the nape of her neck, fanned by the heat of his skin against hers. She mentally followed the points of contact where his body pressed into hers. Cheeks. Shoulders. Chest. Hips. Each point became an epicenter for a new bloom of heat and desire.

When she let go, she grabbed Chance's hand and pointed to the bottles Lautaro was setting out. His fingers squeezed hers sending spirals of warmth up her arm to blossom on her face. She let go slowly, even reluctantly, wishing she had the experience to be flirty or sultry or whatever it was that made men notice women. But she always felt like Switzerland besides her cousins, neutral, unnoticeable.

"I have something to show you." She pulled back enough to where their faces hovered, her eyes dropping to his mouth.

"I can't wait."

Were his words breathy? His gaze lingered on her mouth, that half grin tilting up a corner of very kissable lips that could charm a girl right out of her... Lautaro cleared his throat and Harley pulled back her thoughts.

"I wanted you to be the first to see our new label."

Chance picked up a bottle, turning the clear glass in his hand. The amber tint was no longer obvious once they'd diluted the heart to final proof and the bottle looked almost empty because of the clarity of the liquid. A silver label adorned the front, it's metallic sheen catching the light. When Chance read the label, his eyes widened.

"Diamond in the Rough." He read the words, tracing the lettering much like Harley had done with the business cards.

A lump of emotion welled up in Harley's throat and she had to swallow it down. "I wasn't the easiest client to deal with, I know. But you gave us some good ideas that made today possible, and I wanted to say thanks for getting us here."

His head snapped up, eyes narrowing slightly. "That was all you, Harley. Never doubt that. You and Lautaro got Fortune's Brew to where it is today. I just helped steer you in the right direction."

"But without that good direction," Lautaro added, "We would be driving a very nice car down a dead-end road. Fortune's Brew owes you a lot. And I am very grateful you have been here so everyone can see Harley's hard work as it should be seen."

"Our hard work, Lautaro." Harley amended, nodding to Lautaro. "None of this would have happened without you."

Chance set the bottle down carefully, like one would a priceless antique, his hand lingering over the cap. He cocked his head, a devilish grin adding a light to his eyes. "Kissy might just be impressed with our washbasin moonshine after all."

Lautaro barked a deep laugh, clapping Chance on the shoulder. "You are so right! Let's get set up. I will take the entry to the judges while you two make this pretty."

Once Lautaro disappeared into the crowd, their future in three bottles gripped firmly in his large but gentle hands, Harley and Chance went about setting up the display. As Harley unpacked the boxes, the lump in her throat got bigger. Once again, she'd dropped the ball where the business was concerned.

"The display. Another thing I didn't think about."

She wasn't good at asking for help, preferring to do it herself rather than give someone the ammunition to use against her. But it was hurting Fortune's Brew.

Harley pulled out several large swatches of silver metallic cloth to drape over the pine crates. The analogy of the refined silk over the rough pine didn't escape her.

She realized it also applied to her and Chance. He was a silky damask in the industry; she was more the rough burlap type.

"We would have looked like amateurs today sitting here among the big boys trying to play in the majors. Thank you."

"That's something I wanted to talk to you about, Harley."

He didn't look her in the eye as he aligned the brochures and business cards with the front of the table, even filling a toy pirate's chest with silver wrapped candies. *Here it comes,* she thought. *He's going to tell me I should sell. That I'm bad for the business.*

"I know what you're going to say and you're right."

He paused, his brows drawn together, while he seemed to consider her words. Then he nodded. "You think I'm going to tell you to sell, or that you're messing up your family legacy."

Harley shrugged, keeping her gaze on the bottles of Diamond in the Rough now lined up on the silken draped crates. The display was perfect. The overhead light reflected on the silver labeling and the silver material really highlighted the beautiful clarity of the product.

"Today would have been a disaster. Definitely washbasin amateurs." She tried to smile but found it only pushed the tears stinging at the back of her eyes closer to the front.

Chance took her hands in his and turned her to face him. "Don't let Kissy St. Germaine into your head. That's her specialty." When she didn't meet his gaze, he lifted her chin with a knuckle. That familiar warmth radiated from his touch, but it bumped up against the cold dread of reality.

She'd screwed up. Again. "Besides, the judging is blind. No one knows who wins until the final scores are tallied."

A spark of hope found a home behind the walls of Harley's heart. "But they also judge on design, on how our brand holds up against others in the market. We can't compete with The Gold Standard or Old Barrell. I'm not even sure we can compete with some of the smaller labels."

He turned toward the crowd as if searching for the answer then pulled her forward, their hands still joined. "Let's walk the floor."

Chance escorted her around the ballroom, pointing out the different distilleries setting up their displays. They saw the industry leaders like The Gold Standard and Old Barrell. But also, newcomers like themselves.

Harley was amazed at his knowledge of the people in the industry and again, he was greeted by someone at most of the major players and even a large portion of the smaller distilleries. Where a brand displayed numerous trophies for wins, he talked about where they'd started or how they'd grown.

It was common knowledge, Harley knew. She'd visited most of their websites in the middle of the night when she couldn't sleep because of worry over a decision she'd made about the business. Her brain was like a multiverse at night, playing out scenarios where she didn't screw up her life and that of Granny T.

"What do you notice about every distillery?"

She bit back the first response, a self-deprecating remark about her lack of planning and foresight. That didn't do any good. She was here to learn. If she was going to make Fortune's Brew the success, she knew it could be, she had to fight. That was something she had plenty of: fight.

But Harley needed to take what someone like Chance Diamond had to offer - insight - and put it into action.

"They look organized, professional. Everyone is focused on a job - set up, talk to visitors. I even see some set up to take orders."

She sighed. There'd be vendors at the competitions. They needed to be ready to meet demands for orders... if they ever got any orders.

Chance squeezed her hand, giving her shoulder a nudge with his own. "Stop it." He whispered, as if reading her mind. "You can't do everything. That's what I want you to see. Every brand here has multiple people behind the scenes handling their business specialty. Distillers. Marketing. Customer service. Distribution."

"But I'm sure they didn't start with a staff." Frustration pitched her voice high, and she had to suck in a breath to temper it. "We haven't paid Dean's dad for the corn from last year. We're barely going to pay the vendor for the bottles used today."

"I'm here to help." He stepped closer, reaching out toward her but pulling his hand back at the last moment.

She saw the conflict darken his eyes and felt the same clash in her own mind. This was a business arrangement. Nothing more, she reminded herself. No matter how good he kissed or how comforting her hand felt nestled in his.

"I'm not trying to be arrogant, but I happen to know what I'm talking about. Let me work with you to bring Fortune's Brew to market. And Piper has a degree in marketing and is searching for somewhere to use it."

She rolled her eyes at the mention of Piper's name, but he cut her off before she could protest.

"I know, but she's not Paisley and I think she'd help if

you asked her." At her continued hesitation, he prodded. "At least talk to her. You have to be willing to ask for help."

His words mirrored those of her grandmother and Lautaro. "I guess I'm not really good at that. Granny T swears my first words were 'me do it myself.'"

"I can tell," Chance winked and this time it didn't make Harley's insides want to crawl outside.

She could finally see what made women all swoony over CJ Diamond. The man was hot, yes. He filled out a pair of jeans as well as the charcoal grey suit he'd worn today and looked as comfortable in both as he might in a pair of sweats at home on the couch. But he was genuine in both his praise and his criticism and gave each in equal measure.

"Besides, it's one of the things I like best about you." The words tumbled from his mouth, but Harley could tell by the slight widening of his eyes that he wanted to pull them back immediately. Chance let go of her hands, took a step back, and cleared his throat. "I mean too many of my clients want me to come in and solve their problems. Tell them what to do. I can do that of course."

He cleared his throat again, scratching at the path of his voice like it was suddenly too tight. Now the words rushed like a steam from a condenser, forced in a direction by internal pressure.

"But they just end up in trouble again because they don't know how to make the decisions on their own. You know what you're doing. You and Lautaro. You just need a little fine tuning."

"Chance?" the voice broke the uncomfortable silence surrounding them while Harley figured out how to respond to Chance's speech. She turned in its direction to see a man about their age headed their way.

He wore a white t-shirt beneath a dark jacket, the

contrasting colors deepening the deep walnut of his skin tone and jet-black hair. There was a boyishness in the high cheekbones and exaggerated smile. The obsidian eyes gave no hint of innocence, however. But he wasn't the one that held Harley's attention. It was the woman on his arm.

Her cousin, Paisley.

Chance's brows lifted but there was a shift in his demeanor. "I was wondering when I'd see you."

While the two men shook hands, Harley kept her attention on Paisley who intentionally kept her focus on Chance. Harley wondered why Paisley hadn't mentioned coming to Houston last night or, hell, that she was apparently involved with someone in the industry. They weren't close but Paisley was usually all too happy to tell Harley about her latest boyfriend.

It was like when they were children and Paisley received whatever was the latest, greatest, unattainable Christmas present. She liked to show it off so everyone else knew she had something they wanted. Piper, on the other hand, had always shared. Harley often had the same toy sitting in the box in her room, more interested in watching Lautaro or her dad brew up a special batch of holiday moonshine.

"Leo Quinn, let me introduce Harley Fortune of Fortune's Brew."

Chance moved to Harley's side; the protective gesture not lost on Harley. She knew Leo Quinn's name and distillery and suddenly her aunt's promotion of Lazy River made sense. Why Paisley would want to sabotage Fortune's Brew made more sense.

"Leo owns Lazy River Distillery."

"Always the professional, huh, bro? I've known Chance since college, and we were throwing keggers for the Pi Betas." Leo draped an arm possessively around Paisley's waist but didn't move his gaze from Harley. "Nice finally meet you, Harley. I hear the gators out by Lake Opelousas really like your stuff."

Harley stiffened at the mention of the accident that had cost them so much and put Fortune Brew's future at stake. Leo laughed at his own joke and offered his hand. She reluctantly returned the handshake, his palm clammy, grateful when he broke contact to gesture toward her cousin.

"I'm sure you know this beautiful lady on my arm, Harley." He tightened his grip, nuzzling her ear but Paisley winced, and he pulled back. "Chance you haven't you met my girlfriend. This is Paisley Pallares."

Chance nodded in her direction. "We recently met at Fortune's Brew. Nice to see you again, Ms. Pallares."

"Paisley," Harley folded her arms, surreptitiously wiping off Leo's handshake on her blazer. "I didn't know you'd be here today." Although Paisley obviously knew Harley would be here. And she'd obviously mentioned Harley to Leo before. What else had the two of them been talking about?

Paisley's involvement in the sabotage of the still house distillation tank looked more and more likely but Harley didn't think she had it in her. The desire, yes. Just not the willingness to get her hands dirty. She'd definitely pave the way for Leo if he wanted to do a little midnight *cleaning,* but Leo didn't look the type for real work either.

"I decided to come support Leo at the last minute." Paisley threaded her arm with his and put a hand on his shoulder, tracing a nail down his jawline, but her face remained carefully neutral. "I'm so proud of what he's built with Lazy River. And his operation is growing every day."

A third person slipped into their little group, and Harley almost swallowed her tongue. "Dean?"

Dean's smug expression put a dent in Harley's composure. "Harley." The contempt in his voice couldn't be missed. "Paisley was nice enough to introduce me to Leo. I'm a partner at Lazy River." Leo flinched a little at the mention of Dean's partnership status. "It's nice to work with someone who knows what he's doing."

Harley felt the heat of her anger explode on her face and opened her mouth to cut down the little weasel of her ex, but Chance took her by the elbow. "I'm sure Lautaro is waiting for us at the booth. We'd better go finish setting up, Harley. It's good to see you, Leo. We'll catch up afterward, ok?"

"Of course, lots to talk about. I have more info on that investor we discussed. They're still willing to come on board."

Leo's smirk sparked a thousand questions in Harley's mind, but it was the panicked expression on Chance's face that really sidelined her thoughts. What would cause such a disruption in his normally cool and collected manner? It was the first time she'd seen him anything but certain and it rattled her.

"Now's not the time to discuss personal business, Leo." The warning was clear in Chance's voice, but Leo was either immune or intentionally ignoring it.

"It's a business setting. I'd say that's the perfect place for business."

Chance's brows knitted together, and he motioned for Leo to step to the side. The two of them spoke in harsh whispers, Chance's body a hard plane of sharp and unmovable angles.

"Mommy and daddy really love Leo," Paisley offered, breaking into Harley's thoughts and reminding her she still had an audience.

Paisley smoothed a manicured hand over the edge of her

blouse, an oddly cut piece of material that fell off one shoulder while rising to an old-timey collar style on the other. Harley couldn't figure out how the thing stayed put.

"I guess that explains the product placement on their show a few weeks back. I'm sure it never occurred to any of you to do that for Fortune's Brew. You know...the family brand."

Bitterness razored Harley's words. She'd not watched her aunt and uncle's reality show but had heard through the family grapevine about the endorsement of another distillery. If they were voting to sell out there was no need to promote the family business.

Her cousin reached out with fake compassion to lay a comforting hand on Harley's arm. "They have standards to meet, Har. I'm sure you understand that."

Dean snorted, the smug look on his face jabbing at Harley's pride.

"I do understand standards, Pais," Harley agreed. "It's why I'm single."

Her comment hit its mark and Dean's mouth tightened at the corners as his chin dropped to his chest, a bull preparing to run headfirst at the red cape being waved without noticing the sword waiting for him on the other side.

"You're single because you're a frigid bitch with super glue between your thighs. Maybe if you'd thaw out a little someone would stick around long enough to pop —"

Harley gritted her teeth, tucking her chin until the curtain of her hair fell forward. She fixed Dean with a stare, but Chance was suddenly standing nose to nose with Dean, his shoulders a taut line. "I'd think carefully about the last words you want to speak, Dean. Because if you finish that sentence *ever* in my presence, they will be the last words you speak."

Leo inserted himself between Chance and Dean, shouldering Dean back and taking Paisley's hand. "Let's go. We have business to deal with."

The three of them rejoined the crowds, Paisley and Dean both looking back at the last minute to grin victoriously at Harley.

Chance turned to her, opening his mouth to speak but Harley pivoted and sped away, too embarrassed to face anyone after that little scene. She only hoped it had been private enough that the entire competition wouldn't figure out her sexual history - not that there was one - before the end of the day.

Something burned behind Harley's eyes, and she jabbed her thumb and forefinger into the sockets to tamp it out as she walked blindly through the crowd. But it wasn't tears. It was doubt.

The doubt burned like cheap rye hitting her stomach. Was there anyone she could truly trust with her secrets, fears, doubts? She had Lautaro but everyone else - Uncle Everett, Aunt Elsbeth, Paisley, Dean, even Granny T - seemed to be waiting for her to fail. And if not waiting, then actively pushing for her demise.

She didn't expect accolades from her family for trying to keep the business going. As selfish as it sometimes sounded, she wasn't doing it for them. But her parents had given everything to this business, including their lives. How could she do any less? How could she not fight day in and day out to keep the business, to keep her parents' memory, alive.

And Dean... Harley rolled her eyes and let the regret rumble on the groan that escaped her throat. She didn't regret not sleeping with him. She only regretted telling him she'd never slept with anyone.

The moment the words had left her mouth that night, a night in which he'd made it more than clear he'd expected their relationship to turn physical, she'd known he would use it against her. It was the kind of person he was.

After a brief walk around the facility to calm her nerves and regain some semblance of composure, Harley returned to the booth. Lautaro was already there, engaged in a conversation with two gentlemen. As she neared, she overheard him talking about their distillation process so slipped quietly to the back and fiddled nervously with an extra batch of brochures. Chance, thankfully, was not around.

Business, she told herself. *Focus on the business.*

The marketing materials were great, Harley had to admit. Chance had incorporated pictures of their silly signs - the Drunk Skunk, the Boozy Bear, the Sloppy Possum - and taken the reader on a tour of Fortune's Brew. He had their history and talking points about their process for anyone interested in learning more.

He'd not given a timeline for his work at the stillhouse, but Uncle Everett would start pushing now that they were running enough product to make it to a competition. Regardless of the outcome of today, her birthday was just a few weeks away. Even with Chance's help, could they change the minds of the family and buy more time?

When Chance had arrived, all she wanted was for him to leave. Now, she wanted him to stay. She didn't even try and fool herself that it was for work only. Something had started between them. Harley didn't understand it. But she wanted the opportunity to figure it out.

He made her feel... safe. Even thinking that made her inner warrior woman cringe a bit. She was used to going things relatively alone. Granny T and Lautaro were always standing in the background, waiting to help her pick up the pieces when she fell, and Harley knew that.

But with Chance, it was a different kind of feeling. Chance would keep her from falling apart. He saw through the bluff of her "me do it myself" attitude and when she pushed back, like she always did, he hadn't turned away.

Harley felt Chance's presence before she turned. The gooseflesh dimpled her neck and cascaded down her torso. The warmth at her back slipped around her like strong arms on a cold night. When she didn't move, he slid in beside her. The smoky, spicy scents of cardamon and sandalwood surrounded her, earthy, solid.

"The panel has already started judging and the agenda says the finalists will be announced by three." Chance retrieved a sleeve of disposable shot glasses they could use throughout the day without worrying about washing and sanitizing glassware. Vendors would want to sample the product before ordering. He'd really thought of everything. "There's a reception later for the entrants if you're interested."

She pulled her laptop out of its sleeve and watched as it booted up, grateful both for the distraction and his professionalism at ignoring the little scene with Dean. Her initial reaction to the reception was to say no. She wasn't a mingler, but she knew Chance would think it a good opportunity to meet vendors and other industry players.

"I'm sure you think it's a good idea for us to make an appearance. I mean, I didn't wear this skirt just to show you and Lautaro my legs."

Her face immediately warmed at the suggestive innuendo, but Chance's grin cooled her embarrassment. "I'd heard rumors you had them," he joked, brushing back a loose swatch of hair from her forehead. She leaned into the contact, lifting her chin. "But Lautaro did try and convince me the baseball cap was hiding a bald spot."

"Gasp!" Harley covered her head with her hands. "He's not supposed to spill all our secrets to outsiders."

He was close, only an arm's length between them. The more subtle notes of champagne were stronger now, rich, bursting against her senses, and she looked up to see the honeyed brown of his eyes deepen and darken.

"It's ok. I probably shouldn't mention the social media pics have gone viral. I think they're calling you Misfortune's Follicle now. You give new meaning to 'hair of the dog that bit you.'"

"At least they're not dissing our moonshine."

"Your moonshine is top notch."

"I'm glad you're finally seeing things my way."

"To be clear, I never said you made anything but stellar moonshine."

She simmered beneath the smoldering heat in his eyes and understood how women could fall for the silken words of a man who knew how to weave them.

"Thanks to you, no doubt."

"Thanks to a very smart businesswoman listening to some good advice, it's moved up the ranks."

"I'm not sure I'm such a smart businesswoman."

"Why is that?"

"I did hire Dean."

The flash of anger tightened on Chance's face. "I'm sorry about that. It never should have happened. I should have been there to stop it instead of dealing with my own issues with Leo. It was very unprofessional of me."

"You're a consultant, Chance. Not a babysitter. I can handle my own ex issues." She laughed then paused, surprised at how at-ease he made her feel. She wasn't embarrassed or self-conscious. Well, not about the facts but maybe how he'd found out. "About what Dean said —"

"You don't owe me, or anyone, any explanations about that. Now or ever."

His hand was very close to hers. A magnetic pull arced between them, drawing her closer. All she'd have to do is slide her pinky over a hair and they'd be touching. She'd never wanted to touch, or be touched, as much as she did in that moment.

"Besides, a smart businesswoman wouldn't keep thinking about kissing the man hired by her family to evaluate her business sense."

Chance's eyes narrowed then softened and his gaze lingered on her mouth. His fingers found hers, twining gently before pulling back. "And a smart consultant would remember Rule Three and know that wanting to kiss the client can be bad for business."

Her face scrunched up with the question on her lips but before she could ask, he waved it off. "Never mind. I'll explain later."

"Maybe we're not as smart as we thought we were." Harley swallowed, lifted her shoulders in a noncommittal shrug. "You could stay."

Chance's eyes narrowed and his gaze dropped.

And Harley had her answer.

She just didn't think it would hurt this much.

Chapter Thirteen

Chance lifted his glass as the photographer framed the shot and signaled the three count with a raised hand. "To the best damn team of moonshiners since the repeal of prohibition."

"And to the man who put their Cadillac on the right road." Lautaro added, touching his glass to Chance's, pride putting a steel rod in his spine.

Chance stepped out of the photo a millisecond before the photographer's flash. This was Harley and Lautaro's moment but damn if he didn't feel a touch of pride at seeing their names on the winner's list displayed on the overhead screens.

Craft Distillery - Debut Category
FORTUNE'S BREW
Bronze Medallion

The photographer jotted down their information in a little notebook before diving back into the crowd of people mixing around the winners' tables at the front of the ball-room. The excited murmur of voices ebbed and flowed, punctuated by the clink of glasses being raised and the occasional flash from a camera.

Fortune's Brew had edged out Lazy River Distillery, who'd been awarded Honorable Mention in the category. The fight he'd had with Leo earlier in the day replayed in his head.

"You're supposed to be on our side," Leo accused, his eyes cutting to Harley over Chance's shoulder. "You're getting cozy with the enemy."

"Harley isn't the enemy. If you can't stand on your own there's nothing anyone can do for you."

"Don't count on that." Leo spit out the words and Chance could tell by the way his eyes widened he hadn't meant to say them.

"What's that mean?"

Leo rolled his shoulders, taking his time before responding to gather his thoughts. "I'm going to move forward with A Shot and a Beer with or without you. I have a new partner to consider."

"You partnered with Dean without consulting me?

"I needed the money. I have investors to consider. Plans I've made."

"What investors?" It was the first time Leo had mentioned outside money, but Chance should have known that Leo would tuck his tail between his legs at the first sign of hard work. Why he'd ever considered going into business with the man, he didn't know. "You've already made a deal with my mother, haven't you?"

"No." Disappointment edged Leo's voice and Chance realized that the investment from Sondra was a package deal. Leo got the money if he delivered Chance. "But I will," he lied. Leo and the truth were only acquainted in theory. Chance had learned that in Chicago last year. "She has the connections to make the bar a reality. Don't let pride stand in your way."

Chance bristled at Leo's words. "And don't let ego make you think you can do this without me. You're still an unknown, Leo. Don't forget that. Even without the Gold name, I'm known in this industry."

Leo puffed out his chest at the challenge. "Then let the best man win," Leo snapped as he turned and walked away.

Chance returned his attention to Harley, his own chest puffing a bit at the look of contained excitement on her face. It was one of the things he loved most about his job. The hard work was made worthwhile when an owner saw their efforts pay off and the possibilities became visible through the fog of what had only been defeat.

For now, he ignored his personal feelings. *Rule Three*, he reminded himself. Rule Three was going out the window in a few hours, and he planned to let Harley Fortune know exactly what his feelings were for her.

There had been so many things he wanted to say earlier when she'd asked him to stay, yes being at the top of the list. But he couldn't cross that line while he was on the clock. He needed to finish the job before pursuing anything with Harley.

Harley remained quiet; her attention focused on the certificate announcing their third place finish in the debut category. She'd been in a state of shock the last fifteen minutes.

"It's ok to be excited, Harley." He took a deep breath, savoring the moment.

She shook her head in disbelief. "We actually did it."

Lautaro nudged her shoulder. "Yes, we did. I had no doubt. Now we drink to our success, Harley."

Harley picked up her glass and gulped the drink which made Lautaro chuckle. He propped his elbows on the table, saluting Chance with his glass. "I think one of us will be driving home tonight."

Chance took a modest sip from the liquid in his own glass then motioned to the ballroom where they'd gathered for the awards ceremony reception, but his attention never wavered far from Harley. "The competition has moderators throughout the room ensuring no one leaves here obviously intoxicated. The participants also know that anyone who does get wasted during the event won't be allowed back."

She sat with her elbows propped on the table, hands clasped against her forehead. She'd removed the tailored jacket hours ago, leaving her in only the silk blouse and pencil skirt. That skirt... wow. His libido had played havoc with his concentration all day watching her move around the booth in that skirt, talking with vendors and other visitors. All curves and soft places he wanted to nuzzle and put his hands. It was damn near impossible to remember Rule Three when a woman looked like that in a skirt.

"This is a good rule." The older man spoke as if confirming Chance's assessment but soon it would no longer apply.

Lautaro set aside his glass but motioned with a nod of his head to the dais at the front of the ball room. The Gold Standard had taken top honors, which surprised no one, and Chance glanced around the room searching for their representatives but didn't see the face he was looking for. "Your friend did well today."

Chance dragged his eyes from Harley to Leo Quinn up

on the dais, hoping his face didn't give away the truth of his inner thoughts. Leo stood with three of the judges, including Kissy St. Germaine and Glynn Bowers, taking a picture for his honorable mention in the small distillery category.

Chance had heard about Bowers after Kissy had recommended he replace Chance after his departure the distiller's association. While Kissy draped herself over Leo, Paisley was standing out of the picture looking none too pleased with the situation.

"Leo hasn't figured how to stand out. The market is saturated with small craft distilleries now. It takes more than a fancy label to grab a decent market share." Chance said dryly.

Leo wasn't much into experimenting at Lazy River; it was one of several points of contention between the two of them. Chance knew what it took to make a name for yourself in the business and so far, Leo didn't have it.

Harley on the other hand…

His mind wandered briefly to what would happen if Chance opened A Shot and a Beer with Fortune's Brew as his primary supplier.

The thought was interrupted as another laugh jolted Lautaro's large frame. "Harley, the results are not going to change if you stop staring at the paper. You did it. We must celebrate."

Harley blushed, setting the certificate aside, shaking herself from the deep tunnel of thoughts that had pulled her inward. "I am celebrating, Lautaro. It's just…" She traced the rim of her now empty glass with her index finger. "I can't actually believe it. I was prepared. I'd been preparing the speech in my head for when we returned to ask Granny T to give us more time. To not vote with Everett and Elsbeth or, more likely, to accept that she would vote with them." She finally looked up, the wet shimmer in her eyes making the blue-green ring around her iris more pronounced. "But we did it."

"We are not, as they say, free of the woods, but we can see outside the forest, no?"

Lautaro brightened and excused himself from the table and Chance saw him walk over to join a man and a woman from another distillery. They greeted each other amicably and soon fell deep into conversation. His attention swept back to Harley and the mix of confusion and elation tightening her mouth and tightening her shoulders.

"I can hear the gears churning in your head, Harley," Chance teased but it was gentle, wanting to ease the tension from her body. He couldn't do it the way he wanted – by taking her in his arms and holding her close until she relaxed against him. The heat of her body still branded his soul. He was supposed to leave after today. Could he? Did he want to? So, he was left with words. "Isn't this what you wanted?"

Harley swiped at her forehead, her fingers looking for the absent ball cap, the nervous gesture something Chance recognized when she was feeling conflicted. "I'm not sure." Her eyes widened and she pulled back, drawing her hands into her lap. "I mean, of course. We've been working so hard. I want the distillery to do well."

"But if things had gone differently today, that would have taken some of the pressure off, wouldn't it?"

She tucked her chin, a flush of color darkening her cheeks.

"You wouldn't be the first owner to hope decisions get taken out of their hands. It makes it easier in some regard, especially if they didn't want the business."

She straightened, crossing her legs under the table. "It's all I've ever known. It's everything my dad wanted."

"That doesn't have to mean it's all you want." He started to reach across the table but leaned his elbows against the edge instead. The urge to comfort her tugged at something inside of Chance, that protective instinct. Not because she was weak but because strong people often felt they couldn't lean on others when they needed it. "I think good parents want us to live the life we dream, not the one they dream."

"Are you speaking from experience? I mean, I'm guessing Diamond is a name you use for business. Are your parents involved in the industry?"

Her insight was more on target than he would likely admit, especially to a client. Instead of answering, he side-stepped the question. "I worked for one of the bigger labels after college. When I went out on my own after a few years I didn't want people to think I was still connected to the business."

She didn't want to ask more probing questions, so they talked of the win some more and made plans for the competition in Nashville the following week. The platform would be different than Houston - a vendor driven event which looked at marketability. Chance discussed strategy and Harley listened, much to his surprise.

Chance picked up the last bottle of Diamond in the Rough he'd saved. It was going home with him, a present from Lautaro before the ceremony before they'd known they had reason to celebrate. He only had one other souvenir from work, and that was the framed copy of the first contract he'd ever signed as CJ Diamond.

"Success can be as frightening as failure." He'd realized what was weighing on Harley with her confession. People thought him cocky all the time and it wasn't far from the truth. He'd never really known failure. Not because, as they often thought, of his mother and father standing in the background. But because he worked damn hard.

"When you fail, people admire you when you pick yourself up and start again. But when you succeed," he flicked at random pieces of confetti surrounding the table's centerpiece, "they expect you to do it again. The fall from grace is a lot harder if you've risen a bit with success."

Harley nodded, her face managing to hold both excitement and disappointment. Would she be sorry to see him leave? She'd asked him to stay. Was it only for the business? "At least now I have a bargaining chip with the family. You've given me good advice, Chance. I wish I'd listened a little sooner. I'm sorry about that."

His jaw would have dropped had he not been clenching it so tightly to keep from spilling his guts on how much he wanted to stick around and work with her to bring Fortune's Brew to its full potential. He was coming to the conclusion that he and Leo had different ideas on how business should operate. He would compromise on many things, but his integrity was not for sale. Kissy had tried to put a price tag on it in Chicago which was why Chance ended up walking away. He was still paying for that decision.

He was just a contractor, always the outsider looking in. His role was to coach the owners to success then step back and let them accept the accolades. Being in the background had never bothered him before. It was the first time in eight years he wanted to be there when they crossed the finished line, not for the accolades but to be standing with Harley.

The small taste of whiskey he'd had earlier turned bitter in his stomach at the thought of leaving. "No apologies are necessary. You were protecting your business." He dropped his chin to his chest but looked up at her from beneath the fringe of his eyelashes.

She'd loosened the top two buttons on her simple silk blouse. In the slight vee of cleavage showing, he could see a silver locket. Throughout the day he'd noticed her touch the talisman and wondered what it represented to her. Like with most things in his line of work, he'd never get to find out. His role was always temporary. It had never bothered him much before now.

"You know what you're doing, Harley. Just trust your instinct."

For Chance, his contract said it was time to go. Only his instinct told him he wanted to stay.

Harley's instincts were telling her she needed Chance to stay. It went against her nature to ask for help but Chance had proven himself, both as someone who knew what he was doing and as someone she could trust. And there were other things she wanted to explore. Things she'd not thought she'd find. Things she'd not thought she'd want.

But she'd asked.

He'd not said yes.

She swirled the ice around the bottom of her glass, the momentary warmth the shot of liquor had given her earlier having dissipated with the cold knowledge that Chance would be leaving. A week ago, she couldn't bear the thought of him being in her still house. Now she couldn't bear the thought of being in the still house without him.

Sure, he was a know-it-all pain. The bigger pain was that he was right. The man knew the business. As much as Harley would like to use his cockiness as an excuse to want him gone, she couldn't. Chance didn't make you feel less because he knew more. He was genuinely happy when someone could learn from him. He was even happier when he could learn something new.

Whatever their personal feelings, he was able to keep them separated from their business. She envied that in a way. For her, the personal was deeply tied to her business.

"What's next for you? Another stubborn moonshiner waiting in the wings for you to come in and save them?" She tried to make light of his departure, but the weight of her disappointment made the words heavy on her tongue.

He filled two of the water goblets from the pitcher on the table, sliding one in her direction. She gratefully pulled it closer to her.

Chance took a long drink but kept his eyes on the glass when he put it on the table. He traced the beveled edge absently, distractedly. "I've got a personal venture I may be working on for a few months. I don't want there to be any hint of conflict, so I'll step back from consulting while I do that."

She wanted to ask more but he hadn't offered so she backed off. She suspected it had to do with the argument he'd had with Leo Quinn and the investor Leo had alluded to. He'd been careful not to look at her since she'd hinted earlier at wanting him to stay. Their kiss on the dock had obviously meant nothing to him and now he was happy to use the end of the contract to make his exit. Fine, she thought. She didn't need to be hit over the head.

"I wish you the best and appreciate all you did for Fortune's Brew." Harley pushed from the table, forcing her gaze to the crowd of people as she stood. "Let me go find Lautaro and then we can be on our way. No sense hanging around here any longer."

Chance stiffened, his brows crashing together as he leaned toward her then pulled back as if getting too close had been accidental. "There's no rush. You should enjoy the party."

She grabbed her jacket, draped it over an arm and grabbed the dolly with the booth set up. They'd packed up before the awards ceremony, wanting to make a quick exit. She'd never expected to see Fortune's Brew listed among the winners. Chance and Lautaro had to practically knock her from her seat when her name was called.

"No, I'm done celebrating." She thought of dragging out the night, knowing it would be the last she got to spend with Chance. But he'd still be leaving in the end, and it was better to just rip off the bandage now. "Tomorrow is a workday."

He stood, patting down his pockets as if searching for something, then circled the table to stand near her. She'd become familiar with his cologne, with the scents of smoky cardamon and champagne that would always remind her of him. The five o'clock shadow darkened the sharp angle of his jaw but couldn't hide the pulse point near his chin.

He scratched behind his ear, then ran his fingers over his chin. "You could take the day off. I think you deserve it after the last week. I'll be officially out of your hair tomorrow. I'd think that would be worth a day off to celebrate."

The reminder of his departure poked at the ache in her chest. "Tomorrow is just another workday. We need to prep for Nashville next weekend. I want to read over the rules again."

He just nodded and reached to take the dolly from her, his palms brushing her knuckles. The warmth of his hands wrapped around her heart and slowed the beat to thud. Harley released the dolly and stepped back, not because she didn't like the feel of his hand against her, but because she liked it too much.

"Are we breaking up the party?" Lautaro's voice snapped Harley out of her reverie, and she stumbled sideways trying to avoid touching Chance again. "I will be taking the keys, carina. Too much winning has gone to your head."

Harley handed over the keys without comment then beat a hasty retreat from the ballroom. Outside she paused, breathing deeply to calm her shaking hands and aching heart. She'd worked hard at remaining off-limits to matters of the heart. As much as she understood the nuances of how corn and barley would work together to make the perfect blend of whiskey, how subtle changes would alter the flavor, she knew little about the nuances of relationships.

It wasn't that she didn't want a relationship. She'd just not had much opportunity. Her sole focus had been protecting her family's legacy. For the first time, however, she wished she'd paid a little more attention to men and women rather than corn and barley.

The doors opened behind her and she moved to the side, leaning against one of the large stone columns that marked the entrance to the convention center, as a large group of people exited, noisily chatting and laughing.

She lifted her chin, turning her face to the darkening sky, only the final hint of daylight remaining. It didn't matter what she felt, she reminded herself, tamping down the spiral of lust that tightened in her gut every time she got near Chance. It only mattered what he didn't feel, and he didn't feel anything for her. She was a business for him; nothing more.

Tears stung the back of her eyes, but she willed them away. He was leaving. She was staying. She wasn't going to be a one-night stand, or a weekend stop while he traveled around the country. And he wasn't one to stay still.

Paisley's familiar voice intruded into Harley's pity party and Harley intuitively took a step back, not wanting her cousin to see her lovesick over her boyfriend's best friend. She didn't need to relive this every Thanksgiving and Christmas for the rest of her life.

"I don't care, Leo," Paisley snapped in her bored-to-tears voice, her words spoken in time to the clack of her heels on the sidewalk. "You've been whining about how to finance that lame idea you and Chance have cooked up for months. I brought you Dean and he's happily shelling over his money for this *partnership*."

A heavy dose of sarcasm slurred Paisley's use of her final word, leaving Harley to wonder about Dean's arrangement with Leo.

After they passed by, Harley angled her body so she could see Leo and Paisley. They stopped only a few feet from Harley's location while Paisley searched her purse for her keys.

"But either you and I are partners in this or not. This is a guaranteed win but I need a decision before the family votes on that stupid distillery. Everett isn't smart enough to realize what he has on his hands."

"Then make sure he doesn't find out," Leo grumbled, shrugging deeper into the ill-fitting jacket. He stuffed his hands under his armpits and glanced guiltily over his shoulder. "You have no trouble hiding shit from the rest of the family. I've done what I can with the judging but that won't always be possible. And I'm not sleeping with Kissy. I don't care what she promises."

Paisley lifted her keys into the air, and they continued to walk toward the parking lot. "Yes, but Chance..."

"Chance will come around. He just needs time. He'll be on board, and he'll bring the Fortune..."

Their voices trailed off and Harley was tempted to follow. What did Paisley mean? Did Everett already have a buyer lined up for Fortune's Brew? If that was the case, winning today may have sealed the coffin shut for them rather than pulled them into the light. Winning made them a viable brand.

And what role did Chance play in all of this? His entire job was to show the family Fortune's Brew was worth the effort of saving. Or was the goal of that just to raise the selling price when Everett put it on the market?

She thought back to Kissy St. Germaine and Leo's comments about the judging which led to the biggest question of all. Was Chance's little *disagreement* in Chicago with Kissy St. Germaine a lover's quarrel? And if so, what had Chance gotten for his part?

The questions were left unanswered as Chance and Lautaro exited the conference center, their postures relaxed. Harley had rarely seen Lautaro this happy. He'd poured his heart and soul into the business since her grandfather's time. The man was as much family as anyone carrying the Fortune name.

He'd been with her parents the day they'd died and still blamed himself for the accident that took their lives. After their victory, they'd left to return home, but he'd remained behind to celebrate their victory. He believed fate would have turned differently that day had he been with them in the car. Harley told him - as had Granny T - that was ego talking, that he would have died in the crash as well. But Lautaro could not see it that way.

It was good to see him with hope again. Another reason Harley would be grateful to Chance. But it made the hole he would leave all the bigger and the questions Leo and Paisley's conversation raised all the more troubling.

Right then, Lautaro reared back his head, a roar of laughter echoing in the amphitheater of the conference center's entranceway. He clapped Chance on the shoulder, leaving his hand there as the two of them came to stand before Harley.

"This one, Harley," Lautaro cut a side eye toward Chance. "This one is dangerous to have at a party if the stories he tells me are true."

Chance clasped a hand to his chest and raised the other in the Boy Scout salute. "I swear, I am not the one who put a duck in the oak barrels the distillery was using in their display. But that was one daffy bird after sampling whatever was in those barrels."

Harley smiled at the image before the memory of her questions filled her head. Could this man betray them? Was he just another in a long line of bad decisions for Harley *Mis*Fortune?

"*Mi carina*, you look like you've lost your best friend this evening."

If only he knew, Harley thought dejectedly.

"This is a night for celebration! Have you called and told Trudy --" Lautaro stuttered suddenly, coughing and clearing his throat. "Have you called Mrs. Fortune and shared the good news?"

Chance watched her with his brows drawn into a single curious line, but he remained quiet.

Harley pushed the questions aside in her mind, knowing the answers were not going to be found tonight. "No. If I know her, she'll still be up when we get home, and we can tell her in person."

Lautaro smiled broadly, sweeping his hand toward the car. "Then let's go home."

Hours later, they pulled into the yard at the house and spilled from the car with the same slow *glug* as an overturned bottle of whiskey. Bone tired, Harley stretched her arms over her head, already counting the minutes until she could trade the pencil skirt and heels for a pair of lounge pants and her fuzziest slippers. The lights were on in the kitchen and that meant her grandmother was awake.

Her excitement did a little dance in the pit of her stomach when she turned to Chance, both at the object of her perusal and the request she would make. "Come inside with us to tell Granny T the news."

Before Chance could answer, Trudy Fortune stepped onto the porch. She was wearing a silk robe, the sash cinched as tightly as the arms crossed over her chest. Her glasses were pushed atop her head and the look on her face was one of seriousness.

Harley took the stairs two at a time. "We have good news."

But Trudy's face didn't soften, and Harley felt the familiar dread of incoming bad news. "What happened?"

By this time, Lautaro and Chance had joined them on the porch, Lautaro nodding a greeting in silence. Trudy acknowledged the master distiller, but her attention went to Chance. "You're the consultant Everett hired."

"Yes ma'am. CJ Diamond."

Harley moved closer to her grandmother, nervously twisting her hands against her stomach. "What happened, Granny?"

"Y'all better come inside. I've got tea and biscuits." Without waiting for their response, Trudy turned and entered the house, the screen door slapping against the door frame with a sharp crack.

They followed through the darkened living room, the light from the kitchen slicing its way out of the doorway to carve a path.

The Fortune kitchen was Harley's second favorite place in the world, after the still house. She'd learned most of life's lessons in here with her grandmother, making jelly and jam, doing her homework around the breakfast table while Trudy did her own homework on the business or with one of the many charities she supported in southern Louisiana.

Trudy motioned them into the kitchen, where the familiar faces of Miss Perla and Mr. Shaw greeted them. It was her Uncle Everett's face, however, that stopped Harley cold.

Miss Perla laid out the serviette and a sampling of her jam with some homemade biscuits while Mr. Shaw gathered their coats and bags from the hooks near the door. Even though they lived upstairs, they came and went by the outside entrance daily. Miss Perla said it kept work and home separate. Home should always be a place of escape.

"Harley. Lautaro." Miss Perla nodded once at each of them, her eyes skimming over Chance to return to her grandmother. "Trudy, we'll see you in the morning."

"Thanks for staying, Perla, Shaw. I'll see you tomorrow."

Once settled in the kitchen around the breakfast table, Harley turned down the tea, wanting instead to get to the source of her grandmother's strange mood. Something was wrong.

"How did the competition go?" Trudy's voice lacked emotion, but her fingers trembled around the cup in her grasp.

Everett sighed but went silent at his mother's deadpan stare.

Harley looked first as Lautaro, then at Chance, though both remained silent. They sensed the trouble as much as she did. "We placed third. But I think you already know that." She swallowed the hard lump in her throat. "What's wrong?"

"One of the event organizers called." Trudy licked her lips, then slumped back against her chair, wrapping her arms around her middle. "You've been disqualified. A complaint was filed because you entered in the debut category, and they said Fortune's Brew didn't qualify as a debut distillery since we were in business fifteen years ago."

The words sucker punched Harley. She cradled her face in her palms, deflated, as Lautaro jumped from the table, cursing in a mix of Spanish and English, maybe even a little Creole French as he jabbed at the air.

When Harley looked up, Chance was scratching at the stubble on his jaw, his face neutral. She thought back to Paisley and Leo's words tonight. To the disagreement Kissy St. Germaine alluded to with Chance. Was Chance unsurprised by this news? His poker face was inscrutable.

"I've already told mother but I'm making a deal with Sondra Gold at The Gold Standard. She wants to buy Fortune's Brew."

Harley gasped but Chance went statue still. He leaned back, raking his gaze over Everett, a challenge in the silent perusal. Everett ignored him.

"You can't," Harley sputtered. "I have a few more weeks. And we're meeting the terms of the trust. Fortune's Brew is doing well. We could turn a profit this year."

Everett gave a dismissive wave. "Given the debt you've run up and the limited production, I doubt that."

She snapped, jabbing a finger at her uncle. "You can't let Fortune's Brew disappear into something like The Gold Standard. They'll just steal the name and fill the bottles with subpar liquor. Daddy and granddaddy wouldn't want that."

The first crack appeared in Everett's demeanor. "I loved my brother and father, but it's time to put this dream away. It's cost this family enough. It's time to move on." He reached out to pat Harley's hand, but she jerked away. Everett tilted his head, looking at Harley with a patronizing smile. "I'm doing this to help you, Harley."

Harley deflated beneath her uncle's words but also under the silence of her grandmother and a too quiet Chance. "I don't need this kind of help."

"We don't often know what we need." Everett rose from the table and kissed his mother on the cheek. "I'll talk to you tomorrow, mom."

Once he'd made his departure, Harley looked around the table. She and Lautaro sat beside each other, across from Trudy while Chance sat alone on the fourth side of the table. Three sides of a triangle. Three sides of their business. Three sides of an argument.

Uncle Everett was wrong. Harley knew what she needed. She needed Chance, at least the Chance she'd gotten to know that past week. Only he was leaving, and she'd be left to face the end of her family's legacy on her own. Maybe it was for the best. But the burn in her gut revealed the lie.

"I guess your friend Leo moves up from honorable mention now." Bitterness laced Harley's words. All their work, the leverage she needed to keep the family from voting them out of business, out the window.

Everett dangled a way out for all of them. Would they take it? She wouldn't put it past Paisley to make the complaint to see her own plans win out. Was Chance in on the deal? Harley didn't want to believe it. She couldn't.

Chance nodded. "He does, not that it helps him out really. He qualified for Crescent City on production. This is about something else." Chance turned his attention to Trudy. "Mrs. Fortune, I was hired to give an opinion as to Fortune Brew's marketability so I'm going to give it to you. You've got the best whiskey I've ever tasted."

To say that Trudy Fortune smiled would be generous, but the slight lifting of her mouth barely registered. "You're not the first person to say that, Mr. Diamond. And Harley is not the first person in our family to want to believe it." She leaned across the table and patted Harley's hand. "But something always gets in the way of us getting to market."

"There are operational hiccups that need working out and you definitely need some help with marketing brand recognition but honestly, that's nothing more than the right person focused on the job. You could be top shelf within two years if you give Harley and Lautaro a shot."

Trudy watched Chance with her eagle eye, one brow raised in a look Harley recognized from her childhood when Granny knew you had something to tell her, and she was just waiting on it to spill out. "But..." she prodded.

"Someone doesn't want you to make it to market."

Trudy's brows clashed together. "Everett?"

"No." Chance answered quickly and shook his head, but Harley sensed there was something else behind his denial. "No. He hired me for other reasons."

A coldness started in Harley's toes and worked its way up her body. "What reasons are those?"

Chance hesitated, a debate warring as he opened and closed his mouth but remained silent. "It doesn't matter," he finally said. "My contract with him is complete and as I explained to him after I arrived, I wouldn't help with a deal with The Gold Standard. It's not what I do."

"Why would anyone want to sabotage the business? No one makes money if we go under."

"No one in the family makes money. That doesn't mean that someone else hasn't figured out how to do it." Chance leaned forward, his shoulders stretching the fabric of his tailored shirt taut across his shoulders. "Can I ask how you plan to vote when the trust comes due in a few weeks?"

The older woman sighed and behind that Harley heard the forty years of heart break and disappointment. "I'm sorry, Harley. I just think it's best to call it done. You've sacrificed enough for your dad's dream."

Harley sandwiched Trudy's hands between her own. "It was my dream just as much. I'm just sorry I couldn't do the Fortune legacy justice."

Trudy lifted Harley's hand and kissed it. "You are his legacy, sweetheart. The only one he cared about."

"He cared about Fortune's Brew, too."

"But not at the expense of his family, his happiness. You've sacrificed too much. You gave up college. You practically gave up high school. When was the last time you did something only because you wanted to do it?"

Harley was silent. She could no longer separate what she wanted from the dream her father had spent his life working toward. Was her grandmother right? Was it time to let Fortune's Brew go?

What would she do then?

Chance cleared his throat then leaned over and claimed one of the biscuits, selecting the peach jam. "My contract with Everett is complete. I finished my report on the drive home tonight and will submit it by morning." He split the biscuit and put a dollop of the homemade jam on top. "I'd like to make you a proposition."

Trudy gathered the empty coffee cups and began clearing the table. "I haven't been propositioned in quite some time, Mr. Diamond." As she reached across the table, her eyes cut to Lautaro who was suddenly interested in the rose pattern on the dishes. Harley filed that away for later consideration, more interested, at least for the moment, on Chance's proposition.

Harley jumped up to help her. "Let me do that, Granny T. I'm sort of interested in this proposition myself."

Trudy gave her the dishes and returned to her seat. Harley put the dishes in the sink then turned to lean across the island that separated her from the trio at the table. She'd kicked off her shoes at the door and the cool pine floor eased the ache in her arches from wearing heels all day.

"Go ahead, Mr. Diamond." It was Granny T's placating voice, Harley recognized. The one where Trudy could listen to anything from a story about Paisley's latest fashion find or Harley's newest, greatest idea for making Fortune's Brew number one on the market. Poor Piper, the quiet one in the trio of Fortune grandchildren, barely got a word in edgewise during some visits. "Proposition an old woman."

That genuine flash of pleasure darkened the ridge of Chance's cheek bones as he bit into the biscuit he'd topped with Trudy's peach jam. Harley didn't think Chance forgot he was charming, she just thought he forgot to lay it on sometimes, like now. And when Chance was not being the consummate salesman, Harley could see the charm.

"If you will agree to hold off the vote on Fortune's Brew until after Crescent City, I'd like to stay on as an interested bystander working with Harley and Lautaro to—"

He stopped, searching for the words but Harley's heart started to pound a staccato beat in her temple.

He wanted to stay.

Harley's vision pulsed in rhythm to the beat of her pulse. She watched him search the kitchen for the answer, as if seeing it in the jars of jams and jellies on the shelves.

"—fine tune the recipe and process. Even though today didn't go as planned I think it shows Fortune's Brew as a marketplace contender."

Granny T turned to Harley and asked the unspoken question with a raised eyebrow. Could she accept help?

The loneliness of trying to make the company work while the family remained passive or resistant had eaten away at Harley more than she'd realized. She wasn't sure she could trust Chance, but right now he was the only thing keeping Granny from voting with Uncle Everett.

However, the memory of Leo's words haunted Harley.

Chance will come around. He just needs time. He'll be on board and bring the Fortune...

The Fortune *what*? What would he deliver?

Harley bristled, more out of habit than anything. Her independence streak was a mile wide, as Miss Perla liked to remind her. But Chance saw through to what was beneath and called her bluff. He hadn't disappeared the many times she'd told him to get lost so far. He'd stuck around and helped her, even when she didn't want it, because she needed the help.

She picked at a random spot on the table, looking up at Lautaro under the fan of her lashes. "Are you ok if he sticks around?"

Lautaro nodded slowly before she even finished, not even trying to hide the grin adding a new wrinkle to his lined face. "I am very ok if he sticks around. We make a very good team."

They talked another hour about tentative plans for the Nashville competition the coming weekend, while Chance enjoyed more biscuits and jam. The competition was more critical than ever because it was one of only two left before Crescent City in April. They needed to place in both or they wouldn't be invited to participate in New Orleans.

After a series of yawns from everyone around the table, Granny T ordered everyone to bed. The heat of Harley's blush was instantaneous, and she quickly pushed from the table to head outside. Chance caught up with her at the front door, pushing open the screen and letting her walk out first.

They stopped right outside the door as Chance eased it closed, Harley drawn closer to Chance as the night air enveloped them and the warmth of their bodies gave way to the cooler temps.

"I'm sorry I didn't discuss my proposition first with you in the car." Chance walked to the edge of the porch and leaned against the railing, tilting his head back to stare into the star-filled night.

She stood beside him, following his line of sight out over the horizon. They were far enough from town to where the city lights of Belle Terre barely made the darkness over the tree line a few shades lighter than the sky above.

"You know what my answer would have been then." It wasn't a question. He'd shown he knew her well enough in short acquaintance, understanding her independence and her need to listen patiently to a good argument before weighing in.

He shrugged and angled his body, his attention on her.

"Accepting help can be difficult. Asking for it can be almost impossible when you feel backed into a corner."

She considered the analogy. "There's nowhere to flee in that situation." Would Chance be another of her MisFortune's Follies?

"Correct. I want you to understand very clearly that you are not backed into a corner right now, Harley. There are many options around you."

"We did well in Houston. I think our odds are even in Nashville."

"That's not what I mean."

Chapter Fourteen

C hance reached out without moving another part of his body, not wanting to spook her, and brushed the knuckles of his fingers against her cheeks. Her breathing went from slow and steady to an uneven depth that lifted her shoulders and tightened the flimsy silk shell across her breasts.

She hadn't looked at him yet, but he saw her eyes close, felt her lean into the touch, heard the rush of breath as it exited her lungs. Her shoulders dropped and with it, some of the tension coiled inside her like a rattlesnake waiting to strike eased away, no longer sensing a threat.

He threaded his fingers around the back of her head as she turned to him and lifted her hands between them, putting them on his chest. She didn't push away but held him still, letting herself get used to the space they occupied.

Chance leaned down, nuzzled the hair over her ear, pressed his lips to her temple. "Is this alright?" She nodded hesitantly, cautiously, her breath catching with each press of his mouth, so moved slowly to the other side, offering equal treatment to the shell of her ear. A light nuzzle. A brief kiss.

More of the tension eased from her body and she relaxed, only the width of her hands separating them now.

She started to speak but it took her two tries to give voice to the words. "Back in Houston, you said something about Rule Three. What does that mean?"

Since she didn't move away from him, he was content to stand there in the press of their bodies. His feelings for Harley went beyond lust and some baser instinct to dominate. He wanted to protect her, let her hold onto the innocence that attracted him and shaped her into the woman he held in his arms.

"I have three rules for business. Rules one and two basically say what I do is for the client. I have no personal stake in their wins or losses in theory. I know my reputation depends on the perception of their success but if I can't make my clients successful then I don't deserve any return for my investment in them."

When he hesitated, she pressed her hands into his chest, splaying her fingers in a protective gesture, as if what he would say would hurt and she wanted to protect his heart. And just like that, Chance fell head over heels for Harley Fortune.

It narrowed his sight, blocked out the world as his vision tunneled to encompass only her. Her eyes and mouth, the mole on her neck, where her hands sought to keep him safe. Harley was a fighter. She protected as well.

"And Rule Three?" she prodded. She sucked her bottom lip between her teeth and Chance resisted the urge to brush his mouth over her lips, smooth the worry from the gesture with a kiss.

"Rule Three reminds me to think with the big brain and not the little one."

"The little one?" She snorted the words, covering her

mouth with her hand but he pulled her hand back to his chest, liking the sight of her mouth when she laughed at him, liking the feel of her hands on his body, liking the feeling he got when *she* was protecting *him*.

He lowered his head to rest his forehead against hers, sharing the laugh. Leaning back only enough so he could speak, he explained. "Most of my clients are male but I was surprised to learn the *dedication* their wives often had to their success."

"*Hmm-mmm.*" Her grin was too big for words so instead she lowered her hands and wrapped her arms around Chance's waist.

"There are lines I don't cross, for anyone. I wanted our business concluded before anything else happens... or doesn't." He added the last part at a quirk of her eyebrow, but the smile was still there. "Not that I'm anticipating. Just clearing my calendar in case anything interesting comes up that needs my attention."

His brain shifted into *down boy* mode, trying to think of things that definitely didn't turn him on, because Harley Fortune this close to his body had the opposite effect and he didn't want to grind a hard on against her body. At least not yet. Of course, even trying to think of things that didn't turn him on as much as Harley made him think of how much Harley turned him on.

Then he felt her stiffen and pull back, drawing her hands closer to her body and tucking her chin. "About what Dean said..."

Chance didn't move because he didn't want Harley to think he was stepping away from her. He placed his hands on her upper arms, squeezed gently, then leaned in to rest his chin against her forehead. "I don't care what Dean said."

She visibly relaxed again, the softness returning to her

body but some shadow still lurked behind her eyes. She had difficulty trusting and Chance, maybe better than many, could understand that. He'd show her he was trustworthy.

"Then my calendar is clear as well." She tightened her hold around his body, her hands fitting snugly into the hollow at the base of his spine, her hips nestling closer to the hard on he was unsuccessfully trying to tame. "But I have an early day tomorrow so I can't stand here all night waiting for you to kiss me."

The invitation was all he needed. The space between them was small but enough so that he saw the widening of her eyes in recognition of his intent as he lowered his mouth to hers. He angled his head more to complement hers and she lifted her chin and met him in the kiss, their lips touching once, twice, three times. He hovered, the drive to claim and possess meeting the urge to go slow. He sensed the hesitancy of uncertainty in her kiss, in the slight tightening of the muscles in her shoulders.

He brushed his mouth up the line of her jaw, threaded his left hand into the hair at the nape of her neck, letting the silk spill over his hand. "Good?"

Harley rasped a "Yes" and claimed his mouth, bringing her arms up under his to put her hands on his shoulders and pull him down to her, urgent but still gentle, opening her mouth as she relaxed into his.

Their mouths danced a slow waltz although Chance's body raged to the heavy metal of passion and lust. The kiss deepened on its own, without thought on his part other than wanting to taste more, be closer to Harley. Some hint of perfume ribboned up through his senses, a heady mix of flowers and citrus mixed over notes of vanilla and bourbon both on her tongue and in her hair, on her neck.

A possessive growl lumbered up from his chest and he

tightened his hold around her, lifting and turning to press her backside against the porch railing, wanting a solid foundation with which to claim this woman as his.

He molded her body to his with his embrace, their mouths both dueling and playing a duet of tongues and lips and groans of desire and want. Just as the kiss had deepened on its own, it played to its conclusion in slow, rhythmic pulses. She was liquid in his arms, warm and enveloping.

"If that's how you say goodbye every night we're going to need to start earlier." Harley spoke against his collar bone, her voice a breathy whisper.

Chance gave a single chuckle, too wrapped up in how well she fit against him, her softness and curves melding into his lines and hollows. He didn't feel empty when she stood in his arms. He hadn't realized how empty he'd been *until* she stood in his arms. "As long as Lautaro doesn't expect the same treatment."

"Lautaro is madly in love with my grandmother."

"Then she can kiss him good night."

"I'm working on it."

"Good." He stepped back from her when what he really wanted to do was keep kissing her. And more. But that was thinking with the little brain. She wasn't ready for more. Harley, for all her bluster and bravado, feared the intimacy building between them right now. That was ok. She was worth waiting for.

He cupped her chin, brushed a thumb across her kiss swollen lips, then replaced his finger with one more gentle kiss. "I'll see you in the morning about ten."

Her brows shot up. "Ten? As in ten in the morning?"

Chance took a backward step, shrugged casually. "Well, yeah. I'm not on the clock or anything."

Then he winked, and her face crumpled into disbelief. "You will pay for that."

He winked again, his heart nearly choking off the words as it lodged in his throat. "I look forward to it."

Chapter Fifteen

"You're being stubborn." Chance scrubbed a hand across his jaw then down the back of his neck, hoping to find some patience in the tension knotted between his shoulders. The woman was going to drive him crazy. Or crazier. He had to be crazy to have *volunteered* for this. "More stubborn than usual, that is."

"Did you just meet our Harley?" Lautaro deadpanned, walking back toward the dock to return the second condenser Chance recommended they install shortly after his arrival before sunrise.

Harley stood off to the side, arms crossed defensively like armor. She'd put herself in front of the fermenting vat, as if she needed to protect the product from Chance. Now, she pulled at the hem of the purple t-shirt, smoothing a hand down the wrinkles as if she could smooth out her own frazzled nerves. "You're changing too much. You said yourself our stuff is the best you've tasted. It was good enough to place in Houston so why mess with it now?"

She didn't look mad. She didn't look hurt. She looked sure of herself. It was one of the things that drew Chance to her. She was as confident in her position as he was in his. The only difference was his confidence had been nurtured out in the world. She'd done little but fight every step of the way against the people she should most count on for support.

Breathe. Chance filled his lungs with air, breathing out the frustration. He couldn't blame Harley, didn't want to blame Harley for her resistance. He knew what it was like to be up against the boards while people told you your dream was pointless, useless, ill-conceived, whatever. He knew what it was like to go against someone's advice when they thought they knew more but in your gut, you knew you were right.

Breathe. This time he added a ten count. "Houston and Nashville are different competitions. They focus on different things." He let the confidence of his experience fill his voice and made his way slowly to where Harley stood. "Where Houston was comparing you against market equals, in Nashville you'll be up against the big labels based on product type." Standing in front of her now, he took her hands and released the armor she'd put on in preparation for battle. He didn't want to be someone Harley had to battle. "The judges are trade professionals, and they want to know you can compete equally on the shelf. It's a different mindset."

The problem right now, Chance realized, was both he and Harley were in the same position in terms of being right. She wanted familiarity. He knew they needed risks.

"I'm on your side, Harley."

And he was. Completely. He'd fought with Leo the night before; sure he was the one that lodged the complaint that ended Harley's good fortune before it had really begun. Sadly, it was a purely Leo move.

Chance had always ignored that part of Leo's personality, the win at all costs. He was much the same, but Chance drew the line at taking a win from someone else or doing something underhanded. Leo had no such line. Chance had seen it before in Chicago and reined it in.

Chicago had been Leo's first big competition and he'd had the audacity to hint the judges were open to bribery. One judge in particular, Kissy St. Germaine. And Leo made it clear he was open to meeting Kissy's demands.

Chance knew Kissy had flexible morals, but he'd never been able to conclusively prove she was doing anything against the rules of the association. So he'd written off her meteoric rise to stardom in their industry as luck more than anything. But she'd taken great offense at Leo's suggestion that she was dirty, especially since he'd offered so little in return for her support. Leo didn't comprehend what it meant to play in the big leagues yet.

Regardless, since Chance couldn't prove anything against Kissy it became the classic he said/she said, and Chance knew the association would side with Kissy. He had stepped in and convinced Kissy to allow Leo to withdraw rather than be disqualified, or worse, be accused of cheating.

It was when she'd suggested what Chance could offer in return for her silence that he'd quit, if only to protect his own reputation and that of the competition.

He should have walked away from their business partnership then, but Leo was a friend. Leo's contrition had been slowly replaced by ego the past few months as their venture into A Shot and a Beer had been less than successful.

And of course, now he had to deal with Kissy St. Germaine thanks to Leo.

Chance accepted that, as long as Harley didn't have to suffer for it.

"I'm on your side," he repeated, as much for his benefit as hers.

The slashes of color on her cheekbones, marking her battle ready, diffused. Her shoulders dropped. "I know." It was her turn to tunnel fingers through her hair, reach behind the nape of her neck in search of patience.

He grinned and she raised a quizzical brow at his response. "We have the same tell when in deep thought." He mimicked the gesture. "My dad called it searching for patience."

Chance was close enough now to put his hands to her cheeks, lift her face to him for a quick kiss. The familiar hints of cedar and peach were back, scents he now associated with Harley.

They'd had only a few moments of privacy that morning when he arrived with the sun, once again bearing coffee. She'd practically run him over going for the coffee. Then she'd kissed him.

It had been worth the near head on collision.

The kiss had been spontaneous, he was sure of it. After the first sip of coffee, while still sighing from caffeine-induced bliss, Harley had stretched up on her toes and brushed her lips to the side of his mouth and murmured *thanks*. The contact seemed to awaken her more than the coffee and as she pulled back self-consciously, he wrapped an arm around her middle and kept her close.

"I hope my kisses make you look as happy as that coffee."

Harley *hmmm-mmm'd* deep from her throat, the sound primal and it roused Chance's desire to wrap her in his arms and carry her away somewhere way more private.

He was letting Harley set the pace of things. Like a fine wine or a good whiskey, some things were slow to develop but worth the wait. Harley was worth the wait.

Her passion and commitment to family reached something inside of him.

Something he'd not even known he missed.

Taking another sip of coffee, she swallowed slowly. "It's a close race at this point. I may need to do a little more research before I can say for certain."

A reminder bell dinged in Chance's brain. "Research. When I was looking at your books my first day, I didn't see an invoice for your corn supplier."

Harley stepped from his side and lifted a hand to touch the copper piping that ran from the distillation pot to the thumper, gauging the temperature of the batch by feel. He found her measurement by touch to be as accurate as the legally required thermometer installed to the right.

"We get our corn from a friend of the family. There's never been a need to invoice. Mr. Blanchard just tells us what we owe when he delivers, and we pay it. We owe him for this year, however. The batch that watered the weeds on Lake Opelousas Road would not only have served to qualify us for Crescent City, but it would have given us the cash to pay what we owe for the corn."

"That's an unusual arrangement." That little accident was looking less and less like an accident to Chance. Destroying one batch had done significant damage to Fortune's Brew's viability with a single action.

"He and granddad did some kind of cross-hybridization experiment when daddy was little. They split the costs for growing and the Fortunes buy the corn at market value. The corn isn't available on the market."

"Did they file a patent for the corn?"

"I think so, but Lautaro would know more."

Chance led Harley to the dock area where Lautaro was busy putting the second condenser back into storage, wrapping it to protect from dust. He quickly confirmed Harley's story. The patent was a mystery, however.

"This could be what Everett is after."

"The corn?"

Harley's brow tightened and Chance wondered what heavy thoughts were behind the gesture.

"In an industry where everyone uses the same ingredients for the most part, it's what you do with them that counts. But you've found a new ingredient and it's possibly what gives your product the edge."

Harley paled at the news. "I thought it was our recipe that made our whiskey special. We need to find that patent."

Chance's mind was spinning back to his conversation with Everett his first day in town, and Everett's suggestion that his mother was interested in merging Fortune's Brew and The Gold Standard. His mother wasn't one to share, as Chance had explained to Everett. But she would be willing to buy Fortune's Brew to get the patent. The only loss she had known in a competition had been fifteen years ago to Fortune's Brew.

Now that Everett had revealed his intent to sell to The Gold Standard, Chance's position was precarious. He should have told them last night about his connection to Sondra but had gotten caught up in the planning for Nashville. Keeping his identity a secret was second nature.

He opened his mouth to tell Harley about the conversation then decided to find out more about Everett's dealings with his mother. Chance kept the connection between Sondra Gold and himself as quiet as possible, and this was the reason. People made assumptions once their relationship was known.

"Hello?"

Chance turned at the voice and saw Harley do the same. Her cousin, Piper Pallares, was standing in the doorway, looking very unsure of herself. She wore a pair of designer jeans with a silk blouse beneath a tailored business jacket, her face mostly void of makeup. She was all the prettier for it.

Harley stepped forward and Chance sensed the distrust in the still line of her body. He put a cautioning hand on her arm, giving it a squeeze. He'd investigated the family while researching the business before taking the contract, and Piper's background in sales and marketing could be very helpful.

Harley looked back at him, her mouth firm, but her eyes searched his face and obviously saw his unspoken warning because the lines on her face softened, and her shoulders dropped.

"Hey, Piper. I think Granny T is in the house."

Piper steepled her fingers in front of her body, then clasped them together, repeating the gesture in succession as she looked around the still house. The young woman walked further into the building, the mid-morning sun sweeping in through the open door at the same time. "I came by to see you."

Chapter Sixteen

Harley looked at her cousin's nervous stance, the tremble in her hands as her fingers moved again and again through the steeple to church motions they'd done as children. The first thought to enter her mind was the conversation she'd overheard between Paisley and Leo last night, and Paisley's harsh condemnation of their uncle. *Everett's not smart enough to realize what he has on his hands.* The context became clear given what Chance had revealed moments earlier.

Paisley, either with help from Leo or on her own, had apparently figured out what made Fortune's Brew worth its fortune. The question remained, was Piper a part of her sister's schemes or apart from them?

"Oh?"

Piper's eyes bounced from Harley to Chance to Lautaro before finally landing on Harley again. "First, I wanted to tell you I didn't know about the proxy thing with Paisley. She never mentioned talking with mom and dad about it, and they never discussed it with me."

"Guess we're both getting left out of family decisions."

"Seems that way." Piper squared her posture but continued to fidget. "Can't say I like it. I — I — wanted to see if I could help. Granny sent me an email last night saying my marketing background might be useful. I wanted to see if it was." Realizing her nervous gesture, Piper put her hands behind her, as if hiding them would soothe her. "Useful that is. I'd like it to be."

Her voice lost some of its momentum on those final words.

A year older than her nearly identical sister, Piper had spent much of her childhood trying to mimic Paisley who stole every bit of attention the moment she entered a room. But the precocious toddler had turned into a spoiled tween and then an entitled adult.

Piper, however, didn't have it in her to be a fashionista mean girl. And where Paisley milked their mother's reality TV fame for every ounce of cream, Piper avoided the limelight with the same fervor. She currently made her living as a freelance grant writer. She and Harley had never been close, but would Piper look to hurt Harley and Fortune's Brew to get closer to her sister?

Harley didn't think so.

Last night, the loneliness of fighting for Fortune's Brew had been shared with Lautaro, Chance and Granny T as they laid out a plan on how to get to Crescent City. Harley had gone to bed for the first time in nearly five years with something close to hope in her heart. She wasn't good at asking for and accepting help. But Chance was right. She didn't know the mindset of these judges like he did. She had to be willing to listen if she wanted a chance to save Fortune's Brew.

Harley released some of the air in her lungs, hoping it

eased the tension she felt tightening behind her ears and in her temples. "We'd love some help in that department."

Piper's face fell and she started to turn away, then her eyes widened. "Really?"

"Absolutely." Harley walked toward Piper and motioned her forward with a wave of her head. "These guys were just adding a second condenser to the distillation set up." She looked back and gave a nod and shrug to Chance in silent agreement to his recommendation before turning back to Piper. "Chance thinks it will improve our odds at Nashville this weekend."

The smile on Chance's face was worth the risk she took in letting someone else in to help make decisions on the business. She'd trust him. He'd not given her reason not to. From the side, she saw Lautaro make the sign of the cross and raise his clasped hands to the heavens.

If you're up there, daddy, Harley prayed, *I hope this is the right decision.*

While Lautaro and Chance managed the addition of the condenser to the distillation line, Harley and Piper reviewed the current marketing strategy, which didn't take long because there was basically nothing.

"Word of mouth is all we've been able to afford." Harley sat sideways on the big desk while Piper sifted through a stack of files containing the original label ideas their grandfather had designed more than forty years ago.

"We need to freshen up the look." Piper pulled out the current label and started sketching on the back of one of the folders. "Right now you look like every other bottle out there. We need to make you stand out a little more until the world knows how good Fortune's Brew is on taste alone."

Harley watched as her cousin's hand flowed across the page, a little in awe of the ease with which the design came to life. "I'm glad you're here, Piper. But I have to wonder why. Why now? More than likely Fortune's Brew is going to be sold or broken up for its assets."

Piper's work never stopped or slowed but Harley saw her pull her lower lip between her teeth, her eyes narrowing. "Do you know the thing I hear most often when Paisley and I are together?"

Harley shook her head.

"That people didn't know Paisley had a sister. I'm a year older than her but I'm invisible. And not just with strangers. You remember when we were kids" Piper looked up from the drawing, but her eyes focused on the distance. "It was all about Paisley with mom and dad. I'm over the jealousy." A sad smile touched her lips, then she went back to her drawing. "For the most part, anyway, but I don't want to be in the shadows anymore." She laid the rough sketch of the new label on the desk and turned it toward Harley. "I'm also pretty good at what I do and think I can help."

Harley gasped at the rendering, an aged oak barrel with a skunk peaking over the top. "It's amazing, Piper. I love it."

Piper's face lit up, her dark eyes bright in their intensity and intelligence, and it was easy to see the differences now between Piper and her sister. Kindness softened her features into a familiar comfort that said *talk to me*.

They made a few changes. Piper had added a splash of teal against the silver and black and Harley asked her to change it to red in honor of her mother. Vivienne Fortune had loved the color red, filling their flower boxes with red peonies or begonias and of course, red roses.

"I always loved the story of the drunk skunk and how our great-grandmother took over while her husband was away. It made me think women can do anything."

"We can." Harley leaned forward, whispering conspiratorially. "Especially Fortune women."

As if emboldened by those words, Piper stiffened her back and shuffled the papers into a rough stack. "I want to work on a vendor event next. Maybe in Lafayette. Invite area businesses to taste test the product, have music and food trucks. Maybe even a cash bar and open it to the public. I need to find out the licensing requirements, but it could be a good way for some word of mouth advertising mixed with a targeted market hit. Would you have enough product to support something like that?"

Her cousin's excitement was contagious, and Harley's mind began to spin with the possibility of sharing Fortune's Brew on a larger scale. Their footprint in Lafayette was decidedly small. This event could be instrumental in terms of getting them into the area market. "Let me calculate it out with Chance and Lautaro but I think so. That sounds like a great idea."

Back in the still house, Lautaro and Chance had finished hooking up the second condenser and were starting the distillation when Harley rejoined their team. The two men worked in silent unison, in tune to the needs of the process and what the other was doing without a word between them.

When Dean had worked there, it had been a constant struggle to keep him focused on a task, to instruct him over and over in the right way to set up the distillation tanks or monitor the proofing. Chance had stepped into the nuanced dance without missing a beat or causing Lautaro and Harley to miss a beat.

It left Harley a little rattled at how easy it was for him to move into their lives, as if he'd always been there.

Because he wouldn't.

She knew that on a fundamental level. Whereas in the beginning, his arrival had caused her frustration and unsettled her neat little world, she knew now his departure would do the same. How had he become such a part of her life so quickly? So easily?

Did that mean she trusted him? Leo's words haunted her.

Chance will come around.

But Chance didn't strike her as a person who could betray another. He'd kept the line between personal and professional very clear. His integrity was important to him.

Maybe Harley didn't trust him yet.

But she thought she could.

She wanted to.

Harley slipped into the work Lautaro and Chance were completing, and by the time the sun no longer cut across the entrance to the still house, they had disposed of the head of the run and had a few gallons of the new product spider-legged and waiting for next steps.

"That sits on the tongue really well," Harley said after the first taste, watching as Chance moved the liquid around his mouth.

Chance tipped the last of the liquor into his mouth, letting out a sharp inhale. "Yes it does." He motioned to the end product with his glass. "We should get an equal amount over the next few hours which after we dilute each half to proof will give us more than enough for Nashville. Are you up for a little experimentation?"

Harley's senses perked up, but she tamped down the instantaneous instinct to put up her shields and shy away from whatever Chance would suggest. She had to be willing to listen. He'd been right about the double condenser, as much as she may hate to admit it. He was moving them in the right direction. She just had to stay on the course he was leading and hope he could take them where they needed to be.

"You mean the double condenser wasn't enough of an experiment?"

He narrowed the gap between them but didn't take her in his arms however much she ached to feel safe in the protected circle of his body. It was scary to feel this safe with someone she'd known such a short time.

"I know that was a risk for you and your trust is valuable to me. That's why I want to use the second part of the heart purely as is, like we discussed. What I'd like to do with this part is spice it with some of your grandmother's peach and ginger. Just a subtle flavoring. Like an old fashioned. I thought of it last night while tasting that jam. It's the perfect complement."

Harley looked to Lautaro who'd remained just outside their little circle but still focused on the conversation. "Lautaro has suggested something similar in the past but..."

"You were right not to experiment too much in the beginning. Now I think we have to play it a little risky. Two entries at Nashville would improve the odds if we get the flavors right."

"But it must sit for five days once we spice it," Lautaro reminded them. "That will not give us much time to bottle before the competition."

Harley looked between the two men, seeing their expectant faces, looking to her for the decision, trusting her with the decision. Normally the weight of such a decision would feel overwhelming but today Harley felt lifted by the possibilities presented. "Let's do it. We still have a fall back if it's not what we want."

They moved in tandem once the decision was made.

Lautaro retrieved the peach and ginger from the barn stores while Harley and Chance moved the distillate to a stainless steel container to rest. Within an hour, the spiced shine was mixed and waiting to be tested for proof.

Harley's stomach grumbled and Chance raised a silent, questioning brow. She looked at the Pepé La Pew clock hanging in the office, a gift to her dad their last Christmas. "It's almost five and we have a few hours before this is ready. If I'm going to keep testing the product, I need to grab something to eat. Else Scooter there won't be the only drunk skunk in the still house."

Chance said as wiped his hands on his jeans. "Let's get everyone together and head out to Gastineaux's. I've had a craving for their boudin balls since my first day in town."

It didn't take much convincing for Piper and Lautaro to put away the work in exchange for food. Trudy needed a little more convincing.

She, Miss Perla, and Mr. Shaw were finishing up the day's chores in the house and preparing for a quiet evening.

"I'm going to heat up some leftovers and then Netflix and chill." Trudy tried to wave off Harley as she puttered around the living room, but Harley saw her eyes cut to the window where she could see Lautaro waiting by the car.

Miss Perla harumphed. "You need to get out of this house, Trudy. You're growing into the woodwork."

"Hush, Perla. You and Shaw should go with them if you want."

Mr. Shaw clucked his tongue and shook his head. "Nope. They'll expect me to keep my pants buttoned at that fancy restaurant."

Trudy and Harley laughed as Shaw winked at Perla's horrified expression, her mouth flapping like a landed catfish.

Miss Perla playfully slapped at her husband's arm, but her eyes were filled with love. "I can't take you anywhere, Shaw Duplantis."

Mr. Shaw leaned down and planted a kiss on his wife's nose. "You can take me home, woman."

While Mr. Shaw and Miss Perla gathered their things, Harley returned her attention to convincing her grandmother to go out with them.

"Netflix will be there tomorrow night," she argued. "Besides, Lautaro is going and it's time for you to stop ogling him from afar and ogle him up close, don't you think?"

Trudy's face blossomed red, and her mouth dropped open. "I... You don't.... I...." Her hands conducted an orchestra of explanation as she first pointed at Harley sternly, then pointed out the window, then back to herself. Finally, Trudy dropped her arms to her side. "He's not aware, is he? That I'm ogling him from afar? I'd be so embarrassed."

"Are you aware he's been ogling you from afar for the past three years?"

Harley nearly giggled at the pleased smile her grandmother tried to hide as it tugged up the corners of her mouth.

"He has?"

"Yes. Let's go." Harley ushered the older woman toward the door. "You two are going to have to face each other."

"Does this mean you're going to face Chance?" Trudy shot back, grabbing her purse as they shuffled toward the door.

It was Harley's turn to stammer and blush a solid crimson. "That's completely different. He's so..." She gestured outside as if that explained the miles separating them. "And I'm so..." She gestured to her wrinkled clothing then at her reflection in the hall mirror. Even if he wanted something physical with her, it didn't mean he wanted her. She was holding out for more. She'd had examples of true love all her life. She wanted to wait until she'd found her happily ever after.

"That's easy to fix."

Trudy grabbed Harley's hand and did a quick one eighty in the hallway. In her room she snatched a hanger from her closet and tossed it to Harley. "Paisley gives me clothes every year for my birthday. That girl has great taste for herself but she either thinks I'm a hundred and twelve or thirteen. This year, however, she got me this and it's cute as it can be. Put it on."

Harley pulled on the soft pink chambray top dutifully, staring at the smocked bodice and hem that barely skimmed the top of her jeans in the mirror. "It's short."

"It's fashionable." Trudy dragged Harley closer to the vanity and did some magic with her hair, tugging the stands behind her ear and letting them fall and spritzing something so they stayed there. She added two sparkly bobby pins at her temple.

"It's pink." She tried to untuck the hair back behind her ear, but Trudy pushed her hand back down. Then Granny T pointed the *finger of death* coupled with *the look* and Harley kept her hand by her side.

Now Granny T was swiping stuff on Harley's lashes and then on her lips, thankfully not the same stuff, before she stepped back and did a Vanna White motion to Harley. "It brings out the rose in your complexion."

Harley couldn't reconcile the image in the mirror with how she saw herself. She never considered herself ugly but compared to Paisley and Piper she was definitely the plain one in the family. Whatever magic Granny T had done had made her eyes look large and luminous and her lips more defined and luscious.

"I look like a girl."

"I know this will come as a shock, Charlotte Vivienne Fortune, but you are a beautiful woman." Trudy secured a simple gold chain with a garnet pendant. "Perfect."

"Hardly perfect," Harley corrected, studying the reflection in the antique mirror, looking for the same objectivity she used on a new recipe.

Trudy collected the cosmetics and tucked them back into her vanity. She wrapped an arm around Harley's waist, laying her chin on the flat of her shoulder. "Nothing ever is, but granddaughters come close."

"I wish I was doing a better job for the family." Harley turned in her grandmother's embrace, so many words on the tip of her tongue.

"Stop it, Harley." Trudy put a finger to Harley's mouth and shushed her. "I think holding on to Mr. Diamond was pretty smart."

"But Uncle Everett brought him on board."

Trudy shrugged. "I'm not sure Everett brought him on board for Fortune's Brew or for himself. But you turned the relationship into something really positive for the business."

At her grandmother's hesitation, Harley asked, "What is it?"

"Connie did a little checking on our consultant."

Harley's heart did a two-step. "Oh? What did she find out?"

"Diamond is a name he uses for business, but he was quite in demand on the judging circuit until he walked away last year."

Chance loved his work. She couldn't imagine anything

making him walk away. Unless he'd had no choice. "Why did he walk away?"

"Connie's brother's boss' wife's mother works on the distillery council and said that Chance stood up for a friend after some accusations of blackmail and bribery at a competition. There was no evidence to support either side but since CJ Diamond had a personal relationship with the accused, he walked away rather than let the competition judging be called into question."

Harley turned the new information over in her head while Trudy finished getting ready. It sounded like Chance. He wouldn't want there to be any question about his integrity.

Or he'd wanted to give them no further reason to look into the accusations.

Minutes later the two women exited the house, Harley walking behind her grandmother as they stood on the porch. Lautaro exited the still house, Chance running to catch up, the two men falling `deep in serious conversation.

"Hope you don't mind if I join your group, Chance." Trudy shouldered her purse and walked down the steps to the yard.

Chance looked away from Lautaro toward the women. "Not at all, Mrs. For —"

Harley's head snapped up when Chance's voice cut out, pleasure rocketing up from her toes at his open admiration. He stalked forward, eyes only for her, but held out his hand to her grandmother as she stepped from the porch. Lautaro beat him to the punch, however.

She looked up as Lautaro escorted Trudy to the car and saw Piper giving her the "you're hot" gesture by waving her splayed hand in front of her chest excitedly and simultaneously wiggling her eyebrows. Harley had to look away before she stumbled over her own shadow.

Chance leaned a hip against the stair railing, crossing one ankle over the other. He was dressed as usual since that first day: well-fitted jeans that hugged his hips and thighs, crisp button down tucked in at the waist, shiny brown loafers. Nary a wrinkle or crinkle in sight. Unless you counted the smirk that deepened the dimples at the corners of his mouth.

"Excuse me," Chance tipped an imaginary hat, the sparkle in his eyes brightening the chocolate starburst in the amber. "I'm waiting for Harley Fortune. Have you seen her inside?"

Heat chased the pleasure around Harley's body, finally screeching to a halt in her cheeks and neck. "It was Granny T. She made me do it."

Harley tugged at the hem of the shirt, her fingers brushing the bare skin of her abdomen. She woke up wrinkled and the day didn't get much better from there. She'd never thought about it if truth be told. But Chance made her think of a lot of things she'd never thought of before.

He was up the stairs in two seconds flat, pulling her hands into his and bringing them to his chest. Beneath their joined hands, she could feel his heart thumping, see the jump of it beneath the sharp cut of his jaw.

"You are the sexiest woman on the planet, Harley Fortune. And it has nothing to do with your clothes, wrinkled or otherwise. Or your hair." He caressed her temple with the pad of his thumb, tracing a line down her jaw to the corners of her mouth. "With or without your dad's baseball cap." His hand rejoined the knot of their fingers at chest level. "You're smart and funny and incredibly loyal to those you love. You have vision and determination. And those are just a few of your better qualities. Later tonight, when we're slow dancing, I'll tell you a few more."

His smile exploded but she was certain it was the horror-stricken look on her face. "I do not dance."

"You will tonight."

He pulled her forward, where they joined the others, Harley noting the varied expressions on their faces: curious (Granny T), hopeful (Piper), and full of warning (Lautaro).

"It's my professional opinion that you need to be twirled around a dance floor tonight."

Harley scoffed, but there wasn't much weight behind it. Her mind and body were entirely focused on Chance and the way he kept looking at her as if the rest of the world didn't exist. "Your professional opinion? I didn't realize that was a clause in your contract."

They all piled into the car, Harley somehow ending up in the middle of Chance and Piper in the backseat.

"It's in the fine print," Chance teased, angling his body so he could watch her squirm beneath his appreciative look.

Lautaro cranked the engine to life, putting his arm across the back of the seat where his fingers brushed Granny T's shoulder. Neither moved as Lautaro executed the three-point turn to point the Mercedes down the road.

"Always read the fine print, Harley," Piper chimed in, grinning from ear to ear.

The twenty-minute trip to Gastineaux's was filled with small talk. Granny T shared bits and pieces of info about the history of the area with Chance as they passed landmarks. Piper and Lautaro traded ideas about the vendor event she was planning.

Harley? Harley couldn't get past where Chance's thigh rested casually against her own, the hard line of muscle slicing into her thoughts and composure with equal discombobulation. Along the road, Lautaro hit a pothole hard enough to make the back of the car bounce and in the split second her body left the seat, Chance slid his hand down her back, stopping just above the waist of her jeans, and snuggled her closer to the curve of his body.

Her shoulder fit nicely beneath his arm, as if they were made to fit together. His fingers skimmed the exposed line of skin where the shirt was riding up, and the explosion of goosebumps from that miniscule contact tingled along her flesh.

Awareness flooded Harley's senses; awareness of Chance's breath, the rise and fall of his chest, the fact that the circles he rubbed on her back had a pattern. Circle, circle, caress. A wave of warmth followed each caress, as if she was the tide coming to shore and he was the moon pulling her back out to sea.

Something she would only call surety replaced the awareness. A comfort in knowing he'd stood by her side. Confidence in knowing he'd continue to do so in the days and weeks to come. Because that was Chance. His protective streak wasn't meant to smother her or overwhelm. He was there to lift her up if she fell, not step on her while she was down.

She decided it didn't matter what Leo had said about Chance's loyalties. What Chance had shown her time and time again was all that mattered. In waiting to pursue their personal involvement, in not pursuing her about the recipe. In staying on to help because he believed in her and Fortune's Brew — something not even most of her family could profess to do. Those things showed Harley all she needed to know about Chance Diamond.

The car slowed as it made the turn into the parking lot at Gastineaux's, the motion pushing her further into the crook of Chance's arm. With unspoken welcome he nestled her closer, adjusting his body to fit to hers.

The parking lot was full, diners coming and going from the popular restaurant. Even from outside they could hear the live music leaking out from the open windows and filling the early evening air with the lively cadence of zydeco rhythm and dueling fiddles, piano, and drums.

"Sounds like Les Haricots is playing tonight." Harley kept a piece of her heart for her old band mates from high school. It was one of the only good memories she had from those days.

"We gwan pass a good time tonight, *cher*!" Lautaro sing-songed out into the night. Granny T added an "*aie-eee*" on for good measure to Harley's delight as the group joined those waiting for tables. Within minutes, the hostess Miranda had them seated in the dining room, close enough to hear the music but far enough so conversation was still possible.

At Granny T's encouragement they ordered a range of appetizers so Chance could try out the menu, giving him a sampling of crab and crawfish au gratin, eggplant Pontchartrain, and Oysters Belle Terre in addition to the boudin balls.

The conversation was easy between the five of them as the meal progressed, touching on business, of course, but also circling around to topics like sustainable farming, the seafood industry, last year's hurricane season, and this year's Saints' roster.

Opinions were not lacking on any topic, but even disagreeing with Piper or Granny T, Harley realized how much she had missed being close to her family. She had cut herself off from the others, putting all her focus on the business. Her dad had loved Fortune's Brew, but he never would have let it come between him and his family.

Maybe Chance was right, and Harley wasn't protecting his legacy as much as she was protecting her memory of him.

"Hey Harley!"

The familiar voice pulled Harley from her musing and she looked up to see Les Haricots' main fiddle player and one of her best friends from high school. He pulled her from the chair and wrapped her in a bear hug.

"Seth, it's good to see you." Harley gestured across the table. "Seth Boudreaux, meet Chance Diamond. Chance has been consulting out at the distillery for the family."

Chance stood and the two men shook hands.

Seth grabbed a paper towel from the table and blotted the sweat from his forehead, the moisture glistening on his deep chicory skin in the low light of the dining room. "You gotta watch out for Fortune's Brew. It's a truthteller, that one."

Harley laughed, remembering the night they'd snatched a bottle from the still house and brought it out to the levee where the band had gathered. "You can't keep blaming my moonshine because you kissed Angela Chaisson in front of your girlfriend that night, Seth."

"I most certainly can." Seth didn't even try and hide the contented smile that took over his face. "It makes for a good story when Angie and I go out for our anniversary dinner each year."

Harley looked around Seth where the crowd had started to thin in the back room, the band absent from the stage. "Everything alright? Y'all took a break about twenty minutes ago. Is the set done already?"

Seth's shoulders dropped. "Nah. Our keyboard player's

not feeling good and the backup can't be here for another hour. Since that would only give us an hour left in the set we decided to call it a night instead."

Granny T perked up, having been sitting silently during the conversation so far. "Why don't you fill in Harley? You know the music."

Before Harley could utter the denial that jumped to her tongue, Seth's head snapped to Harley, curiosity lifting his brows. But it was hope that filled his voice. "It would mean we wouldn't have to lose the gig tonight. And Mason will use it as an excuse not to hire us again."

Harley knew that Seth and the band played because they loved it, but she also knew, as you know things in a small town, that the money came in handy. But Harley also hadn't played publicly in fifteen years, not since her parents had died returning home for her recital. Was it time to take a chance?

Speaking of Chance, she glanced over at him as he watched her, his eyes assessing and full of questions. But she also saw answers. Chance hadn't hesitated to offer his assistance when Harley needed it. How could she do any less for a friend in need?

"I'd be happy to, Seth. I may be a little rusty."

"Pfft," Seth waved her off, pulling back her chair as she stood. "'Metal rusts, music lasts forever.' Come on back and I'll get you set up."

Harley laughed at the familiar quote from Seth's favorite author as he loped back through the crowd, a bounce in his step as he waved to the band and announced the music would be back in a few minutes.

She hoped Seth was right and the music was forever. Already her palms were sweating at the thought of playing in front of a crowd.

Granny T beamed. "I'm proud of you, sweetheart. They would be too."

The twist in her gut was there at the memory of her parents, but not as sharp as she would have thought. Her mother especially loved to listen to Harley play piano in the afternoons, sitting in the living room and working on her needlepoint or putting away jam in the kitchen. It was why Harley loved to help Granny T make jam. Where being in the still house reminded Harley of her dad, the familiar melody of clinking jars and rattling pot lids made her feel close to her mom.

Piper reached over and squeezed Harley's arm. "You got this, Harley."

Lautaro made a show of breathing in, then breathing out again. "Piper is correct."

Chance now stood next to her; he leaned down, his breath a warm whisper against her ear. "I can make an excuse if you need it, but I don't think you do."

Harley nodded. She was grateful he'd offered to get her out of the situation but also willing to let her make the choice. Chance did that with most things, she realized. Let her know he would be there to protect, but also letting her know she didn't need it, that she was fully capable on her own.

"Thanks." She pressed a kiss to his cheek, the world narrowing down to the two of them for that heartbeat.

On stage, she settled behind the piano, adjusting the bench, testing the keys with a quick run of scales, looking over the notes for the set list. Even those simple notes pulled at something inside of Harley. Once, she'd considered music her first love.

Her parents had taken her to a Broadway musical one summer, and she'd been mesmerized to think people got to write new songs and play music all day. When her parents were killed returning early from a business trip to attend one of her recitals, the love of music had gone out of her, drowned beneath the sorrow of loss. Like so many other things, Harley had not found balance with her sorrow and her love.

It was what Chance had meant the other night when he told her she could live her dream and not the one of her parents. That she could choose what made her happy and not be disloyal to the memory of her parents by choosing herself. He was the first person to understand the conflict that raged inside of her.

Harley looked out to the crowd and saw Chance leading Piper, Lautaro, and Granny T into the back room, the four of them scooting into a vacant booth as a waitress cleared the dishes. The murmur of voices had risen since the music stopped, a hum beneath the buzz in her ears.

She'd made Fortune's Brew her life out of a sense of loyalty to her parents' sacrifice but in doing so, she'd sacrificed what she wanted. What would they think of that?

The band joined her on stage and the noise of their tuning up brought her back to the present. As Seth tucked his fiddle under his chin, he winked at her. "Things haven't changed that much since you left. Just jump in and we'll see where she goes."

On the three count, the music started and Harley remembered what it was like to be free.

Chapter Seventeen

I n the time it took the opening notes of the music to jump start the crowd, Chance witnessed a rebirth of Harley Fortune. She gave in to the temptation of the music, closing her eyes and letting it carry away the tension in her shoulders and that stressed little v-shaped furrow between her brows. He'd seen her focused and determined and even enthusiastic during their hours together in the still house.

But this.

This was happiness to Harley.

Chance had known a few days ago he was falling for the amazingly complicated woman at his side. He thought of all the cliches: yin to his yang, fire to his ice, sun to his moon. There was something about Harley that made him better when they were together, that made him want to be better when he was around her. He couldn't explain it, but he liked the feeling.

He had especially liked the press of her body against his on the car ride over. She fit perfectly against him and while he felt protective, he also knew she was strong enough not to need his protection. Harley Fortune would be just fine with or without him.

He hoped he could figure out how to make *with him* happen.

There were things he hadn't told her yet, things he'd kept to himself for professional reasons. At least that was what he told himself in the beginning. He didn't share his family history with clients. It created too many uncertainties and Chance liked surety in business. On his own, he never had to question whether a client was hiring him or the potential to curry favor with his mom and dad.

It was time to tell Harley exactly who he was.

He just hoped she didn't hold it against him.

The crowd from the dining room had made their way into the back and filled the tables around the perimeter of the room. A few dancers were circling the center, showing off their two-step to the lively tune Les Haricots was playing.

Piper pushed her chair back raising her glass of wine to the table. "I'm going to dance. Who's coming with me?" She took a big sip, her eyes jumping between the three others at the table.

"I'm up for it." Chance stood and held out his hand to Trudy. "Come on, Mrs. Fortune. Show me how it's done."

Trudy blushed and stumbled over her words. "I haven't... no... I couldn't..." But she gazed at the dance floor and raised a questioning brow. "Well, maybe I can."

"That's it, Granny T!" Piper grabbed her hand then hauled Lautaro to his feet. "You're not sitting here by yourself. *Allons!*"

Lautaro had the good sense not to argue and soon the four of them were sweeping around the dance floor with the crowd and moving their feet to the impossibly quick tempo of the Zydeco music. Chance danced just as often with Mrs. Fortune as he did with Piper, learning to merge his two-step into the Cajun jitterbug under their patient tutelage.

When the music turned to the slow walk of a waltz, Lautaro held out his hand to Trudy who shyly put her hand in his and let him lead her away.

Piper wiped away the sheen of sweat with the back of her hand. "It's about time."

She led Chance back to their table and the two of them signaled the waitress for more ice water.

Chance laughed as he gulped the cool liquid, leaning forward so he could be heard over the din of music and conversation. "So, it wasn't my imagination. Your grandmother and Lautaro?"

Piper blotted her forehead with a napkin. "They've been simmering like that for years. Granny T thinks she's too old for a second chance at love and Lautaro's too honorable to go where he thinks he's not wanted."

She went on to explain Lautaro's guilt over the death of Elias and Vivienne Fortune. Chance knew what guilt could do. His dad's sense of guilt after Sondra abandoned their family had been a third member of their family in the early days after her departure.

Chance thought at first that was why Isaac Gold had remarried so quickly, only six months after the divorce. In the end, Chance realized it was a match based on love and respect. And Evie had been a fierce protector and friend. He only hoped he could find the same one day.

The expression on Piper's face morphed into wariness and Chance followed the direction of her gaze to see Dean Blanchard propped against the door at the entranceway, nursing a beer and a grudge if the pinched look on his face was any indication.

"I know I shouldn't ask," Chance began, right before he asked, "But him and Harley?"

Piper gave a dismissive wave in his direction. "I think she dated him out of some sort of obligation. He'd had a crush on her since we were kids, so she finally said yes last year. It lasted about four dates."

Chance recognized the look of jealous rage, remembering the bite of the man's words about Harley in Houston. It wouldn't surprise Chance now if the accident on Lake Opelousas Road when he'd first arrived in town had been intentional. Things may be over for Harley, but it wasn't over for Dean.

The music stopped and Seth lifted the microphone from its stand. "Help me thank Harley Fortune for filling in with us tonight folks. The woman makes great whiskey and beautiful music!"

Harley waved away the compliment, her face flushed from the sudden attention, and exchanged places with another man making his way on stage. They shook hands and hugged briefly, their expressions the relaxed familiarity of old friendships.

Within seconds the band was counting into their next set and Harley was sliding into a chair at Chance's right. Piper accepted an invitation to dance and quickly disappeared into the crowd twirling and swirling around the center of the room.

"You were phenomenal." Chance poured her a glass of water and slid it to within reach.

Harley swiped the hair on both sides of her face behind her ears, struggling to contain the elation dimpling the corners of her mouth. "It was good to play again. I'd forgotten..." She let the sentence trail off beneath the rising chorus as the audience joined in with the band to sing the refrain.

They waited in comfortable silence for the noise to die down. Harley leaned back in her chair, playing with the condensation on her glass, but her eyes avoided everything around her. When the music again shifted to something slower, Chance offered his hand.

"Dance with me?"

Harley's head snapped up, looking to see who Chance was asking. He grinned and asked again. "Dance with me?"

She hesitated but started to reach up. "I don't really dance."

Chance took her hand. "It's like making whiskey, Harley. It's all about the timing and the touch."

They blended into the crowd, Chance wrapping Harley in his arms and pressing his cheek to her temple. Her body was a line of tension at first but as they moved, she relaxed into him, letting him lead and set the tempo. The first slow song melded into another and neither tried to release the embrace as they continued to make their way around the dance floor.

The rhythm was easy, their bodies in tune, similar to their movements in the still house each day, each knowing where the other would be, anticipating the next step as if one had the thought and the other needed to put it into action. Seamless. Fluid. For Chance, most of his clients were like the boulder he had to move around. Harley was another body of water that just flowed into his without interruption, two becoming one.

"You know you don't have to choose." He whispered the words against her ear, pulling her tighter into the hard line of his body, wanting to shield her but mostly wanting to be something she could lean on in her uncertainty. "Music or business. Your passions for your father's passion. It's possible to do both."

Harley lifted her head from his shoulder but kept her body pressed against his. "It doesn't seem like it most of the time."

There was a heaviness to her words that settled around Chance's heart.

"Uncle Everett and Aunt Lisbeth have been pushing to sell since mom and daddy died. Granny T wouldn't even talk about until I reached eighteen. Then it felt like she needed me to keep the place alive, but I think after the last five years even she's doubting my ability to make this place profitable."

Chance squeezed her hand. "She doesn't doubt you, Harley. I think maybe she fell into the same trap, thinking it was all or nothing. She wanted to make her husband's and son's dreams a reality but forgot about her own."

His own memories crowded into the conversation. Hadn't he done the same? Run away from his father's business to avoid his mother? He'd always blamed a need to keep his interests separate, not wanting to use her notoriety to benefit his consulting but in doing so, he'd also sacrificed his love for his father's world.

"I think we all do it to some degree," he confessed.

She tilted her head back so she could see his face, her eyes searching his. "What are you trying to balance?"

"You know about my friend, Leo." At her nod, he continued. "We're supposed to open a bar together in the French Quarter, but the financing is not working out as planned. The building's owner is getting anxious, and Leo wants me to use some personal connections I have to make it happen."

"But you're reluctant to mix business with personal business." Harley paused. "Once you do that, it changes a relationship, no matter what."

Her quick understanding shouldn't have surprised him. "It's more than that. I cut ties with those connections Leo wants me to use many years ago, but in doing that I also sort of walked away from someone I love a great deal. That was never my intent, but it became a sacrificial byproduct."

"Is that the *all or nothing* you were hinting at? You thought you had to walk away from both in order to walk away from one?"

"At the time, yes. But looking back I didn't."

"Can you repair the relationship?"

"Absolutely. It's more blocked by pride than broken."

"Then break down the wall. If the only thing keeping your from being with someone you care about is pride, then that's a stupid thing to let keep you apart."

Chance huffed a laugh. "Speaking from experience?"

Harley shrugged. "Mine isn't so much pride as self-preservation. There are ulterior motives at play with my family that I can't figure out. Like with the corn. Is that what Everett is looking to do with The Gold Standard? Or is there something else I'm not seeing? It makes it doubly hard to trust anyone that wants to help."

The heaviness of his deception stuck in his throat, crowding out the words he wanted to utter. Would she walk away once he told her? Would she send him away?

"Sometimes secrets are kept for a good reason, Harley."

"Does this go back to mixing business with pleasure? Because you can talk to me. Since I'm no longer a client it's not breaking Rule Three to get personal."

Chance leaned forward and brushed a wisp of hair behind her ear. "Tomorrow is for business. Tonight is just for pleasure."

He'd tell her tomorrow, he promised himself. If she kicked him out of her life, then at last he had tonight.

The song wrapped up and Harley and Chance made their way back to the table where Lautaro, Piper, and Trudy waited, faces flush, smiles bright from the music and dancing.

"Time to get this old woman home, Harley, dear," Trudy sighed, brushing back the sweat-dampened curls from her temple. "I fear what happens when the clock strikes midnight."

Lautaro held out the chair as Trudy stood and offered his arm. "You will still be a queen, dear lady."

When the two walked away, Piper and Harley exchanged looks then broke into non-stop laughter.

Catching her breath, Piper finger-combed the loose strands of hair from her eyes. "Geez, they were bad enough when they were ignoring each other. Now that they are out of the closet, so to speak, it's going to be insufferable."

Chance watched Harley watch her grandmother and Lautaro, her face softening, the corners of her mouth lifting in a wistful smile as she said, "I think it's sweet they're getting a second chance at love. Some of us are waiting on our first shot."

Her head snapped up as the last word left her lips and her eyes widened, as if the confession had startled her. Chance pretended to be occupied with the bill, realizing Trudy had paid while he and Harley had been dancing. Regardless, he added a few bills of his own then joined Piper and Harley as they weaved through the thinning crowd toward the front door.

The ride back to the Fortune's was quiet, the fivesome lost in individual thought. Chance had pulled Harley against him as soon as they settled in the backseat, more comfortable with her body pressed against his than not. He didn't have to spend much time deciphering that little detail. It was easy for him: he was better with Harley in his life. He hoped once he came clean about his connection to The Gold Standard she would let him stay.

As Lautaro guided the Mercedes down the final stretch of road, the older man suddenly sat tall in the driver's seat. "*Madre de dios.*"

Chance leaned forward to look over his shoulder, seeing the smashed back windshield of his car illuminated by the Mercedes' headlights. The spiderweb of cracks reflected the bright light like a star in the night sky.

"The still house." Harley's voice drew Chance's attention to the open door of the still house. Lautaro parked the car and they scrambled out, Harley flinging open the door to the still house as Chance warned, "Wait, Harley!"

He followed on her heels, finding her in the dimly lit interior, searching the seemingly undisturbed equipment with a slow turn of her head. The sharp smell of fertilizer filled the room and their eyes fell on the vat of product they'd left resting before dinner.

"No!"

Harley and Lautaro ran to the vat, Chance not far behind. Dirt and other debris floated on the top of the vat's surface; the discarded fertilizer bag tossed on Harley's desk just a few feet away.

"Son of a —" Harley slapped her hand against the ruined vat, pushing away to pace like a caged animal. Her eyes were wide, fists clenched at her side as she stalked the length of the room.

"Harley." Chance wanted to calm her down but knew that telling someone to calm down was a decidedly inappropriate way to get them to calm down.

Lautaro, Piper and Trudy had joined them around the ruined vat, Trudy and Piper looking at Harley with worried expressions.

Lautaro cursed under his breath. "I saw Dean at the restaurant. He did not look happy to see all of us, but he left, so I thought that was the end of it."

Chance had moved closer. "Harley. Look a little closer at the vat please."

Harley held out her hands. "Why? So I can see Dean's handwriting? My future, along with Fortune's Brew, going down the drain? No, thanks. We're out of mash. That was the last of it."

Chance let her vent, knowing sometimes you needed to get to the bottom of the barrel to find what you were looking for.

"There's nothing left for Chicago or Nashville now. And that means we can forget about New Orleans." Her voice broke. She stopped, back turned to her family. "Granny, you were right. It's time to sell."

"Harley, no." Trudy reached out to Harley, a gentle hand on her granddaughter's shoulder. "Not like this. This is not what I wanted."

Harley turned, falling into her grandmother's arms. "Me either. All I wanted to do was see their dream come true."

Trudy leaned back and captured Harley's face in her hands. "I keep telling you. You were their dream. This was their business."

"But they died —" Again, Harley's voice broke and tears leaked down her cheeks. Trudy dashed them away with the pad of her thumb. "They died coming to my recital. They sacrificed their dream for mine. The music just got lost after that."

Lautaro stepped forward, wrapping his arms around

Harley's shoulders. "They were going to your recital, Harley. Whether they had been coming from the competition or the grocery store, they wouldn't have missed that for the world because they knew how much it meant to you."

"And the business meant that much to them."

"Yes, but not more than you. You do not have to give up everything in order to make them proud. They would be proud no matter what, as long as you were happy."

"Fortune's Brew does make me happy. I loved working here with daddy when I was a little girl. I still had my music so I could feel mom close whenever I played." Harley tilted her head to the side, as if the weight of her realization tilter her world. "But daddy gets further away every day. I don't want to screw up everything he worked for."

Trudy stepped forward, back stiff, a determined look on her face. "If Dean is responsible for this, we'll deal with him tomorrow. What's important right now is you. You are not responsible for this. You are not failing anyone because of what that boy did."

"I'm the one he's mad at. I thought changing the locks would be enough, but I didn't think it through. He probably purposefully wrecked the original shipment of Fortune's Brew that would have qualified us for Crescent City. If I hadn't sent in the last of our money for the competition, we'd have enough to pay off the Blanchards and some of the others."

Harley sank onto the retaining wall around the propane tanks, elbows propped on her knees. She tunneled her fingers through her hair then clasped her hands behind her neck. "We're going to go under, and it is my fault. Those are all decisions I made."

"Technically, yes, you made those decisions." Piper had crossed the room to stand near Chance, and he liked having her on his side. She was smart and forward-thinking and probably a little ignored in the family because she wasn't flashy like her sister or balls-to-the-walls like Harley. She was a perfect business partner.

All eyes were on Piper, who looked to Chance with a lifted brow. He nodded. "It was your idea. Take credit for it."

Piper took a deep breath. "The bank was willing to extend us a line of credit based on the showing at Houston, considering it an investment to keep the business running rather than, and I'm sorry for insinuating this Granny, us going under and them losing both the business and family accounts. I negotiated with the vendors to give us a ninety-day extension in exchange for advertising and booth space at the vendor event after Nashville in a few weeks. We can use the line of credit to pay off the vendors but since they're happy to wait right now, I say we hold onto the cash in case we need it for additional inventory. I went ahead and paid off the Blanchards and prepaid for next year's crop."

Crickets.

Harley stood, jaw slack, between mirroring bookends of Trudy and Lautaro. No one moved. No one spoke. They barely blinked.

Piper rocked forward on her toes, then crossed her arms at the weighty silence that followed her speech. She finally turned to Chance, concern deepening the familial 'v' in between her brows. "I'm not sure — *oomph*." Piper finished as Harley launched herself at her cousin and wrapped her in a bear hug.

As the cousins hugged, Chance looked over the duo to Lautaro and Trudy. "I know I should have double checked with management before okaying those changes, but things were happening fast and nothing is final without your signatures on the purchase orders. It's still all in theory. But it was a good theory, and I didn't want Piper to lose the momentum she had going."

Harley pulled back from the hug, dashing away the shimmer in her eyes. "That's amazing, Piper. I can't... I don't know what to say."

Piper looked away from the intensity of Harley's gratitude, sweeping the hair brushing her jawline back behind her ear. "Anyone could have done it Harley."

True, anyone could have done it, but no one had. Harley hadn't. She hadn't even thought to ask for the help, fearing what someone would do with the knowledge she needed help. People could take advantage of your weaknesses like Dean had done. She looked at Piper and then Chance. People could also surprise you.

"But I didn't even think of it. You probably saved us. At least in the short term." Harley gestured at the ruined tank. "We still won't have any product for Nashville this weekend. That means we're out of the running for Crescent City."

It was Chance's turn to rock forward on his toes. "Have you looked closer at the tank?"

Harley inspected the tank closer, Lautaro joining in as they circled the ruined vat.

"This is not the vat we finished earlier." Harley traced the noticeable dent in the side and the sealed off transfer valve. "This is the extra vat from the storeroom. The one we couldn't use."

Chance couldn't help the self-satisfied smile. "I switched out the tanks earlier, worried if no one was here there might be another *accident* in the stillhouse. It seemed like too good an opportunity to pass up. I also set up the webcam to record so we should have video of our saboteur for the sheriff if you want to press charges."

This time Harley launched herself into Chance's arms.

He wrapped his arms around her waist, his hands feeling the soft skin of her obliques and back as her blouse rode up. She smelled of cedar and peach and felt like heaven against his body.

"I don't know how to thank you."

"Consider this payment in full."

The trio behind them laughed.

"But your car..." Harley began as she pulled away, pointing to the ruined windshield. The culprit had managed to smash in the front windshield as well, leaving the car undriveable until he could call for repair in the morning.

"It won't be the first time Goldilocks has been roughed up a bit."

At the round of giggles Chance explained. "Goldilocks was a consultant." When their faces remained blank, he explained. "She shows up in someone else's house, proceeds to try out two-thirds of what's there and declares it unfit before leaving to let the family deal with her mess."

Everyone groaned, but it was more in relief, and they set about putting things right.

Luckily, the still house was mostly untouched except for the ruined vat. A quick look at the door found it jimmied but not destroyed so Trudy recommended they wait to call the sheriff until the morning. Lautaro and Chance maneuvered the tank to the dock while Piper swept up the fertilizer and Trudy and Harley checked on the vat Chance had hidden in the storeroom.

Chance found them testing the proof, a look of surprise widening Trudy's features.

"You changed the recipe." She sniffed the small sampling of moonshine Harley had given her in a glass then took another small sip, swishing the liquid around her mouth.

Harley replaced the cover on the vat. "Not really. Chance had us put a second condenser inline. It lowers our output by about twenty percent, but I think the result is worth it."

Trudy tipped back her head and drained the glass. "Definitely worth it. Well done, you two."

Harley beamed beneath the praise. "Let's hope it makes a difference in Nashville this weekend. We'll be competing against The Gold Standard head-to-head. It'll be the first time since mom and dad beat them fifteen years ago. I'd really like to do it again, especially if Everett is planning to sell to them. I can't stand the thought of Fortune's Brew ending up as another part of the Gold dynasty."

The twist of guilt made Chance suck in a breath. He needed to tell Harley the full scope of his involvement with The Gold Standard but also had an obligation to Everett under his original non-disclosure beyond the scope of the original agreement.

"Harley —" he started but Trudy interrupted.

"I wish I knew the right thing to do, Harley. Just remember I love you." Trudy smoothed a hand over Harley's head, cupping her granddaughter's chin. The familiar v creased her brow, sorrow deepening the shadows in her eyes until the pupils disappeared into a pool of darkness.

Harley took her grandmother's hand in her own. "I know, Granny T. I think for the first time I'm doing this for me, not just because I want to keep Fortune's Brew going."

"I think you've got a good shot, Harley," Chance offered as the three of them returned to the main area of the still house. He'd tell her soon, he promised himself.

Chance grabbed his satchel. "I'll need to leave my car until I can get a windshield repair vendor out here. Can someone give me a ride back to the hotel?"

"I'll do it," Piper, Lautaro, and Harley offered simultaneously.

Harley stepped toward Lautaro, taking the keys from his hand, a slight tremble in her fingers as she clutched her fingers around the keychain. "I don't mind, y'all. Piper, it's in the opposite direction of you and Lautaro, maybe you can finish the proofing on the vat in the storeroom if you don't mind. Besides, I'd like to talk to Chance about the plan for Nashville."

Everyone said their good nights. Lautaro and Granny T hovered around each other like a blind date that had ended well but unsure what they should do next. They were still staring at the walls when the others walked out of the still house.

Chance escorted Piper to her car then joined Harley in the Mercedes. Piper led the way back to the main road and turned right, while Harley turned left and began the familiar drive back to Belle Terre.

The car's headlights made little work of the thick darkness that swallowed the car. Harley was glad for the shadows inside the car, however. Hopefully, Chance couldn't see the nervous tremble in her hands on the steering wheel, or the way her left knee bounced like it was spring loaded.

From the corner of her eye, she could see him staring out the passenger side window, his right arm propped on the door, body angled slightly so the broad plane of his chest could distract her. The long legs that had whirled her effortlessly around the dance floor tucked in the space beneath the dashboard, ankles crossed, his body closed off unlike the open, relaxed posture he'd held earlier. She wondered what had changed to make him shut down.

He turned suddenly to face her, catching her open perusal. Chance smiled, the now familiar uptilt of his mouth knocking up the rhythm of her heart. "You wanted to ask about Nashville."

Harley snapped her eyes back to the road, thoughts jumbled as she tried to refocus on the driving, the competition, anything but the desire to know what it felt like to be with Chance as any woman would want to be with a man. Sure, they'd spent nearly every waking moment together the past weeks, but this felt beyond Harley's communications skills.

Chance knew her lack of sexual history and didn't seem to care. She'd never considered her virginity an obstacle until Dean made it the center point of their brief and failed excuse for a relationship. It was just a fact. Waiting for the right person made sense for her, so it was easy. Harley didn't pretend to know that Chance was her forever person, but she knew he was someone she could trust.

Suddenly, waiting was no longer easy.

"Uhh, yes... Nashville. I, uh, looked up the entry form. I wasn't sure if we should go with bourbon or stick with moonshine. I didn't know if the classification would help us or hurt us. Some vendors still think of moonshine as lower quality."

Chance scratched at the day's growth of bristles on his jaw. "I always say stick with what you do. Both are corn based, but moonshine is unaged while bourbon is aged. Technically we could age this batch for a week, but that seems to go against the spirit of the spirit."

Harley nodded, liking Chance's nod to integrity. "I agree. I'd rather lose with the truth than win with a lie."

"Do you think we stand a chance against someone like The Gold Standard or Old Barrel?"

Chance pushed up straighter in his seat. He sat the satchel on the floor but focused his attention on the darkness. "They hold the number one and two spots in the market for a reason, but sometimes that reason is because people don't like change. People buy what's familiar to them because they know what to expect.

"Your advantage here is the blind tasting. The judges won't know which product belongs to which distillery. That's your advantage. I meant what I said. You have the best moonshine I've ever come across, Harley. I can't imagine that not standing out when judged equally."

"I never thought I'd say this but I'm glad Uncle Everett hired you." She reached over and put her hand on Chance's, twining her fingers with his. "I think if I stand a chance of convincing Granny T that this can work, of keeping Fortune's Brew out of the hands of someone like The Gold Standard, it will be because of you."

Chance squeezed her hand, traced hesitant circles on the back of her wrist. "All I did was fine tune the signal, Harley. You were playing the right notes all along."

They crossed the bridge, the after-midnight streets of Belle Terre nearly deserted except for the occasional car or semi. Within minutes, Harley had pulled into the parking lot of the hotel.

She left the car running, scared that if she turned it off, she'd be tempted to join him in his hotel room.

"I want you to know I'd like to ask you inside," Chance said hoarsely. His thumb made little circles on the back of her hand and when she looked at his face, she saw that he watched their hands with an intensity she found mesmerizing. When he looked up, his eyes were hooded, as if cutting off her view inside his mind. What was he holding back?

"But you won't." Her head snapped up. "Are you married? Involved? Emotionally invested in someone you swiped right on?"

Chance laughed, a brief chuff of air. "Nothing like that. There are business reasons. Professionalism." He cleared his throat, finally looking up to meet her gaze. His eyes searched hers. "But there are also things I need to tell you first. Things I don't want between us."

Harley debated pushing him, both appreciating his honesty and hating the integrity that kept him from her. "So, tell me."

"I can't. Not yet. I want to, but there are things I need to deal with first."

She nodded. "I understand." She didn't. The pulsing need in her body interrupted rational thought.

His hand cupped her jaw, held her face as he leaned forward and pressed a gentle, chaste kiss on her corner of her mouth. "I'm glad you do because my body is going into rebellion at the thought of leaving you alone tonight."

"Guess it's cold showers for the both of us then."

Chapter Eighteen

Harley exited the bath, tightening the towel wrapped around her body. Water still beaded on her skin as she padded to the dresser to find a night shirt, noting for the first time her serious lack of anything remotely qualifying as sexy or even feminine. Her night clothes consisted of over-sized t-shirts and lounge pants for the cooler evenings.

She picked out her favorite shirt, the words *My imaginary friends think you have serious problems* emblazoned on the front. Geesh. If she ever did manage to bring a man into her bedroom, she'd better hoped he liked *Dr. Who* and sarcasm.

She tossed the shirt onto her bed with more vehemence than needed.

She'd taken a quick bath, the cooler than normal water not taking the edge off her frustration or the pulsing beat between her legs. She grabbed her jeans to toss into the hamper, her phone falling from the back pocket. Great. All she needed was another phone in the spin cycle. What was her problem with phones, anyway? Paisley was right. She was the only twenty-something that hated the stupid things.

As she bent to plug it in to recharge, Harley saw the three little dots in her text messages from Chance. He was still awake. Was he as wired as her or was his brush off just a polite way to say he wasn't interested? She thought of the kisses they'd shared, the way their bodies fit together in the car while driving to the restaurant earlier. She may not be the most experienced woman on the planet, but she wasn't a complete moron.

No. He wanted her as much as she wanted him.

How could one of the things that attracted her most - his integrity - be the thing keeping them apart? His message beeped at her.

Just wanted to say good night again.

See you in the morning.

She scrolled through her recent calls and hit his number before she thought about it much.

"Hey." His voice sounded hoarse, strained, and she could picture him lying in bed, bare chested, perhaps only a pair of boxers riding low on his hips as the covers bunched around his thighs.

"What are you wearing?" Holy shit. What was she doing?

A cavernous silence on the other end of the phone echoed in her ear, then his harsh breathing filled the void like the roar of the ocean in the night.

"Not much. You?"

Her skin tingled with the warmth of his breath in her ear. She traced the edge of the towel. "Even less."

"You'll get cold."

"Do you know something that could warm me up?"

His voice rumbled against the side of her face and in the

background she could hear the covers rustling, could picture Chance laying sprawled on the bed, those long legs slightly bent. "I have a few ideas."

She cradled the phone closer; heard his breathing change as things rustled on the other end of the line. Harley slid deeper beneath the covers on her bed, letting the weight of the duvet become the weight of Chance as it covered her, warmed her. "I hear skin to skin contact is essential for sharing body heat."

"I'm feeling plenty warm right now."

Harley's eyes fluttered close as she trailed one finger over the areola of her nipples. "I must be cold then because I'm feeling rather... perky... at the moment."

He murmured words of encouragement as she pinched each nipple and brushed the underside of her breasts, cupping their weight and lifting them as he talked about kissing and sucking on her flesh. She, in turn, had him trace the muscled plane of his stomach to the juncture of his torso and thigh, pulling his legs further apart, but never letting him touch the aching part of his body.

"You don't play fair," he growled in frustration.

She laughed; a throaty sound foreign to her own ears. "I didn't realize we were supposed to."

He retaliated then, having her brush the fingertips of one hand over the outer seam of her body but refusing to allow her to part the flesh and find the throbbing bundle of nerves where her heart now pulsed. Would he be so cruel as to build up her need then keep her waiting?

"Now put the other hand to your lips," he directed, his voice getting lower with each command to slowly insert one finger, then two, to swirl her tongue around the tips while gently pistoning them into the cavern of her mouth.

She coated her lips in the warm saliva, her body arcing

beneath the want and need. Harley rasped out her next instruction. "Push your hand down your stomach - imagine it's my mouth."

It was his turn to groan, and she drowned in the sensation of his pleasure as it filled her senses and rushed over her body like waves of heat and electricity.

"Touch yourself like I want to."

"Please."

Then words ceased. Only need filled the space between them and as her body moved on its own in a rhythm both known and unknown, Harley gave into the break of release with a shudder and a cry as Chance's voice seized and sighed her name with his fading breath.

Chapter Nineteen

Walking into the crowd for the Nashville Craft Distillery Competition mirrored the tailgating party at a Sugar Bowl game to Harley. The atmosphere couldn't have been more different from Houston's reserved professionalism.

The competition had taken over the Vanderbilt football stadium. Tents of every shape, color, and size dotted the horizon of the parking lot and field, little islands of food, music, and whiskey. In the stands, small groups gathered to escape the throngs on the field.

Unlike Houston, the Nashville event would open to the public after the initial judging. There was an underlying competition among the distilleries to see who could get the most mentions on social media or the biggest crowd for marketing pictures.

Like Houston, Chance had helped Harley and Lautaro prepare appropriately. They'd added to their display, bringing a supply of Granny T's jellies and jams, cured meats and cheeses, and a bubbling vat of Lautaro's gumbo.

The vat, the size of a Smart car, was currently being

stirred with a boat paddle by no-nonsense barista Bex from the coffee shop Beans and Bubbles. Barista Julie had also been offered a job but declined and Harley thought Julie was a little nervous about being around Chance after the coffee shop fiasco his first day in town.

The primary attendee at this event was vendors like Mid-South Beverage whom Harley was shaking hands, swamped with the elation that they would start carrying Fortune's Brew in their distribution rotation starting in July. Now all Harley had to do was get the company to survive until July. Oh, and make enough product to meet demands.

She scooted to the back of the tent and grabbed her water bottle, tucking the business card from the VP into the glass jar of business cards they'd collected so far. "That's four so far."

Chance beamed at her, his body lining up with hers from shoulder to knee, and it stoked the fire of adrenaline and excitement doing a slow-burn in her gut. "Amazing, Harley. I'm so proud of you. You knew when to listen and when to pitch to that guy. You were perfect."

It was natural for Harley to want to brush off such praise but for once she basked in the glow of success. "It felt right talking to him. I gave him the production info and our capacity. He wasn't deterred so that made him easier to talk to. He didn't care that we were small and new. In fact, he liked it."

It made Harley think of the growing relationship between her and Chance. They'd still not sealed the deal, although they'd come close in the office this past week. Had Piper not returned to pick up the inventory reports, Harley wasn't sure what would have happened.

There was still something Chance couldn't tell her and it

weighed on him. He'd spent time going over his contractual obligation with her uncle but whatever it was had kept him silent – and fully clothed – for now.

Chance joined her as she set up more bowls and dished rice for Bex to ladle on the gumbo. The spicy scents of andouille sausage and the Cajun holy trinity swirled around the inside of the tent and reminded Harley of weekends when the family would get together, and her grandfather and dad would feed the army of folks out in the still house.

She liked having that sense of family again, working together with people other than Lautaro. As much as she loved the man, she'd missed the circle of family and friends that had grown smaller over the years.

"It's why this competition got started," he explained, adding spoons and napkins to the set-up Harley was making. "Vendors want to find the next rising star, be the first to introduce them to their customers."

"*Aie-eee!*" Lautaro cheered as he two-stepped to the rear of the tent, dropping another business card into the jar. "I think the Boozy Bear will need a bigger cave very soon, Harley."

"And more corn," she added. Her words dampened Lautaro's cheery demeanor and Chance raised his brows in silent question. "I called Mr. Blanchard a few days ago but hasn't returned my calls about the corn. He keeps the overflow from the harvest in a grain silo the families built but I wanted to discuss increasing the next crop. See if we could turn over some acreage to him where our properties meet. Just in case."

She added the last bit, feeling the optimism in her words leak out. It was an unfamiliar emotion to Harley who'd become almost comfortable with the expectation of failure.

It wasn't that she liked failing, only after so many unsuc-
cessful attempts at getting Fortune's Brew going again, she'd
resigned herself to seeing her father's legacy disappear.

For the first time, she thought maybe they both had a
chance.

Chance.

He suppressed most of the tell-tale grin as he sidled over
and wrapped his arm around her shoulders, even the arrogance not bothering Harley at the moment.

"Go on," she prodded, finding her grin mirroring his.
"You can say it."

He kissed her temple, lingering, and Harley leaned into
his solid form. "My only comment is we make a damn good
team."

"Yes, we do!" It was Piper's turn to dance into the tent,
her laugh and excitement infectious. Reaching into her
pocket, she withdrew two handfuls of business cards.
"Thirty-seven." She let the cards waterfall into the jar to join
the others then pulled out the reservation forms she'd
created and slapped those against her palm. "Twenty-three
confirmed for our event over Memorial Day. We have
ourselves a party folks."

Harley's head spun a little at the news. "Piper, that's...
that's... incredible."

"Wait," her cousin went statue-still, her face losing the
excited flush evident seconds earlier. "I hope you say that
after I tell you what I did. Sort of an executive decision."

At the group's silence, Piper continued but Harley's
heart was beating almost loud enough she had to ask her
cousin to speak up. "We're going to have a mini-competition
for a showcase cocktail with Fortune's Brew. A monetary
prize, trophy, picture in our quarterly newsletter."

"We have a newsletter?" Lautaro asked.

"We will by the time the event is over." Piper answered, her infectious grin spreading faster than spilled peach jelly on Miss Perla's linoleum.

Harley got stuck on two words, however. "Monetary prize? Piper, I love the idea, but we do we have the capital to offer anything significant in terms of prize money right now?"

"We do with the line of credit I secured from the bank. I think the publicity will be a great return on that investment."

Harley looked to the faces surrounding her and let their optimism boost her own. "OK. I trust your judgment." She'd not uttered more difficult words but also realized how true they were. She trusted Piper. "Let's get back to it. We have a few thousand more vendors to impress before the judging at noon."

The four of them worked like a well-oiled machine with barista Bex keeping the machine both fed and hydrated. Lautaro delivered their entry an hour before judging was to begin, Harley as nervous as a first-time mother sending her precious bundle of joy off to the front lines.

They had a lull in the booth traffic, something Harley had not thought she'd be happy about. The day had gone a hundred times better than she ever expected. When Chance had pitched the Nashville vendor competition, she'd initially declined thinking they weren't big enough to warrant anyone's attention. Add in the judging against the big houses and she'd seen disaster written all over the day.

Their success had been two-fold. Chance was right and the mere thought returned the cheek-splitting grin to her face. Vendors here were looking for the next big thing.

Harley hoped she could be one of them. But the four of them had worked so well together it had pulled some of the stress off her shoulders. Their strengths complemented each other, and everyone worked at one hundred percent to make sure their side of the boat didn't tilt or rock unsteadily. For the first time in years, Harley could breathe when thinking about the business.

Which of course made her wonder what they would do when Chance inevitably left. His time with them had an expiration date. She'd known that from the beginning but since the first *anonymous* night of phone sex she found herself wanting him to stick around more and more. Not just so they could put away the phone – luckily, her cell had unlimited minutes - but she found herself thinking of more with Chance blended with her future. Was that even possible?

She'd never considered it before.

A tall shadow blocked the sun from her eyes, drawing her attention to the handsome man who'd walked up to their tent. The head of silvery hair put his age at sixty-some-thing, she guessed, but the comfortable smile reached light brown eyes and took years from her estimation of his age. The name badge pinned to the crisp plum-colored shirt read —

Oh boy.

"Mr. Gold." Harley held out her hand, stiffening her back and squaring her shoulders. You didn't slouch in front of the owner of the second biggest distillery in the nation; one of the top ten in the world.

As much as she resented the bigger labels, she had to admit Old Barrel was different than most. They were Louisiana locals originally and unlike The Gold Standard had stayed small rather than sell out to the lure of quantity over quality.

Isaac Gold took her hand in his, covering it with his other hand in a warm handshake. "Please, I'm Isaac. You must be the Fortune behind Fortune's Brew."

"Yes, sir, I am. Harley, uh, Charlotte Fortune."

"It's a pleasure, *Harley*."

Isaac's eyes went over her shoulder to the back of the tent where Bex was working on the gumbo, and he scratched at the shadow of a beard already darkening his jaw. A tingling started at the back of Harley's neck.

"I think this is your first time at Nashville."

"It is." Harley gestured to the gumbo. "Could I offer you some of our master distiller's gumbo? It might be the second-best thing Lautaro makes after our secret recipe moonshine."

Isaac rubbed his hands together. "I can't say no to that."

Bex was bringing a fresh bowl, napkin and spoon before Harley could turn to ask for it. "Thanks, Bex. You're always a step ahead of me."

The teen nodded once but gave Isaac Gold a head-to-toe perusal that left a tight line to her mouth.

While Isaac tasted the bowl of gumbo, Harley collected some of the new literature Chance and Piper had designed showing Fortune's Brew and their operation. Harley traced her fingers over the smooth paper of the colorful brochures, still amazed to see the professional images with her name emblazoned in silver below. Looking back to Isaac, she was pleased to see he'd already consumed half the bowl.

His eagerness gave birth to a blossom of pleasure and pride. "I told you it was good."

Isaac had the good nature to laugh at himself, wiping the

napkin across his mouth. Harley watched his movement, that tingling sensation back, something she could only call familiarity. She knew Isaac Gold had started in New Orleans but after his very public divorce and his wife's betrayal he had moved to Memphis and built Old Barrel. The better distribution hub in that area had done well for him. Maybe he'd known her dad and their paths had crossed when she was a kid.

"I have to be honest; I have tasted Mr. Sanchez's moonshine and his gumbo does his skills justice. I can see why the circle's buzzing about Fortune's Brew."

Harley's eyes widened. "There's buzz about us?"

Isaac put aside his bowl, wiped his hands. "Absolutely. Many of us knew your parents."

Even the mention more than fifteen years later still gutted Harley and Isaac reached out, pulling his hand back at the last second, as if hesitant about the intimacy of the gesture.

"We knew back then Fortune's Brew would be big. I know how proud they would be to see you carrying on their legacy so successfully."

"You knew my parents." Maybe that was it, Harley realized. He'd come to their funeral.

The church had been packed, and they'd had to move the service outside to accommodate the overflow crowd. That was why he looked familiar. The day remained a blur in her memory, barely holding on to the faces of her family and friends who'd come by to pay their respects.

Harley had gotten mad the night before the service and cried she didn't want to go. Granny T had tried to explain that people were coming by to pay their respects. Harley had tearfully asked if people paid their respects so that death didn't choose them next. She'd been ten but she'd learned early the cruelty of death's randomness.

Isaac made a side-to-side gesture with his head, shrugging wide shoulders and that familiarity deepened in Harley. "We traveled in the same circles because we were both small distilleries in Louisiana. I'm afraid I didn't have the pleasure of their friendship, only their acquaintance over business. I did find a bottle of Lucky Lady last year in Lafayette while I was traveling, and the product is as good as always."

Harley sucked in a breath, releasing in a measured sigh. "Thank you for telling me that. About my parents, and about the business. It's nice to know people still remember them. I'm also glad to know I'm living up to the memory they left behind."

"My pleasure, Harley. Perhaps there's a way for our two distilleries to join forces." Isaac reached into his shirt pocket and withdrew a business card and pen, then scribbled a number on the back before tucking the pen away. "If you're interested... I understand you have a consultant working for you."

Harley eyed the business card as both the Eden's apple of temptation and the Holy Grail it was. Partnering with someone like Isaac Gold could put them on the map ten times faster than she could manage it alone. She wasn't naïve to the power of a top shelf label. It depended on how much of her soul she'd have to sell.

"Yes. CJ Diamond. He's been a tremendous help maximizing our production and fine tuning our process. He's —" Harley pointed to the mass of people churning behind Isaac between the hundred tents lining the field.

"It's ok. I'm sure he and I can catch up later." Isaac assured, handing over the card. "We have some distribution channels that could be helpful to you."

Her senses went on alert. "Why would you want to help

us?" The words escaped before she considered their bluntness, but the truth remained: Isaac Gold stood to gain nothing from helping the competition. So why would he?

He laughed, a good-natured sound he accompanied with a casual lift of the shoulders. "We all start at the beginning, Harley. I'm paying forward some kindness that was shown to me in my early days by a few old timers, I guess you would call them. They shared their experience with me." He scratched a finger through the grey at his temple. "I'd like to do the same now that I qualify as the old timer."

"But we're competing against each other."

Isaac gestured to the vast field of vendors. "I think there's room on the market for both. And if I can't hold on to my customer, it's not your fault." He pointed to the business card he handed her. "My cell is on the back if you or your consultant need it. Talk it over with your team then call my office if you want to set up a meeting."

Harley had to nail her feet to the ground to keep from dancing across the fifty-yard line. "We'll discuss your offer. Thank you." She surprised herself at the smooth professionalism exuded by her words because inside she was streaking naked across the end zone.

Chance plowed through the crowd of people walking like they had all the time in the world to get where they were going, trying to elbow his way toward Harley without actually using his elbows. The knot in his gut tightened with each breath until the pain danced before his eyes.

He'd known his father's brand would be at the competition. He just didn't expect his father to accompany it. Isaac Gold was usually happy to let his marketing and PR folks handle these types of events. He preferred the business side of things, which is probably why Chance loved it as well. How many nights and weekends had he spent in his father's office doing homework or waiting while his dad finished up work? Then how many nights and weekends had he spent there when he didn't have to, just because he loved the place and loved spending time with his dad?

How long had it been since Chance had been in the same room with his dad, afraid to use his dad's influence, afraid to let others think he was willing to cash in on his dad's success to further his own goals?

Just like his mother had done.

No, it had been better this way, Chance continued to tell himself. Staying away, making sure his business didn't cross with his dad's was best. When he finally caught sight of the Fortune's Brew tent, the knot of tension eased a bit. Harley, of all people, would understand the weight of a family legacy.

As he stepped inside the tent, he saw Lautaro, Piper, and Harley bent over something in Harley's hand, her face lit with excitement, her body practically vibrating.

"He wants us to set up a meeting." Harley tucked the card back into the jar and Chance saw her fingers tremble slightly.

"This is incredible, Harley." Piper hugged her cousin, giving her an excited shake.

"I did not think you wanted to sell Fortune's Brew, *carina*." Lautaro looked up, worried.

At Lautaro's statement, Chance wondered if Everett and the rest of the family had made a decision about the trust and the fate of Fortune's Brew. Trudy said they had until after Crescent City, but it wouldn't be the first-time owners and investors changed their minds. The possibility of not losing your shirt in a business deal often pushed one side to act hastily which is why the other side often pushed.

"The decision may be out of my hands. But Mr. Gold mentioned distribution, not buying out the company."

Chance lunged forward, reminding himself to temper his reaction at the last second. He was supposed to be a neutral party where her business was concerned. "Isaac Gold was here?"

Harley's head snapped to him, her smile wavering slightly at what he could only imagine was the look on his face. He'd wanted to be the one to tell her about his parents, explain why he used the name Diamond. Had his dad... no, his dad wouldn't do that. Chance was certain of it. His mother wouldn't hesitate. She hated that Chance had cut ties with her but only kept their relationship a well-guarded secret on the off chance he would change his mind eventually.

But Harley didn't look mad.

"Yes." She handed him the business card. "He asked about you." Harley gave him a high-level breakdown of the conversation and Chance was sadly relieved his dad had respected his wishes to stay in the shadows of the Gold name. It would have solved the problem of how to tell Harley about his true identity. But it was the coward's way out and not how he wanted Harley to hear the truth.

Chance nodded as Harley relayed the information. "It would be a good business connection. They've already created the distribution in Memphis."

"Would you come with us to the meeting? Help me figure out if it's a good proposition or not?" Harley asked, tapping the edge of Isaac's business card with her finger.

"You and Lautaro can handle this. If there's anything to discuss, I'm happy to be a sounding board afterward."

Lautaro eyed the business card with skepticism. "But why would he want to help us?"

Harley explained Gold's reasoning. "I admit though, I feel like there's more to it. It seems odd for him to come to us out of the blue."

"You're making a name for yourself," Chance offered but he couldn't fault her thinking the way she did. Her own family had been looking to sabotage her. Why should his be any different? "That's what the meeting will tell you. If he has an end game, you can decipher it then. But right now, we need to get to the judging."

Chance and Piper gathered up stacks of brochures and business cards for the judging tent in case they met with a vendor while Harley put out a sign that said, "Back in an hour" and went over the details of manning the tent with Bex one final time. To the teen's credit, she listened attentively even though she'd been a part of the routine all morning.

As they exited, a familiar voice greeted Chance. "I thought we'd see you here. On your way to the judging? Hopefully, it goes better for you this time."

Leo walked up to Chance and extended his hand, but it wasn't Leo that grabbed Chance's attention. It was the woman with him.

She'd traded her bottle auburn waves for a chestnut closer to the natural color Chance remembered, the light brown eyes a mirror to his own. They studied each other silently and Chance knew his time to come clean with Harley had run out.

"Hopefully, the cowards that couldn't face the competition in Houston stayed home this weekend." Piper bit out sharply, stepping forward but Lautaro put a restraining hand on her shoulder, whispering under his breath.

Standing behind Leo, Dean snickered. "You're up against the real distillers now, Harley. You won't make the cut."

Chance leaned in close to Harley's ear. "Harley, I need to speak with you a moment, please."

She ignored him, distracted by Dean's taunts.

It was Piper that responded to Dean, however. "Is that why you're still working elsewhere when your dad owns a business, Dean?"

Dean's face flushed red, his mouth a pinched line of anger. "My dad likes to be taken advantage of by the Fortunes. But that'll be changing soon."

Harley pushed forward from the protective wall of Lautaro and Piper. "What's that supposed to mean?"

"It means —"

Leo held up his hand to Dean, silencing Dean. "Where are my manners? Harley, have you met my business partner?"

Chance's stomach dropped. "Leo." He put all the warning he could into the name. Leo knew Chance's secrets. They knew each other's secrets, they'd been friends since junior high. Would Leo sell him out now?

"This is Sondra Gold, Chance's mother. She owns The Gold Standard."

Apparently, the answer was yes. The betrayal knocked Chance cold, spinning his world on its axis.

But not as much as Harley's world was spinning. Twin spots of color darkened along the ridge of her cheeks; her mouth parted as if testing out the words on her tongue.

"The Gold Standard." Harley's eyes pinged between Sondra, who's face morphed into a casually evil grin, to Chance, who felt the blood drain from his entire body. "Sondra *Gold* is your mother. Then Isaac Gold..."

"Is his father, yes." Sondra purred. "It's such a nepotistic little world we live in."

Harley turned to Chance, the questions and confusion written on her face, but she held her tongue and Chance watched the steel walls slam shut behind her eyes. Harley turned to Leo and Sondra. "It's a pleasure to meet you, Sondra. If you'll excuse us, we have to get to the judging."

Harley could see the faces of people she passed, the tents and stadium a peripheral blur. She knew she was walking because they were all moving. She just didn't know how because there was nothing beneath her feet. The world had dropped out from under her.

Piper tried to keep up but Harley was huffing it. In back, Lautaro was a silent, blank wall. The very fact he had not urged her to remain calm, to breathe, to consider all the angles told her his thoughts circled the same conclusion as hers.

Chance had sold them out.

Everett's deal with The Gold Standard had obviously been orchestrated before Chance had arrived, or Chance's arrival had sealed the deal. Either way, he'd been fattening them up for his mother to feast on.

Harley groaned. *Stick a fork in me, I'm done.*

Once again, she'd picked the wrong person to trust. Made the wrong decision. Now it would cost her everything.

Even the man she loved.

Even thinking the words put a bitter taste in her mouth and she swallowed hard to rid herself of the cocktail of betrayal and despair with a chaser of humiliation. He'd been sent to spy on her. Sent by whom was unclear. Sent to find out more about Fortune's Brew.

Especially their corn.

It was what Harley had thought that first day out on Lake Opelousas Road when she'd encountered Chance looking every inch like a salesman. Everyone knew they used a unique variant of corn. People had tried to buy it in the past. How could she have been so naïve?

Already her body felt the emptiness that would greet her in bed tonight. Not that he'd ever actually been in her bed, thankfully. She'd wanted him enough. Had shared with him things she'd never shared with anyone.

"Harley!"

Piper grabbed her arm and Harley spun toward her cousin, obviously having missed previous attempts to get her attention while she wallowed in well-deserved self-recrimination.

"I'm fine, Piper." Harley assured her, resuming a more sedate march toward the judges' tent set in the end zone.

"I don't believe you." Piper matched her step for step. "Chance would not sell you out. Whatever this looks like, it's not that, okay?"

Harley chuffed her disbelief. "He had plenty of chances to tell me about his parents."

"Not everyone wants to live vicariously through their parents' fame."

The truth of her statement hit its mark. Harley knew the struggle Piper had to maintain a distance between her mother's reality TV life and her own. The bleed over made it almost impossible for Piper to get a job at a reputable marketing firm without the firm wanting to cash in somehow on her tangential notoriety.

The first crack splintered her resolve to stay angry. "It's still a lie by omission."

"Maybe there's another reason."

"The corn. He needed more info on the corn and our

patent." She didn't want to think about the nightly phone calls, the intimacy they'd shared.

The trio weaved through the judging tent and found seats in the fourth row. Isaac Gold sat a few rows back, his head bowed toward the man with whom he was talking.

When Isaac's marriage fell apart and his wife had stolen their business, he'd not fought for it. He'd let her walk away with the recipe, the name, *his* name, everything. Why would Isaac Gold give up something he'd built and put his name on so easily?

Harley couldn't have done it.

Maybe Isaac's current interest in Fortune's Brew was intent to sabotage Everett's deal to get back at his ex-wife. But that would hurt his son and Harley couldn't see the man she'd met doing that.

Seeing her attention, he winked and grinned, and Harley felt the recognition to her toes, the smile one she'd grown to love. Harley only nodded in acknowledgment.

She tried to focus on the things around her because thinking about Chance knotted something in her chest and made it too difficult to breathe.

Earlier rounds of judging had narrowed each category's field down to seven finalists, though no one knew who they were; all judging was done blind. Each contestant's entry was transferred into an identical decanter, the distillery's identity in a wax sealed envelope attached to the front.

Harley studied the seven trays, her eye pulled to the tall shot glass of colorful swizzle sticks that accompanied each decanter, wondering if Fortune's Brew was among them. She'd have thought after a lifetime of watching the product be made, she'd recognize it anywhere, but they all looked alike. She could no more tell which one was hers than she could tell which person to trust apparently.

"And you've told him everything about yourself already?" Piper interrupted her thoughts.

Chance's words chased the heels of Piper's statement.

There are things I need to tell you.

I want to tell you some things about myself. Things that are important.

Had he been trying to tell her the truth?

"I've told him the important stuff. Hell, he knows as much about our business right now as Lautaro and I do."

"Oh, you've shared the recipe with him?"

No, it was the one thing she'd held back. The one thing she'd held back from everyone except Lautaro.

"That's what I thought." Piper turned in her seat, placing a comforting hand on Harley's shoulder. "I understand why you're mad. But maybe give him the benefit of the doubt right now. At least allow him to explain. He's earned that."

Lautaro suddenly stood, adding as he crossed in front of Harley and Piper. "He has earned the right, Harley."

Looking up, Harley realized why Lautaro was changing seats. Chance was waiting. He settled in beside her, their arms brushing shoulder to elbow in the close confines of the theater row seating. Her world narrowed down to each point of contact. Arm. Hip. Thigh. Heart.

How had she let herself fall for a man like CJ Diamond, knowing his name was a falsehood. Didn't it seem likely other things were also a lie?

In the silence that lingered she listened to the deep breaths that filled and exited his lungs, the scratch of his nails against the soft denim of his jeans as he fisted his hands. He'd rolled up the sleeves of his dress shirt, the cuffs tight where the muscles rolled and bunched beneath his skin. Finally, he stretched out his fingers and with that motion his breathing eased, as if the tension flowed out of his body.

"I'm sorry I didn't tell you sooner. I wanted to but there was a non-disclosure with Everett I needed to respect. I use a pseudonym for business because I don't want clients hiring me because of my parents but I actually think Everett found out and it's why he hired me. Only when Everett revealed the deal with The Gold Standard, I wasn't sure how to tell you without it seeming like I was…"

"Spying."

"Yes."

The one word was heavy between them. Harley studied the explanation in her head, held it up to the light, passed it over her tongue like she would a new distillation. Testing. Tasting.

The judging started, the panel going to the first tray as one assistant poured a taste for each judge while another assistant added ice to a glass and poured another shot on top, finally spearing the tumbler with a red swizzle stick. The crystal of the glass magnified the red plastic, reminding Harley of the walking stick used by the Sloppy Possum at the still house.

"I think it's why Everett hired me in fact. I almost didn't take the job once he let me know he'd been in some sort of talks with Sondra, but I was pretty sure he was exaggerating. Sondra does not share or play well with others."

A resigned huff followed those words and Harley wondered what had put such distance between a mother and son. She'd give anything to be with her parents again. She remembered Chance's earlier words about sacrificing a relationship with someone he loved very much. He'd walked away from his dad. His mom had walked away from him. Did it make it hard for him to trust?

Regardless, he'd lied to her. You didn't build trust with lies.

From the corner of her eye, she saw him look at her, but she kept her eyes forward, following the movement of the judges. Ice. Pour. Blue swizzle stick. The minutiae of the world around kept her from thinking too hard on the feelings Chance aroused. The desire. The want. The hope. She could handle losing anything but the hope.

"And I wanted to meet the woman behind the label. If I haven't said it before, you make a damn fine moonshine."

She smiled before she knew it. "That we do."

The panel of judges finished working their way through the silver tray of decanters, conferring quietly at the back of the dais before one walked forward with four honorable mention ribbons and three prize medallions, one each for bronze, silver, and gold.

As he placed the honorable mention ribbons, polite applause rippled across the audience. With each medallion, the applause increased until the final medallion was placed around the first tray with the red swizzle stick.

Harley eyed the ribbons and medallions, her attention hyper focused, her breath suddenly thick in her lungs. They needed a win today. Everything rested on them getting a win today. Without that, it was all over. Granny T would vote with Uncle Everett and Aunt Elsbeth to sell, and Fortune's Brew would disappear.

Harley would have no purpose left. She would disappear.

One of the assistants began to work their way across the table, removing the wax seal and turning the envelope over to the judge who read the entrant's name and location. Harley had heard of some of them. Some, like her, were still new to the business. Even the honorable mention at this level was exciting and their excitement translated to cheers and whistles as the owners and distillers made their way forward to accept their prize.

At the last honorable mention, Leo's Lazy River Distillery was named only he showed no excitement as he stalked forward to take the certificate and ribbon from the judge. He didn't even wait for the customary picture or join the other winners at the front of the room. He exited the tent, sullen and pouting.

The judge accepted the next envelope, announcing, "Our bronze medalist today goes to... Fortune's Brew Distillery. Owner Charlotte Fortune. Master Distiller Lautaro Sanchez."

Piper and Lautaro were on their feet in an instant, hugging and cheering, but the noise became a loud buzz in Harley's ears and the world slowed to the eternity of moments between a heartbeat. She waited for someone to correct the mistake. *Heartbeat*. Would they be disqualified again? *Heartbeat*. Had they really done it? *Heartbeat*. Could the man she loved really betray her trust? *Heartbeat*.

Chance tapped her on the shoulder, snapping her from the swirl of thoughts. "That's you."

Harley lifted her hands to her mouth to cover the gaping hole of surprise. Lautaro took her hand and they walked to the front, Harley's vision a narrow tunnel leading her where Lautaro pointed. On the aisle she noted Isaac Gold, who took to his feet and extended a hand as she walked forward.

"Well deserved, Harley. Congratulations." He seemed genuinely happy for her win, his eyes a mirror to his son's when they held true happiness. A little hitch caught in Harley's gut.

Harley's head was still spinning as the silver medalist, Isaac Gold's Old Barrel, joined them and she looked up in time to see the judge walking toward the red swizzle stick tray and announce The Gold Standard as their top winner that day. Harley's eyes cut to Chance, who watched her, then to Sondra, who watched her son.

As the final pictures were taken, Harley's attention returned again and again to Chance and the way his eyes hooded whenever he caught his mother looking his way, or the way the tension eased, and regret softened his features when he met his father's gaze.

He finally joined them at the front and for the first time Harley sensed uncertainty emanating from him. He stood with his arms crossed, chin down.

"Congratulations, Harley. Lautaro." He nodded to Isaac, extending his hand. "Dad. It's good to see you."

"I see you're still picking winners." Isaac gestured toward Harley and Lautaro.

Sondra wormed her way into their circle, tugging at the long strand of pearls cascading over her breasts. She toyed with one of the turquoise stones nestled among the pearls. "Isn't this a lovely little family reunion?"

Chance and Isaac shared a stony expression, but it was Isaac that broke the awkward silence. "Sondra, congratulations. First place, as always."

Sondra gestured vaguely to the tent and people around them. "We are the gold standard, Isaac. It's why I've started to branch out, acquire some smaller distilleries. Share our *good fortune*."

Sondra's attention zeroed in on Harley with those final words and Harley stiffened. "I'm sure the smaller distilleries that want to be acquired feel the same."

Sondra's lazy chuckle chased a ribbon of gooseflesh around Harley's flesh. "It's not always about want, Harley, dear. Sometimes it's about necessity."

"It's about control." Chance interjected, his pulse a ticking fuse beneath his jawline.

His mother lifted a hand, palm upward, her brows arcing in a forehead too smooth for a woman her age. "Of course it's about control, Chance. Everything is about control. And only a child or a fool believes otherwise."

Chance spun away from the group, disappearing into the crowds which had started to multiply. Harley watched him go.

The public was streaming in from the gates in the end zone, eager to share in the tailgating atmosphere. A handful of vendors and food trucks had been permitted to secure a liquor license for the day, allowing the event to become a huge private party.

She, Lautaro, and Piper returned to their tent, but traffic was light since they weren't one of the tents offering liquor to the public. The sign advertising the upcoming event in Lafayette drew attention and Piper was able to distribute more tickets. They had a promising venue lined up.

Harley's thoughts swirled about the connection between Chance and industry icons Isaac Gold and Sondra Gold. Her initial reaction had been one of caution and that had emerged once again at Sondra's comment about necessity being the motivator for her to acquire a small distillery like Fortune's Brew. But necessity for which side?

Fortune's Brew was struggling financially but today's showing, and the attention of dozens of vendors put the promise of future business close enough to touch. Would the new line of credit Piper secured be enough to see them through? She'd have to talk to Mr. Blanchard about doubling their corn crop next year. There was enough in the silo to meet the demand even with the new orders. But if things progressed as she hoped, they'd need significantly more.

That also got her to thinking about production capabilities next year. Maybe Chance would...

Harley cut off the thought sharply, sadly. Chance would not be with them next year. He probably wouldn't be with them next week. Maybe not even tomorrow.

Could she trust him?

Maybe it didn't matter anymore. Everett had his deal to dangle like the proverbial carrot before the family. Whether Chance worked for or against her, there was little she could do to change that fact.

She tried to reconcile her feelings over the man. Her confusion about the information he'd withheld about his parents, especially given the potential for Everett to sell the business.

Chance lived by his three rules and at the heart it was always about the client. Being a corporate spy didn't fit into that mindset. He'd been hired by Everett, not Fortune's Brew, but Chance had done the best he could for Fortune's Brew. Not The Gold Standard. Not anyone else.

He was, in his heart, a protector. He would not sacrifice someone he'd been charged with protecting. She thought of Leo, of what Chance had sacrificed for the worthless little snit. He'd given up part of his career for friendship.

Chance was not for sale. Not at any price. Not even to his mother.

Piper was right. Chance wouldn't sell them out. He put himself into his work. He didn't do that so a business could just hand over the reins to someone else. If that were the case, he wouldn't pick the clients he did: struggling businesses with the promise of success within reach. It was just as easy to sell out at that point. No, Chance enjoyed the success too much.

If it was about control, as Sondra admitted, what did she hope to control by getting her hands on Fortune's Brew? There was the corn, of course.

But was there more?

Harley wondered if Chance had a clue as to the answer.

Chapter Twenty

"You're still letting her push your buttons."

Chance looked up to see his father standing a few feet away, the brightness of the sun an aura around his silhouette. He held a briefcase in one hand, a satchel identical to the one Chance carried, and had the other stuffed into the pocket of his pants. The familiar image jerked Chance back to his childhood, of the times his dad would pick him up at school or from soccer practice. He always had the briefcase because he'd always come from work.

Chance scrubbed a hand over his jaw, leaning back in the hard bleacher seat as his dad closed the distance between them, propping his frame against the metal railing on the stairs. "She knows what buttons to push."

Isaac put the satchel at his feet and speared Chance with a knowing look. Chance sighed. "I know. She does it on purpose. I hate that I feel like I'm eight years old when she shows up. You'd think I'd have outgrown being mad at her by now."

It was Isaac's turn to sign. "I don't think a child ever outgrows a mother's betrayal."

"What about a husband?"

Isaac let his gaze wander down to the field, to the top of the stadium, out to the parking lot. Anywhere but Chance.

"She betrayed you too," Chance reminded him, as if he needed reminding. But his dad has always focused on protecting Chance after Sondra walked away. Not on himself.

"Yes, and I've been happily remarried for almost twenty years."

"Happily?" he challenged. "Would Evie agree with that assessment?"

"You two always did talk too much for stepmother and stepson."

"We are pretty close in age." Chance teased, the joke old and loving between them over Isaac's new wife, barely twelve years older than Chance.

"I came up here to talk about you. Not my marriage."

Guilt prodded Chance to say, "I'm sorry. You know why I walked away. I couldn't stand the thought of using your name like she did."

The memory soured in Chance's gut. His mother had stolen not only his father's business but his name as well.

Isaac was already nodding. "You are my son, Chance. My name is yours. She stole my business. That I can replace anytime and if I can't replace it, it's no great loss. You on the other hand, are irreplaceable. I've given you the space you wanted, and you've built a fine reputation all on your own. If you want help with the business in New Orleans, I can help make that happen. And if you still don't want my help, I'll stay out of it."

"The New Orleans venture won't be moving forward, at least not with me. My partner sold out to Sondra."

Isaac dropped his shoulders, resignation tightening the

lines at the corners of his eyes. "I'm sorry about Leo. He always wanted the easy route to success."

Chance thought back to the turquoise and pearl necklace he'd seen his mother wearing earlier in the day and the one he'd seen on the woman with Leo on their video call when he'd first arrived in Belle Terre. If Leo was sleeping with his mother, Chance wanted nothing more to do with him, as a friend or a business partner. "He's always had a price on his soul."

"Miss Fortune, on the other hand, doesn't seem to be willing to sell out at any price. That can be detrimental as well."

Chance pushed to his feet, his eyes searching the field for the familiar black tent. He couldn't see Harley, but he could feel her presence. "Harley just wants to know she's taken every chance, given it every opportunity to succeed. She's willing to listen... eventually." He grinned on that last word.

Isaac met Chance as he exited the row of seats, putting a hand on his shoulder. "Just remember Sondra will do anything to win. Even hurt those closest to her. And you are her biggest unclaimed prize. If she thinks she can get to you through Harley, she won't hesitate. If she can't absorb Fortune's Brew, she'll try and destroy it."

Chance stiffened and met his father's warning gaze. "I'll do whatever it takes to prevent that."

"The price will be high. She'll make sure of it."

"It'll be worth it."

C hance was the first to arrive at the still house the morning after their return from Nashville. He sat at the cluttered desk in Harley's office, going over the invoices and paperwork for Fortune's Brew. During the night he'd lain awake in his hotel room, shifting around the possibilities for his mother's games like pieces of a puzzle in his head. She didn't do anything without planning three steps ahead. So, what did she want by buying out Leo?

She had to have known Chance wouldn't agree to partner with Leo on the New Orleans business if she was in the picture, so that removed that from the picture. Sondra wasn't interested in Leo's recipe - it was moderate at best in Chance's professional opinion. Even if his mother and Leo were lovers, Sondra wasn't sentimental. She wouldn't invest her name or her money without the intent to get more in return.

What did Leo have or have access to that Sondra wanted?

"You're here early."

Harley's voice pulled Chance from the path of his thoughts. Her presence warmed things inside of him he'd not known had grown cold over the years. His mother's betrayal, he'd come to realize, had not only stolen the family business, but had stolen Chance's belief in marriage and love. Could Harley be the one to give that back to him?

"I am." He shuffled some of the papers spread out before him, wishing he could organize his feelings as easily. Chance knew he owed Harley an explanation for keeping things from her. "I was glad to see you hadn't changed the locks."

She blushed, scrubbing her hands against her jeans as she sat in the chair by the desk. She tilted her head, shoulders shrugging slightly. "I thought about it. That was quite a day."

They'd returned in separate vehicles, having needed Lautaro's pick up to haul the trailer with their supplies, and hadn't had an opportunity to talk to her. Lautaro hadn't asked him any questions. His repaired vehicle had been waiting at the house when they arrived so there'd been no reason for Harley to drive him back to the hotel. When his repeated calls went unanswered, he sat with his phone in his lap for hours, hoping she'd return one of a dozen messages he'd left between voice and text.

Chance laced his fingers behind his head, leaning back in his chair. "What I told you is true. My parents had a difficult divorce. The marriage wasn't all that easy either. They'd been working for years to get The Gold Standard off the ground with little luck. Finally, mom said she'd had enough and walked away. Within a week, dad received divorce papers, but he also found out she'd incorporated the business name and stolen the recipe they'd developed."

"Didn't he have a patent or a copyright on the recipe?"

"It's almost impossible to protect a recipe, and he hadn't trademarked the name yet because of money. So, she got away with it."

Harley's eyes widened and she huffed out a long breath. "That's... brutal. That must have made it hard for you as a kid going back and forth."

Chance shook his head slowly. "Not really. When Sondra walks away, she walks away clean. I didn't see her again until I was in college."

She looked down at her hands crossed in her lap, then up again at him, the compassion a wetness in her eyes. "I'm sorry, Chance. My family's a mess but I've always had them around."

"The business thing gutted dad. Sondra found the right partners and The Gold Standard shot to the top, without him. It was bad enough she stole the business. But his name..."

"And that's why you use Diamond for business purposes."

"Mostly. The association with dad is positive. He's well respected. But with Sondra... her business ethics have been rumored to be flexible. Mine aren't. I don't want any confusion. And I don't want anyone to think business with me is a pathway to business with her. Everett and I had already signed a contract when he revealed the deal. I should have walked away then."

"Names are tough, aren't they? They define us from birth. We either spend our lives trying to outrun them or live up to them."

Chance thought about that. He'd spent his adult life wanting to hide from his name, hide from his mother but in doing so he'd sacrificed his relationship with his father. He was no longer willing to make that sacrifice.

"It's not all bad. They give us a tribe of people who accept us and usually we can count on them." He looked at Harley, knowing her own struggle with her name and the baggage that came with it. "I'd also like to think we can live up to a name without letting it decide how we do that."

Harley pulled her hands in close to her body, her thumb rubbing little circles on the back of her fist.

"I changed my name because I wanted to escape. We can see that was a monumental failure." Harley chuffed and Chance leaned forward, resting his elbows on the desk. "You're diving into a business I'm not sure you love because you don't want to lose your dad. The thing is Harley, I couldn't escape by changing my name and you won't lose your dad's memory if you don't keep his business. They're still our parents. I can't imagine your dad would have loved you any less had you gone into music or become a chef or even a used car salesman. And I think your grandmother is waiting on you to figure that out, so she knows how to vote on the business."

"Excuse me." The female voice interrupted Chance and Harley and the two of them turned to find a young woman in a lab coat standing outside the office. She pushed the tortoiseshell glasses up her slender nose and offered up a nervous smile. "I'm looking for Mr. Fortune."

Harley stood. "Everett Fortune's not here. I'm his niece. Can I help you?"

The woman pulled a folded piece of paper from her lab coat pocket. "I'm Lindsey from Louisiana Ag Lab Services. It says here I'm supposed to get samples to test the moisture content from a silo of corn at the Blanchard farm, but I was just there. There is no corn in the silo. My paperwork didn't have contact info for Mr. Fortune, and I saw the sign for the distillery and thought maybe he was here."

Harley's face paled and she put a steadying hand on the desk. "What do you mean there's no corn? There's a massive silo that should be at least half full. And why are you testing our corn?"

Lindsey shrugged. "I don't know why the corn is being tested and there was only one silo, and it was empty. Unless I was at the wrong place." She looked at the paperwork in her hand as she pulled out her phone and swiped her GPS to the screen. "32650 Highway 1, Belle Terre. Blanchard Farm. There was nothing else in that general area, so I don't think I was in the wrong place. No one answered when I knocked."

Harley thumped a fist against the desk, closing her eyes as her chin sank to her chest. "That son of a —"

"Let's head over there." Chance quickly stuffed some papers from the desk into his satchel and thanked Lindsey, telling her they would call to reschedule then ushered Harley toward their cars.

Harley was a tense line of silence in his passenger seat, arms crossed tightly across her chest. "We never called the police after the vandalism in the still house."

"It's going to be ok, Harley."

She shook her head *no* in short, jerky motions. "I should have known Dean would do something to the corn after the wreck out by the lake. He's mad at me. He likely sabotaged the stillhouse. It shouldn't take a genius to connect the dots."

"If you're handing out doctorates in ignoring the obvious, put my name on one. I didn't think about the corn being the prize. I was focused on the business as a whole, not its components. The corn is what makes Fortune's Brew special."

As they were making the three-point turn to exit, Lautaro arrived and Chance explained the problem.

"That son of a —"

Chance laughed and held up his hand. "Harley beat you to it."

Lautaro nodded, his mouth set in a firm, grim line. "I think it's time to teach Dean you do not mess with Fortune's Brew."

Harley leaned over from the passenger seat to look out the window. "What happened to breathe in, breathe out, and all that Zen stuff you've been teaching me over the years."

Lautaro revved the truck's engine. "There is a time for

peace, love, and compassion. And there is a time for kicking butt. We have reached the second."

～

H arley jumped from the car before Chance had come to a full stop, pleased with the look of panic on Dean's face as the sheriff pulled in alongside their vehicle. He turned but Sheriff Guidry was already calling his name in warning.

"You lying little sack of uselessness!" Harley ground out between clenched teeth and Dean had the good sense to look more scared of her than of the sheriff walking calmly toward him. "You destroyed that pallet of Lucky Lady on purpose, didn't you?"

"That was an accident. I didn't do anything wrong, Harley," Dean whined, then added, "You have no claim to that corn if you can't pay for it. I can do what I want with it."

"You might want to check with your parents on that, Dean. The corn's been paid for. We have the invoice." Chance came around the front of the vehicle as Leo and Paisley emerged from the building that operated as the still-house at Lazy River. Regret twisted in Harley's heart at the look on Chance's face as he studied Leo.

"My parents are in Jamaica," Dean sneered but he sidled toward the sheriff.

"Not anymore. Apparently, you're no better at picking out hotels than you are picking out business partners. The hotel was condemned." Harley held out the papers Chance had shown Mr. and Mrs. Blanchard when they'd caught up with the couple at their farm an hour ago. The couple had returned late the night before from an unexpected vacation, a gift from their son's new employer. "Your business partner used you."

"I don't know what's going on here," Leo walked toward the sheriff, palms out in a gesture of surrender. "I trusted my junior partner with securing a vendor. If he's made some sort of illegal purchase, I'm completely shocked and unaware."

Dean's jaw dropped while Chance only shook his head, his eyes hooded as he watched Leo's performance for the sheriff.

"That corn is owned by the Fortunes. The Blanchard's partner for the maintenance and are paid at the end of the season. With the cost of commodities now that theft puts you in felony grand theft territory, Dean, and it's not the one on your video game console."

Dean's mouth opened and closed as his gaze jumped between Leo and the sheriff. "There's no contract that says that. I checked dad's files for the paperwork." But he looked uncertain now and Harley took the stack of documents Chance held out.

"You didn't check with your dad. It was a gentleman's agreement between our grandfathers, an agreement our fathers respected. Piper paid him for the corn. Your dad and I signed an official contract this morning. I also own the patent."

Chance had discovered the paperwork her grandfather had filed in the sixties, apparently never sharing the info with the Blanchard family. If her father had known, he'd died before sharing the information.

"Add to that the video surveillance of you breaking into the still house and vandalizing the property. Although I'm sure you had help on that." Harley gave a hard look at her cousin who had the good sense to keep her mouth shut.

Leo cleared his throat, taking Paisley's hand. "Dean, when I took you on it was because you were bringing certain assets to the business. You failed to disclose those assets were not yours. I don't do business this way. I'm sending you notice of my intent to dissolve our partnership for unethical business practices."

Chance gave a derisive laugh, but Harley sensed the deep hurt Leo's actions had inflicted. "I'd get used to that speech, Leo. Did you tell my mother you could get the corn so she'd help with the New Orleans investment?"

Leo squared his shoulders, puffing out his chest. "We're going to lose the property at the end of May. You weren't doing anything to help."

"We still had other options. Regardless, there are some lines you don't cross. Sleeping with a friend's mother is one of them."

"What?" Paisley screeched, shaking loose from Leo's grasp.

Leo sputtered a denial, but in the end he deflated, swallowing loudly. "How did you find out?"

Chance worked his jaw back and forth. "The woman in the background during our video chat. I recognized the necklace." He rolled his neck and shoulders, a sign of tension Harley recognized. "Why do you think Sondra is interested in you? She thought with Dean and maybe even Paisley you'd have access to Fortune's Brew's corn which is probably what she really wants. It's why she's hinting at a merger with Everett. She's covering her bases. She leaves nothing to..." he scoffed "chance."

Harley went to him, putting a hand on his arm. She knew Chance's trust was not something he gave lightly, and Leo had traded their twenty-year friendship like a business commodity. "I'm sorry."

He looked to her, his pupils barely visible in the chocolate and amber starburst of his eyes. "It's nothing I don't expect from her."

"Maybe from her, but Leo—"

Chance tipped his chin to his chest. "It doesn't matter." A deep breath raised his shoulders, brought some of the color back into his face. "Let's get the corn back to Fortune's Brew. We have a lot of work before Chicago in a few weeks."

"We do have a lot to do," Harley repeated, the emotion leaking from her face. "And I want you to know I appreciate all you've done to date to help us get here. But you're fired."

Chapter Twenty-One

Panic clashed with the icy dread in the pit of Harley's stomach like oil and water. She looked to Piper and Lautaro, each lugging a dolly loaded with supplies as big as the one she pushed. "Shouldn't there be a table for us to check in?"

Already sweat pooled in the small of her back as she led their trio through the packed crowds in Chicago's largest convention center. They'd gotten lost in the traffic around the center. Then they'd gone to the north building first but discovered the event had been moved to the west due to construction. An email had been sent out, but Harley wasn't one to check email on a regular basis; one of those pesky details of business she tended to ignore. Another mistake. When she went down, she went down in flames.

"Maybe they closed since the show officially started." Piper offered reluctantly, wiping back the hair that draped in front of her face. She'd taken off her shoes somewhere along the way, the sensible heels hanging over the handle of her dolly.

Lautaro searched over the crowds, his height an advantage but he shook his head. "Stay here. I will see what I can find out." He turned and was swallowed up by the shoulder-to-shoulder crowd.

Harley pressed her thumbs against her eye lids, pushing back the pain of the burgeoning headache. They'd driven through the night to reach Chicago an hour before opening, giving themselves added time with the insanity of traffic in the Windy City.

She should have gotten hotel rooms like Chance had suggested, but the cost worried her. She didn't want to dig any deeper into the line of credit Piper had secured from the bank.

Fortune's Brew was hanging on by a thread. With so many people swiping at that thread with battle swords, she feared what would happen when the business fell, and she was left with nothing but the leftover bills. Had Everett thought of that in his attempts to sell out their prized asset to Sondra Gold? Had anyone thought of what happened to her after Fortune's Brew was gone?

Anyone but Chance?

Piper thumped her on the shoulder. "Stop it, Harley."

Harley slid her hand behind her neck, massaging the knot of tension that had taken up residence moments after she'd fired Chance. "What? I have a headache."

It was a lie. Not about the pain. The pain was all too real, but it came from somewhere other than the tightness behind her eyes or the thud in her temples.

It originated in the hollow ache of her heart.

"Uh-huh." Piper nodded, arching one eyebrow. "Granny T would say your heart's knocking, but your brain refuses to answer the door."

Harley groaned. "My brain is the only thing I can count on."

She felt bad firing Chance. But it made business sense. First, he'd withheld information about his relationship with Issac and Sondra Gold which put his loyalties in question. Then, just when Harley felt like she understood his reasoning behind the deception, they discovered Chance's best friend had been trying to sabotage them and steal Fortune's Brews assets.

Chance had told her the second time they met he didn't believe in coincidence. Neither did she. And Harley couldn't risk another bad decision.

She couldn't take a chance with her future. Even if the future was dull and lifeless because it wouldn't include him.

"Your brain is getting lost in the geometry of relationships."

At Harley's puzzled expression, Piper continued.

"Geometry's transitive property says that if a equals b and b equals c, then a equals c. Both Dean and Uncle Everett used their inside knowledge of your business against you. Outside of Lautaro, I doubt there's anyone you've trusted with more inside knowledge of Fortune's Brew than Chance.

"You've been waiting on him to betray you. Even though you're not sure he actually did — and for the record, I don't think he would do that — you're assuming he has or will so you're just going to cut him off now because it's safer for you."

"Do I look safe to you Piper? The business is hanging by a thread. I'm back to screwing up every decision concerning said business because I'm trying to figure out which way the axe will fall. If Chance is selling us out, do I use the new line we created and potentially risk furthering his mother's interest in us? If I don't use the new line, am I lessening the value of Fortune's Brew so if Granny and Everett do sell out, we won't get what the family needs to pay off the debts I've created." She slumped against the dolly, the loneliness a heavy weight on her shoulders. "Things were going well with Chance, but he was going to leave eventually. I may as well sink or swim on my own now."

"The registration is on your phone." Lautaro slipped from the crowd and rejoined Piper and Harley. "There is a, how you call it, app to download." He pointed to the overhead banners which, sure enough, described the online registration.

"I didn't even look at those." She yanked the hated device from her pocket, relieved she'd at last remembered to charge it in the car on the drive to town.

"Most have not. Apparently, half the entrants have had trouble. The committee was trying something new, and it has not gone well."

"How did you find that out?"

Lautaro looked over his shoulder and Harley saw Chance standing there. He greeted Piper with a nod, his eyes immediately going back to Harley.

"They decided on the app at the last minute. It wasn't in any of the planning materials sent out," he explained, as if knowing her brain had already gone to self-recrimination for not knowing the process. She hated that he was right.

Harley swiped through the registration, cursing herself for not paying more attention when she and Chance were signing up for the competition. "It says we need to deliver our product to the mixing station for the judging, but we only have a half hour to set up before they begin." She looked at the three dollies.

Chance stepped forward. "I can be trusted with physical

labor Harley. Let Piper deliver the product. I'll help get your set up materials to the ballroom."

She hated the thought of relying on Chance for more help, but they were short-handed. Chicago's competition occurred during the week rather than on a weekend and Barista Bex had been unable to join them because of school. Harley didn't want to need him. She didn't want to rely on him. But Fortune's Brew needed her to think rationally, not emotionally.

"Thanks." She nodded; the relief immediate. Chance had a way of doing that. Protecting her without making her feel weak. Helping without making her feel helpless. Why couldn't it just be about that?

Harley got Piper situated with the product and pointed in the right direction before following Chance toward the ballroom. The organizers had already set up tables and booths so all they had to do was personalize the area with their own brand items. At least they didn't need to set up the overhead canopy.

She'd brought a crate of peaches from the orchard to go with their signature cocktail and within twenty minutes, they had an old-fashioned bar set up to deliver their redesigned Old Fashioned. Mirrored panels provided a backdrop to the bottles of Diamond in the Rough and Lucky Lady with their new spiced line of Luck of the Draw, while a towering display of tumblers adorned with spears of peach, mint, and ginger waited to be filled.

"I'm going to get ice," Lautaro announced, grabbing the small ice chest and disappearing out the back of the booth.

Chance had moved to watch Harley as she worked slicing peaches and setting up the bar. Harley's fingers trembled beneath his perusal, but her heart pounded in her chest. Words of apology warred with words of reasoning.

She didn't want to believe him capable of betrayal, but Piper was right. Experience had taught her everyone was capable of it. Most didn't even need a reason.

"When the owners are coming around with the bartenders," he started, reaching out in the space between them how he usually did: with information. "Talk to the owner. They need to feel like the focus is on them usually. But try and gear your demonstration to the bartender. They'll want to see the detail of the prep."

Harley nodded once as she cleaned up her table, wiping the curls of peel into a bowl. The spicy scent of the infused peach reminded Harley of her nights in the still house with Chance when they were developing the recipe. Of the kiss they'd shared. The way her body reacted then pale in comparison to the heat whirling through her system now as he stood close enough to touch.

Chance signed. "I'm going to let you finish getting ready. Good luck. I know you'll do great."

Again, panic jolted through Harley. There was too much left to say. Too many chances she hadn't taken and now he was walking out of her business. Her life.

She looked up in time to see him turn away, sadness crinkled at the corners of his mouth and eyes. "Why didn't you tell me sooner? You must have known about Leo and your mother after Nashville."

Chance turned, edging back to the booth. He planted his hands on the table, leaning his weight on his arms. "Rule Three. I kept trying to talk myself out of feeling something for you. It wasn't professional. I shouldn't be falling in love with a client."

The jolt of panic solidified into an electric zing through Harley's system. She had to swallow hard to make her throat work. "Love?" Her thoughts scattered around the word, and she closed her eyes to try and pull it all together.

Chance closed the distance between them, looking to the floor before squaring his posture and meeting her gaze. "I know. My timing sucks. You've got lots of people who say they love you, looking to help you with the business but no one is thinking about you. They're really thinking about themselves and what's best for them. Love feels that way when money and business are involved. I wouldn't trust it either."

He cleared his throat, scrubbing a hand across his jaw then sliding it around to massage the back of his neck. "Except your grandmother. I believe she's thinking about you and for what it's worth, she and Lautaro have only your interests at heart."

Harley knew that to be true, just like she knew everything else Chance was saying to be true. Their relationship started as purely business, a reluctant partnership on her part. She'd wanted nothing to do with Chance in business or her personal life. But like him, things had started to change.

"I started falling for you after that first kiss. Maybe even before that if I'm honest. Why didn't you tell me then?"

"Your uncle was talking about selling out to The Gold Standard and I worried what you'd think about my connection with the label."

"And then your dad offered to help us with the distribution channels in Nashville."

Chance gave a sad laugh, lifting one shoulder in a half-hearted shrug. "You're not the only one who struggles with why people love you. My own mother chose business over family."

Harley took a step closer, drowning in the scent of cardamon and champagne. "Just so we're clear, I'm falling in love with you for you, not your father's distribution or your mother's label. For your intelligence and humor and your great taste in whiskey. How you never let me give up on myself, but you don't believe in false praise. You've always told me the truth about the business, even when it might hurt a little in the beginning. And I'd love you if your last name was Trinkenschuh or Ythiervelkersone or Sallow-Dankworth."

Chance straightened, his brows widening in surprise. He brought up his hands to cup her face, tracing the bow of her mouth with his thumb. "And just so you know, I'd love you if you were a tone-deaf piano player or a chef who routinely mixed the salt and sugar or a woman who knitted cardigan sweaters for alligators."

"So, if we can't trust what the other one is feeling or why they are feeling it, what do we do?"

"I honestly don't know. Take a leap or walk away."

"Neither of us is a leaper."

The admission broke something in Harley's heart. She wanted to trust Chance as much as she loved him but doing so risked her future and the future for her entire family. And he apparently couldn't trust her not to cash in on his family business connections to improve her own standing in the industry.

Chance's face looked as blank as her own heart felt. "I guess not. Good luck Harley. I hope you get what you want with the business."

Chance turned away and Harley watched as he walked away into the mist that tunneled her vision. She pushed away from the front of the booth, desperately trying to catch her breath as her lungs shut down and rebelled at breath.

Her eyes were already on strike, clouding the world in a wet haze.

It didn't matter, she told herself, dashing away the tears that had started falling down her cheeks. He was never going to stay. She was just a client, and he was there for the job, nothing else.

Even if it hadn't felt like nothing.

Then Lautaro's arms were around her, cocooning her in the warmth of his unconditional love and Harley leaned into that and let herself cry.

At the final round judging later that afternoon, Harley felt drained. Physically she felt nothing. She'd turned off the part of her heart that was broken in two and let the numbness surround her, instead throwing herself into the tasks at hand: saving Fortune's Brew.

Emotionally, she was plumb tuckered out, as her Granny would say. Harley had never been one to examine her feelings all that closely but today she'd held them all up to the light. What she'd seen left her more than sad.

Trust. It all came down to trust and neither she nor Chance had that to spare.

As she, Piper, and Lautaro settled into their seats, Harley let her gaze roam around the room. She'd gotten to know several other distillers over the course of the competitions and nodded a greeting at those who caught her eye. But if she was to be honest with herself, she was looking for one person in particular.

And he wasn't there.

The announcer introduced the judges and Harley recognized a few of the names. Kissy St. Germaine preened for the spattering of applause, lifting her hand in a controlled princess wave as she nodded to the crowd. Her gaze fell on Harley for a second and her smile tightened at the corners, highlighting the wrinkles that bracketed her mouth.

As the judges began their work, Harley's focus pulled back. Piper sat beside her, arms crossed tightly, her foot bouncing wilding where it dangled over her knee.

"You ok, Piper?" Harley asked.

Piper grunted something non-committal but avoided looking at Harley. She even angled her body slightly away and Harley's senses went on alert. "Piper?"

"I'm not talking to you."

Harley scoffed. "Are you going to steal my toys next and hide them in the orchard like you and Paisley used to do?"

Piper cringed. "You know that was all Paisley."

"I know. What's going on?"

"You're being unreasonable with Chance and it's going to cost you Fortune's Brew and I can't believe you're willing to lose everything because of pride."

It was Harley's turn to cringe. "I'm trying to protect the business. If he's here to dig into our business just so he can turn that over —"

It was Piper's turn to scoff. "Please, Harley." The half-smile lifting her mouth shared space with a look of incredulity. "You are one of the best distillers out there, but you are the worst businesswoman ever. Do you really think someone would need to send in a corporate spy just to find your weaknesses?"

Surprise dropped Harley's jaw. "I can't believe you just said that. I've kept the business going for five years."

Piper was shaking her head before Harley even finished her defense. "Does the phrase *a wing and a prayer* mean anything? If our corn was bought any other way, you'd have been out of business. If we had any customers, you'd have been out of business. If Lautaro ever once cashed a paycheck —"

"Wait, what?" Harley looked to Lautaro who delivered Piper a death stare.

He crossed his arms tightly over his chest, tilted his chin back and focused on the judges still making their way down the line of finalists. "I have been paid. I have the checks. What I do with them is my concern."

"Was everyone just placating my sense of guilt while I played businesswoman? Did no one think I could do this?"

Piper threw up her hands. "It's not that the family doesn't think you can do it, Harley. It's that no one is sure you want to do this. Fortune's Brew has become this ugly shirt you wear because you think you'll hurt the person who gave it to you if you don't. Like granny with those awful blouses Paisley gives her. Sometimes a gift can be returned when it doesn't fit or if you don't like it."

"But this was dad's legacy."

"If your dad had owned an auto shop, do you think he'd want you to spend your life fixing cars if you didn't love it?"

Chance had told her basically the same thing.

"If your parents were here, they wouldn't love you any less for following your own dreams." Piper reached over and took Harley's hand in hers. "Your parents did not die because of you. You don't have to sacrifice your entire life in their memory."

Harley squeezed her cousin's hand. "I know that some-where deep down. I just forget."

Piper flipped her hair over a shoulder, puffing out her chest. "That's why you have an incredibly insightful marketing and publicity VP to remind you."

"Vice President?"

"Yes, I decided I was due a promotion."

"I'm not sure we can afford a vice president."

"I haven't been paid either. That's something we'll have to discuss after you win Crescent City."

Harley wrapped Piper in a hug. "Thanks, Piper."

"You're welcome. I'm right about Chance as well. I don't think he was keeping his identity a secret because of your issues, or this thing with Leo and his mother... please... who wants to think about their parent's sex life? Sometimes you don't want the obvious thrown in your face. Why do you think I never watch television?"

"May I have your attention please?" The announcer and panel of judges were gathered around the microphone. Three of the bottles had been moved to the front.

The judge began to read off the honorable mentions between the polite applause of the audience. When he announced third place and didn't announce Fortune's Brew, Harley deflated a little.

Her dreams of Crescent City were fading, along with the $5,000 entry fee she'd paid. Even if she decided to sell the business like her aunt, uncle, and grandmother wanted, her competitive spirit still didn't want to miss out on the final competition because she hadn't been good enough.

"Second place this year goes to a new entrant," the judge began. "Fortune's Brew. Master Distiller Lautaro Sanchez. Owner Charlotte Fortune."

Piper and Lautaro leapt to their feet, dragging Harley with them. As the three embraced Harley's heart soared and sunk in rapid succession. They'd done it. They'd made it to Crescent City. All their hard work and sacrifice had gotten them to the final race. Only the entire team wasn't there to celebrate. The victory felt hollow.

As the judges congratulated her and Lautaro, the announcer called out the winner: The Gold Standard.

Harley watched the business representatives come forward, but her eyes were on the tray containing the first-place winner. That, and the red swizzle stick in the shot glass.

Chapter Twenty-Two

Harley gritted her teeth in frustration, feeling the tension reverberate from the tips of her ears to the balls of her feet. There were just too many places to be, too many places she couldn't go.

Her birthday last week had been the official deadline for the family to vote on dissolving the business but true to her word, Granny T had bought them one more week. It all came down to today. To Crescent City and whether Fortune's Brew could show as a contender.

But Harley had to make sure they had a fair shot.

She weaved into the Mardi Gras-like crowds at the Superdome, where the Crescent City MicroLiquor Spirits Competition was hosted, passing yet another moving brass band blasting jazz against the concrete walls that made up the avenues leading to the gates taking spectators to the seating area.

Lautaro and Piper thought her nuts. Granny T just looked at her in that way she had, a half-smile that conveyed a desire to believe while reserving actual belief. As much as it pained her, Harley understood.

She had no actual proof of cheating.

But the coincidences it would take for The Gold Standard to win all three competitions Harley had attended and be the only finalist to have a red swizzle stick were too astronomical to calculate.

And it was a brilliantly subtle tell. Who noticed swizzle sticks?

She wouldn't have if they hadn't been red. It was like a message from her mother to pay attention.

She descended to the intersection of Claiborne and Poydras on the ground level, the area more deserted than the rest of the corridors. Harley was still searching for the area where they stored the entrants' reserve for the finals.

If someone was playing fast and loose with the blind part of blind judging, that was likely where it would happen. After a full day of judging, the ten finalists had been selected and the final round judging would begin in a few hours. If she could just prove that The Gold Standard was the identity of the bottle with the red swizzle sticks before it was revealed, someone would have to believe her.

"Harley, what are you doing down here?"

Harley spun on her heels, colliding into a broad chest she recognized instantly. Heat rushed at her from all directions, attacking the empty places left by Chance's absence in her life. She breathed deep, filling her heart and lungs with the spicy earthiness of his cologne, letting the warmth of his breath against her cheek chase away the chill of his absence.

She wrapped her hands in the material of his shirt, hanging on for dear life while still pushing back from the solidity of his body. It was the hardest thing she'd ever done because... dammit... she wanted to hang on. Wanted to pull him closer. She needed Chance more than she'd needed anything: air, food, music. He was what gave it all texture and context and poured the life into her life.

And it scared the hell out of her. Because if his presence gave her life meaning, what was going to happen now that he was no longer around? She'd fired him. How would she survive it?

The cold slap of reality made it easier to step back from him. Harley tugged at the hem of her blouse. "Chance. I'm, uh, looking for..." Her brain went into shut down. She couldn't lie to him. She hated liars, hated the belief that you could lie to someone for their own good. It was never true. But she also knew that if Chance was working against her, she needed to know once and for all. Then she could move on.

She cleared her throat, pushed a curl of hair behind her ear. "I was looking for the reserve room."

Chance's brows narrowed into a tight v over his nose, and he looked over her shoulder. "The reserve room? You know you can't be there. It's off limits to contestants."

"I know but I needed to check on something." Harley deflated. It was pointless. Even if she was right and Sondra Gold was cheating, it still wouldn't solve her problem of saving Fortune's Brew "Never mind. I'm not sure it matters anymore."

"Of course it matters. If you're worried about something, tell me what it is. Maybe I can help."

Help. Such a small word loaded with big meaning. Could she do it? Could she ask Chance to help her? He probably had a better knowledge of what she needed to do than anyone.

But what if he...

No. It wasn't in him. She'd always known that. It wasn't Chance she didn't trust.

It was herself.

He held out a hand. "You and I've always made a really good team."

Harley's heart leaped at the chance before her brain could rein it in. He was right about that. The two of them had worked well together. When she'd been foolishly stubborn, he'd called her on it. When she needed to hear the truth, he'd told it to her, not to be cruel but because he knew she could take it. Everyone else had wanted to protect Harley from failing. Chance had been willing to stand by her side and wait, then either move forward with her or help her pick up the pieces and try again.

"You're not going to like it."

She was about to declare war. On Sondra Gold. On the industry itself. Nearly every bar in America made its decision on top shelf liquor based on what came out of these regional and national competitions. If Harley showed them to be rife with scandal, what would that do to smaller distilleries like hers? Would it even impact the bigger ones?

"Would this have anything to do with red swizzle sticks?"

Harley's jaw dropped. "You know?"

Chance shrugged, using the motion to stuff his hands in the front pockets of his jeans. "I suspected in Chicago last year."

"That was what you and Kissy St. Germaine had a falling out over."

"It was one of the things, yes. In Nashville I noticed the red swizzle sticks were only on Sondra's brand, so I went back and checked some photographs on websites and in the competition archives. Then this morning I had a conversation with Kissy St. Germaine. She's still denying it, but her face isn't really great at hiding the truth even with all the Botox. I guess I've had more practice with lying."

The short distance between them suddenly felt like a mile wide chasm and Harley knew it was going to take a leap of faith to cross it. Could she do it? Did she have it in her to fully trust another person?"

"You're a lot of things, Chance Gold. But a liar is not one of them. I'm sorry I ever doubted that. Or you. The truth is the only person I've ever doubted was myself. The only person to ever really lie to me was myself. About the business, about not wanting it. I've never wanted anything more in my life, but I was scared to say it, to acknowledge it.

It was like if I put it out there in the universe, someone could take it away. I wasn't sure I was strong enough to survive another loss. At least not until you came along and showed me I could."

Chance had been stealing the distance between them in small steps and now he was an arm's length away. He reached out, cupped her face and she melted into the warmth of his touch.

"I won't sacrifice your dream for mine. I won't trade Diamond Consulting or A Shot and a Beer for Fortune's Brew. Helping me could be the end of your work. It could hurt your dad. I can't live with that."

He leaned in; his mouth dangerously close to hers. "As long as you can't live without me. Because I can't live without you, Harley. Nothing else really matters. If I never get the restaurant off the ground. If the entire world knows Sondra is my mother and Diamond Consulting goes away. Nothing else really matters if you're not there to share it with me."

"You showed me I could survive the worse, Chance. That doesn't mean that's all I want to do anymore. I think I've forgotten how to do that."

"You're a fighter, Harley Fortune. I've known it from the

first time I saw you. You don't know how to quit. I think the only thing you need to remember to fight for is yourself."

Harley had to force the air into her lungs because her heart had swollen in her chest at his words. "And you. I'm going to fight for you too because that's what you do when you're in love."

"You still love me?"

"For a man who sees everything, you didn't see that?"

"Good because I'd hate to be the only one still in love here."

And before she could think, he claimed her mouth in a kiss that left no room for doubt. He pressed her back to the wall, bracing a hand over each shoulder as he nibbled the corners of her mouth, stopping only when she was breathless.

"The only reason I'm stopping," he panted in her ear, the heat of his breath searing her skin. "Is there's work to do."

"So now what?" she panted back, wanting to release the fabric of his shirt from her fists but scared she wouldn't be able to stand.

"I think it's time to knock the industry on its ass."

"I'm going to call Piper and Lautaro. We need more help down here. The place is too big to search."

While Harley fumbled with her phone, he started trying doors, listening carefully before actually pulling open the door in case there were people inside. At the last door, they found a stack of boxes inside from various entrants. Chance and Harley slipped into the room, finding the usual set up of finalists in identical decanters on silver trays with sealed envelopes, rows of shot glasses with stir sticks.

They'd found it.

~

Voices rose from the corridor and Chance pulled them behind a stack of folding tables, pointing Harley to a secure corner further hidden by a stack of boxes while he stretched out on the floor. His eyes widened, immediately recognizing Kissy St. Germain. He angled his body to watch the conversation between a gap between two stacks of tables.

Chance recognized the man with Kissy. Glynn Bowers. He was the one who'd replaced Chance after he'd left the judging panel. He'd been pictured with Kissy and Leo after the Houston event.

"I'm telling you, he knows." Kissy opened and closed some of the boxes as if looking for something. "He's known since Chicago. I was able to control the damage thanks to that nasty little friend of his, however. One should never mix friendship and business. It's a recipe for disaster."

"What does it matter what he knows?" Glynn retrieved a matching finalist's envelope from an inner coat pocket. "It's only what he can prove and he can't prove shit. That's the beauty behind blind judging. Now hand me the bottle of The Gold Standard."

Kissy set her phone on the center table and retrieved a bottle from one of the boxes stacked on the side of the room. Her co-conspirator pulled one of the labeled bottles from the tray, ripping open the sealed envelope. "Sorry Shiner's Delight. No finals for you."

He tossed it in the trash bin then slapped the new sealed envelope on the bottle from Kissy and plopped it on the tray, putting a handful of red swizzle sticks in the shot glass. He looked over the row of trays. "Ok. That covers it. The Gold Standard does it again at the final tasting. Ugh." He sneered at the bottle; face wrinkled in disgust. "Have you tasted this stuff lately? She's not even trying anymore."

Kissy crossed her arms, hugging herself as if she felt a chill. "I'm done with this. I'm retiring from the circuit after this year. Sondra can find someone else to manipulate the scores for her or she can start making better whiskey."

"Yeah, right." Glynn scoffed, kicking a few empty boxes back to the corner of the room near where Harley and Chance hid. "And she starts calling in her funding sources and your business goes poof. Ask that kid Leo about that."

Chance held his breath at the mention of Leo.

"The noob thought she would actually get him an in with her capital investment buddies. All Sondra wanted was back up access to that corn. If the Fortunes didn't sell, she figured she could get it through his girlfriend or that idiot junior partner he brought in. Of course, he thought the same which is why he kept them both around."

"Why not just take Fortune's Brew out of the running here rather than some bystander?" Kissy ran her fingers along the decanters, tracing the seal on one of the envelopes. "It would be easier than all this score manipulation she has me do."

Glynn scoffed. "For the same reason she doesn't eliminate Old Barrell. She enjoys winning. Fortune's Brew is the only distillery to ever beat her. Even if it was fifteen years ago, that bitch does a grudge better than anyone. She wants to be the one to shovel the final dirt on their graves. Besides, if Harley doesn't take top three today her family will vote to sell and Sondra will be there to pick over the bones. She'll get what she wants. She always does."

The mention of graves set off a tsunami of goosebumps on Harley's skin, but the cold rush quickly morphed to the heat of her anger on her face. She stiffened, and Chance intertwined his fingers with hers. A heart's sorrow darkened her eyes, and he brought her hand to his mouth, pressing a gentle kiss on her knuckles.

Kissy patted the neat sweep of her hair then waved her hand in the air. "She can do it without me from now on. I don't need her good word any longer. My books sell millions of copies. Retired judges are in demand for the consulting field. I'll just put my name out as a consultant and be done with it."

"You may not need a good word from her but a bad word from her will sink whatever you think you have."

"And I have the evidence that she's been cheating all these years." Kissy lifted one of the silver trays and checked her reflection, touching the corner of mouth with the tip of one finger. She put down the tray, putting the labeled decanter back on the surface. "Sondra and I will call it a stalemate and go on with our lives and business." Kissy shooed Glynn toward the door. "It's time for the announcements. Let's go."

When the door clicked shut, Harley made to stand but Chance signaled her to wait. Within seconds, Kissy returned. From the clutch she retrieved her cell phone and quickly took pictures of the discarded envelope from the bottle they'd replaced then stuffed it further into the trash bin.

"Maybe not exactly a stalemate."

She turned but spun around as Chance stepped from his hiding spot, fists clenched at his side. "You should have retired after Chicago, Kissy."

Kissy gasped, lifting one hand to her throat. "You frightened me, Chance. You shouldn't be down here. You know that. What would the association say?"

Chance crossed his arms and shrugged. "Let's find out.

How about you call the director down and tell him you found me in here. I'll wait while you make the call."

A hint of hesitation lifted the corner of Kissy's brow. "Don't be silly. I don't want to get you in trouble. After the way things happened in Chicago it would be bad for business if you were associated with another scandal."

Chance narrowed his eyes as Kissy moved around the table to stand closer to him.

"And what would happen to your little washbasin moonshiner friend if the industry knew her consultant was found sneaking around where he wasn't supposed to be."

It was a well-aimed swipe and Kissy knew it. Chance had risked everything to save Leo last year. With Harley, he'd risk even more.

"She was smart enough to fire me weeks ago after Sondra manipulated Leo and Dean and Paisley into doing her dirty work. Harley Fortune is a better distiller than most of those here. She can survive anything you do to me."

Did she know that? Had he had time to convince her that she was strong enough to withstand anything and everything the family or this industry or life threw at her? No one should have to go through it all alone. He'd walked that path and nearly gotten lost.

It was Chance's turn to twist the knife. "Do you think you can survive the investigation after I tell the association you've been fixing their competitions? What about Sondra? There's enough animosity against her people will easily believe she's cheated all these years."

"Don't be stupid, Chance." Kissy waved at the row of decanters dismissively. "Sondra always wins, no matter what she has to do. You and your father should know that better than anyone else. If I wasn't helping her win these silly little competitions someone else would be. It's smart business on my part. Do what you need to get ahead and stay there. You'd best remember that. She wants to destroy Fortune's Brew. You may be her son, but she'll still take you down with them if you get in her way."

"I'm willing to take that chance." There was confidence in his words, but Chance wasn't so sure. They were David going up against Goliath. It would not be a pretty fight.

"Really?" Kissy challenged, but her confidence was leaking out. "You think you can stand against me when I tell the association I found you here in the reserve room, especially after last year's incident with your friend? Now I've found you doing the same for your mother."

She held up her phone as if it held the secrets to the universe. "The original scoresheets will support The Gold Standard is not a true finalist, not unless I make her one. When we all come forward - your best friend, your mother, your colleague – and say how you acted alone, you think your integrity will save you? You think the Gold name will save you?"

"I'll start over." His dad had done it, so could he, Chance reasoned. As long as he had Harley.

"And Miss Fortune. Will she start over with you?"

Kissy's words raked him raw. Chance was willing to throw his career away. He'd enjoyed success. But Harley was at the beginning of what Fortune's Brew could become. He couldn't take that from her.

Kissy went in for the kill. "Don't be a fool. The philosophers are wrong, Chance. Sometimes it is too late to start over. Sometimes, the end is just the end."

She turned, heels clicking against the hard floor as she exited, leaving Chance to stare at the closed door.

∾

H arley dropped her phone as she emerged from her hiding spot, her movements lethargic from the weight resting in the pit of her belly and on her shoulders. She'd always been somewhat of a pessimist. Even when she'd argued with Granny T or Lautaro that she was a realist, she knew they were right when they called her a pessimist. Harley wasn't someone who expected things to work out in her favor.

She still worked for what she wanted. She fought the good fight when it needed fighting. She put forth the effort. She even kept smiling. But deep down, she just didn't expect to win. She'd been a Misfortune rather than Miss Fortune for so long, she didn't know how to be any other way.

Until Chance.

He'd done the one thing her grandmother and Lautaro had failed to do in the last five years while she struggled to get the business going. If she was really honest about it, they'd been trying since her parents had died. He'd taught her to see the possibilities.

And now, dammit all to hell, she'd had hope.

Hope that she could keep a business she never knew she wanted. Hope that she could make her father's legacy into her own. Hope that she could make a little happiness with Chance by her side.

But doing any of that meant that Chance would have to give up his dreams. And that was something she could not ask him to do, would not ask him to do.

"Harley?"

The sound of his voice sapped the last ounce of strength from her body. She'd been running on adrenaline and caffeine the entire day but now, the energy just melted away like butter on a hot skillet. She bent and picked up her phone, the screen cracked down the middle.

She opened her mouth to speak, to tell him she was alright — which was a lie he'd see through right away — but her voice got stuck behind the lump of emotion in her throat. Then the stupid lump in her throat pressed against her eye sockets and suddenly tears were clouding her vision.

Harley blinked the offensive things away, rubbing at her eyes with the tips of her fingers while clearing her throat. Finally, she shook her head as if to clear her thoughts and reset her brain. "I'm okay."

"You're a terrible liar." He cupped her face and brushed at the ridge of her cheeks with his thumbs.

A faint smile tugged at Harley's mouth. She placed her hands atop his and leaned into the touch. "I'm a very good liar. I've been telling Miss Perla I like her coffee for years and no one has questioned it."

He planted a soft kiss on the corner of her mouth lifted in the weak smile. "I stand corrected. You're only a terrible liar about things that actually matter to you."

"You may have something there."

Chance looked at her with such intensity, as if he could absorb the contours of her face, see what was hidden behind her eyes or in her brain. Normally it would have made her feel vulnerable, exposed. But with him, she felt safe. As if she could allow him every dark secret and shadow and he wouldn't use them against her.

"Kissy —"

He pulled her forward now, the soft concern in his eyes replaced with determination that darkened his eyes to a hard oak. "We need to get to the award ceremony. Stop them from announcing the winners until we can talk to the sponsors and organizers. Get them to recheck scores —"

"You know we can't do that."

His brows arched like two angry felines. "I don't know any such thing. I'm not letting Sondra get away with this. Or Kissy. I should have said something when I suspected in Chicago last year, but I thought Leo was a friend and I worried what would happen to my own reputation when it was all said and done."

"It doesn't matter now. Uncle Everett and the family will vote to sell. If I'm lucky, I can keep the corn patent out of the sale and maybe sell it to someone else, maybe even your dad."

Chance shook his head. "You're not giving up."

"It's not giving up. It's finding a new path. You're the one that told me that was how business worked. When one thing didn't work, you built a new road, found a new product or service. That's all I'm doing. Our best asset is that corn."

"You're being stubborn. Obstinate, even." The smugness of his expression and tone reminded her of their first day working together. She didn't like it any better now that she loved him.

"Excuse me?"

"Which word didn't you understand? Because I'd think you'd be familiar with both."

"I am not."

He rolled his eyes, the whites showing for longer than really was necessary. "If you think Fortune's Brew's best asset is a field of corn, you're being obtuse."

"I'm really not liking you calling me names over and over."

"Then start acting like a smart businesswoman."

"I'm being a *responsible* business owner and looking at my assets. That corn is probably worth a fortune."

"The only fortune your business has that's worth anything is you, Harley Fortune. You are your company's biggest asset. Your passion and determination. Your fierce willingness to do what it takes, even when everything is telling you to turn and run.

"I think most people would call that foolishness.

"I call it stubbornness."

"You can be a little stubborn yourself," she insisted.

"That's why I recognize a good thing."

Panic nipped at her heart. "She'll destroy you, everything you worked for the last eight years."

"It doesn't matter, Harley." This time he took her in his arms, staring down in her eyes with absolute certainty, face determined. "My dad showed me you can overcome any set back, no matter how big. If he can build a life and brand after she stole everything from him, including his name, I can too. I won't let her bury you in the process. There is one thing you're going to have to put up with however."

"What's that?"

"Me. I'll likely need a job after this. Know anyone hiring?"

"I have a few positions in mind."

"*Aie-eee!*"

Chapter Twenty-Three

For someone as astute in their industry as Chance, not to mention brilliant about business, Harley thought to herself, he was being monumentally stupid. He was totally breaking rules one and two. The thought of how often they'd broken rule three could still bring a blush to her cheeks.

Focus! Her mind ordered, and Harley did just that as she followed Chance's back through the shoulder-to-shoulder crowd in the pre-function area of the Great Hall where the finalists and winners would be unveiled. When the crowd had been dispersed over a half million plus square feet of the first floor, they hadn't seemed quite so intimidating.

Now, however, all crammed into a measly fifty thousand square feet, Harley felt like a fly trapped in a spider's web. The best and brightest of their industry were here tonight. Crescent City was the biggest event in North America and while it still didn't earn an international ranking, contestants from the European and Asian markets were beginning to show up. Whatever happened in the next hour would spread like wildfire.

Harley couldn't let Chance be caught in the afterburn.

But she also couldn't take the chance of leaving him. She needed a wingman.

Pulling out her phone, she hunt-and-pecked a quick text message to Piper while trying not to trip over her own feet or the feet of the other twenty people in her personal space.

Czm u dp smthg w tjis?

Dammit. She really hated typing on this thing.

She was about to erase the text jumble and try again but crashed into Chance, who'd stopped at the doors to the Great Hall. Looking down at her phone, she saw the word *Sending* pulsing across her screen while the little blue line slowly crept across the top. Harley would resend the corrected message in a minute. Maybe she could talk Chance out of cashing in his career to save her dying distillery.

Chance was peering over the crowd, something she had no hope of doing, so she just gazed at their shoulder blades and asked, "Who are you looking for?" as she stuffed her phone into her blazer pocket.

"A member of the staff. I need to get to the director before they get up on stage."

"Chance, we really need to talk about what you're going to do. You can't just go threaten to expose your mother, not to mention the integrity of the entire competition. Think of the repercussions."

Chance whirled on her, and she'd never seen a more serious look on his face as he cupped her cheeks between his palms and devoured her mouth with his.

Because devour was the only word that came to mind as his lips played over hers, not crushing or whisper light, not invading or tentative, but playful one second as he nibbled her lower lip then leaned in closer to sweep his tongue across the seam of her mouth and encourage her to open to his exploration.

And open she did because as much as he devoured her, she was consumed by the ribbons of pleasure and heat and plain old lust curling around her insides. When he broke from the kiss, Harley had to close her eyes and breathe deeply to stop the earth spinning on its axis.

When she was sure she wouldn't fall to the floor, she opened her eyes to find Chance only inches from her face. He leaned his forehead against hers, turning slightly so he could whisper in her ear.

"I've been thinking about repercussions since I was eight, Harley. And I'm done. I want the world to know that I, Chance Gold, love you Charlotte Fortune. I want my name back. I want my life back, not CJ Diamond's life. *My* life."

It was her turn to cup his face, to trace the pulsing staccato beneath his jaw to the thump in his temples. She massaged the heavy rhythm with the pad of her thumbs, wanting to ease away the turmoil filling him within.

He pulled her hands to his mouth, kissing her palm. "I've been trying to plan out every thought and action to account for each possible outcome, thinking if I played the game right, if I followed the rules, the worst would never happen. My father wouldn't lose his business. Clients wouldn't look at me as a conduit to my parents."

"Your mother wouldn't leave you."

He nodded and it broke something inside of Harley. All of her love for the man in her arms tightened in her embrace and she pulled him against her until there was no space between. They moved as one, breathed as one.

"It wasn't your fault." She pulled back enough to see his face, plant tiny kisses on his cheeks and nose and eyelids with each word.

"I know. But I've lived in a sort of limbo thinking if I just did all the right things, it wouldn't happen again. But I can't take that chance. I can't let her destroy you."

"She won't. Not as long as I have you. Maybe Granny T won't vote to sell. We could keep marketing the new lines. We've made good contacts and I think those will turn into contracts. Between that and the loan at the bank, I can probably convince Granny T we're headed in the right direction. I think Piper is going to make a huge difference."

"Of course I'm going to make a huge difference." Piper emerged from the crowd with Lautaro at her back. The two of them looked smugly at each other, then at Chance and Harley. "Have you two confessed your undying love for one another yet because., seriously, I'm not sure how much scarcer I can make myself around the office so you two can fool around on Harley's desk."

Harley's gasp came from her toes but the heat infusing her entire body incinerated the air in her lungs to ash, so it came out as little more than a wheeze. "Wh... I.... you!" she turned and punched Chance on the arm.

Chance had the good sense to rub at the spot Harley had punched. "What? It's not like I was the only one there. I had an accomplice."

Harley floundered like a catfish on the shore, her mouth opening and closing but little oxygen going in and fewer words coming out. Finally, she just crossed her arms and leaned into Chance. "I'm getting a door for my office first thing Monday morning."

A chorus of chimes rippled across the pre-function area and into the Great Hall, the sound rising like a tidal wave as heads swiveled then ducked in orchestrated perfection. Harley's own phone buzzed in her pocket. Chance's dinged in his pocket.

Piper looked over her shoulder to Lautaro, her own phone suspiciously silent. "That took longer than I thought."

Lautaro shrugged. "The file was large. And I'm sure the network was slower than usual given the size of the distribution."

Harley felt the blood move through her body, first the cold withdrawal then the hot rush of its return. "What did you do?"

"What I'm good at. Publicity."

Chance had already opened the email sent to his phone and hit play on the video file attached, holding his phone out so she could see. Harley glanced around the meeting space, so had nearly everyone else in the crowd. The chittering of conversation stopped, replaced immediately by the buzz of the video feed.

"And I have the evidence that she's been cheating all these years. Sondra and I will call it a stalemate and go on with our lives and business."

After a heartbeat of silence, the collective swell of outrage swept across the space with hurricane force winds.

Harley looked to Piper who just shrugged and held up her phone. "I speak Harley." She said, indicating Harley's phone. "I knew what you wanted. But I did edit some of the video. I hope that's alright. I didn't think Chance should go down with the Titanic that is going to be his mother's life over the next few hours. If he wants the world to know she's his mother, he can send out a press release. I wasn't going to spread the news."

Harley threw her arms around Piper and felt Chance wrap them both in his embrace followed by Lautaro who enveloped them all in his bear hug. "Fortune's Brew... where good Fortunes are made of great families."

Chapter Twenty-Four

Harley traced her fingers over the silver medallion from the Crescent City competition, still lost in the dream that had been the last week of their lives. She cradled her phone against her shoulder and ear, nodding before remembering she couldn't do that without dropping the phone. She'd already lost her new phone in a vat of brewer's beer.

"Our production is maxed out through the end of the year, Mr. Gold. We can't handle any more orders. Even with the increase in acreage over at Mr. Blanchard's farm our estimated yield wouldn't cover that much in added orders for the new year."

She leaned over Piper's shoulder as Piper clicked over to the Excel spreadsheet that charted their yield against production. They were solidly in the green with Chance's new plan and the new infused lines he'd talked her into adding, but the new still house would take another few months to complete. Lautaro and their new junior distiller, Hudson, were going to pick up the new copper tanks next weekend. The expansion more than tripled their capacity.

Even that was proving to be insufficient.

"What if I could set aside some space here at Old Barrel? Let you use our distillation tanks until your new production set up is ready. We could team up, create a line between the two distilleries called Fortune's Gold."

Harley smiled. Isaac Gold had the same charm as his son. And the same great vision.

"I'd love to talk about that more, but our limitation is the corn right now."

Chance suddenly filled the doorway, leaning against the brand-new door Harley had insisted be installed first thing the Monday after they'd returned from New Orleans. Her body reacted first to his presence, a visceral response that tightened things and warmed things and tingled along nerves she'd never thought about before. But it was her heart that she paid attention to because it fell in line with her brain in thinking, *I can love this guy forever.*

He flashed her his usual smile, the one that said he was glad to see her, but his eyes darkened and reminded her of what they'd done last night in his hotel room. Finally.

"Mr. Gold... yes, Isaac... I know, you've told me it's just my Granny has told me something different for twenty-five years and she's scarier than you. Chance just arrived. Can I call you back later? Great... talk to you then."

Chance plucked the phone from her fingers, swiped off the phone and dropped it without looking onto her desk as he crowded into her personal space, pushing her against the desk as he slid his arms around her waist. She didn't mind a single bit.

Piper shut the brand-new laptop and shoved a stack of papers on top. "Along with a salary I'm really going to need my own office very soon." She winked at Harley and Chance as she scooted out of the room, closing the door behind her.

"I really like that new door."

"I really like your dad."

"I'm starting to remember how much I do too."

"Do you get your stubbornness from him?"

"It's not that my dad won't take no for an answer," he explained, his smile turning to a grin she was starting to be familiar with when he talked about his dad. "It's just not his favorite word when it comes to business."

"Like father, like son, I take it."

"I did learn from the best."

"I saw Everett's car up at the house. Is he still upset about losing the vote?"

"No. When Piper and I showed him the prospectus with the new production and lines, he realized what a crappy deal he'd made. He even came clean about Sondra's offer of a board position. He's been almost contrite since then, even offering to help with the business."

"Can you afford him?"

"When I told him none of us had taken a salary yet and probably wouldn't for another two years, he still said he'd like to help. That he was a Fortune. Besides, his husband is worth a fortune so it's not like he needs to money. I want to make sure Lautaro cashes all his back paychecks and get Piper on the payroll next."

"You're a good boss, Harley Fortune."

"But I'm not always a good businesswoman."

"Are you kidding? You're an exceptional businesswoman. You hired me after all."

"Actually, I fired you."

"Oh. Then maybe you're just a great businesswoman."

"But I did hire you back. And shared my super-secret, seven generation moonshine recipe with you."

"We're back to exceptional."

Harley lifted her hands in surrender then met Chance halfway as he leaned forward for a kiss. They'd been doing that a lot since returning from New Orleans. Chance split his time between Belle Terre and his place in New Orleans, exploring his options.

He pulled back reluctantly; his face serious. "The association called this morning."

Chance had been in talks with the North American Distillers Association since the debacle at Crescent City. Once the video went viral, every competition Kissy St. Germain had ever judged was filing a complaint and a lawsuit, in that order, against the woman. The only one doing worse than Kissy was Sondra Gold. Stock in The Gold Standard was hovering just below a dollar a share and her investors were not a happy bunch.

"I'm going to be deposed in their lawsuit against Kissy."

Harley nestled her chin in the crook of his shoulder, planting a kiss on the column of his neck. "But you couldn't prove anything back then."

"They know that. It's more as a witness to the conversation with Glynn at Crescent City." He nuzzled her temple, the pressure of his lips sending tendrils of warmth down her arms. She felt rather than witnessed the smile widen on his mouth. "Then they offered me a job. They're looking for someone to manage the judging in North America. Help organizers keep things above board so this doesn't happen again."

Harley tightened her hold around Chance, steeling her face to neutral as the world fell out from under her. She'd known this was a possibility. Her life was here in Belle Terre, with Fortune's Brew. His life was...everywhere else. He had plans and no roots. He'd done that on purpose. She'd known going in she would lose him eventually. It didn't make it any less painful.

She forced a smile, tilting her head back to meet his gaze. "That's wonderful Chance. I'm so proud. You'll have no issues getting an investor for your restaurant now. The kind of connections you'll make through that work will be just what you need."

"I turned them down."

If Harley thought the world had fallen out beneath her feet before, now the oxygen was sucked from the space around her. "I don't understand. It's everything you wanted. Your restaurant. The job. Your name. You earned this. You can't turn it down."

"It's everything I used to want. I talked to my dad last night and he made me realize that my name was mine. No one could assign a value to it but me. Working under a pseudonym didn't change my value, it just changed who people wrote their checks to. All I've ever wanted was to build something. I'm hoping I can help you build Fortune's Brew."

"You want to stay here?"

"I can't think of anywhere I'd rather be for the rest of my life. As long as you'll have me."

"I think the rest of your life is a good start. Think you can put up with me for the rest of mine?"

He tightened his hold and Harley welcomed the security of her place in his arms. "I think it would be my good luck to have you at my side, Harley Fortune."

THE END

Thank You For Reading

Reviews are the lifeblood of an author. Please consider leaving a review on any of your favorite review sites.

If you enjoyed *Love and Miss Fortune*, keep reading for a sneak peek from book four in the Hearts of Louisiana series, *For the Love of Sam*.

Subscribe to the newsletter for release day information, prizes, and more!

For the Love of Sam

HEARTS OF LOUISIANA, BOOK FOUR

Prologue

Sam Girard sprawled lazily on the broad leather sofa in his spacious living room, a bottle of Fortune's Brew's best whiskey in one hand and the baseball from his World Series ninth inning grand slam home run in the other. He traced the laces of the ball absently with his thumb, a gift from his teammates when he'd crossed home plate.

On the TV, the female reporter's voice droned on like a mechanized kewpie doll with a bad southern drawl. But he couldn't find the remote, so he was stuck with her. It was his second longest relationship to date.

"And now for an update on a story we've all watched with great interest over the past few weeks. Memphis Mayor Richard Barrington honored hometown hero Sam Girard today for his part in saving twenty-two children after the November sixth accident trapped them on a burning school bus."

Sam put the bottle to his lips. Three long pulls. That ought to do it.

"Mayor Barrington, seen here surrounded by members of the city council as well as the grateful parents of the rescued children, presented Mr. Girard the Medal of Freedom, the city's highest honor to a civilian. But the real tribute came from the children themselves who had this to say their hero:

"We love you Sam."

"Sam Girard, voted MVP after leading the Memphis Blues to a World Series championship, is recuperating at his home in Belle Terre, Louisiana from injuries sustained during the rescue and could not be present for today's--"

The large screen TV exploded in a boom of shattered glass, the electrical circuits hissing and spitting against the sudden interruption. Sam slumped on the sofa and flexed his pitching arm by lifting the bottle of whiskey to his lips. Fleeting satisfaction raised the corners of his mouth. It was good to know he could still hit the broad side of a barn.

Even if he couldn't see it.

For the Love of Sam will be available soon!

About the Author

Maggie Preston is an award-winning author of contemporary romantic fiction. She fell in love with romance before she knew what it was, stealing paperback novels from her grandmother's closet when her mother wasn't looking.

She loves to travel and tells people that anything and everything they do could end up in her next novel, so if you recognize yourself in the pages of her books, remember you were warned.

Maggie currently balances her life between the right brain and left brain, quality consultant and technical writer by day, romance writer by night.

www.AuthorMaggiePreston.com

Follow Maggie on Social Media

Facebook:
www.facebook.com/MaggiePrestonAuthor

Twitter:
@maggie_preston

Instagram:
@authors_maggie_and_selena

Bookbub:
bookbub.com/profile/maggie-preston

Goodreads:
www.goodreads.com/goodreadscomauthormaggiepreston

Also by Maggie Preston

Hearts of Louisiana

Sex and Insensibility

Second Chance Romance

Hearts of Carolina Anthology

Two If by Sea

Back Home Again Anthology

Dance of the Butterflies